Lark, in Her Element

Lark, in Her Element

A Soul Set Free

Angela Brackeen

WestBow
PRESS
A DIVISION OF THOMAS NELSON

This book is a work of fiction and is a product of the writer's imagination, a creation of her mind, in its entirety. All characters, all names, happenings, businesses, and locations (with the exception of major U.S. cities or national landmarks) are also fictional and products of the writer's creative ability. Any resemblance whatsoever that the characters bear to persons living or dead is entirely coincidental.

Scripture taken from the HOLY BIBLE, NEW INTERNATIONAL VERSION. Copyright © 1973, 1978, 1984 International Bible Society. Used by permission of Zondervan Bible Publishers.

Quotations from, or references to, other works are cited on the last page.

WestBow Press books may be ordered through booksellers or by contacting:

WestBow Press
A Division of Thomas Nelson
1663 Liberty Drive
Bloomington, IN 47403
www.westbowpress.com
1-(866) 928-1240

Because of the dynamic nature of the Internet, any web addresses or links contained in this book may have changed since publication and may no longer be valid. The views expressed in this work are solely those of the author and do not necessarily reflect the views of the publisher, and the publisher hereby disclaims any responsibility for them.

Any people depicted in stock imagery provided by Thinkstock are models, and such images are being used for illustrative purposes only. Certain stock imagery © Thinkstock.

ISBN: 978-1-4908-0381-4 (sc)
ISBN: 978-1-4908-0382-1 (hc)
ISBN: 978-1-4908-0380-7 (e)

Library of Congress Control Number: 2013914062

Printed in the United States of America.

WestBow Press rev. date: 8/21/2013

For souls who whisper words of grace, and

for those who are,
like I was once,
seekers of approval in others' eyes.

Dear kindred soul,
there is only One whose love we need …
and His love is already ours.

*"The noblest spirits are those which turn to heaven,
not in the hour of sorrow, but in that of joy;
like the lark, they wait for the clouds to disperse,
that they may soar up into their native element."* (Richter 1876)

Contents

Acknowledgments

Thanks *especially* to my husband who is ever patient and ever supportive ... *my* 'Hart.' And thanks to my children, who have shared their mom with this work for several years now, and who are our reason for *everything*.

I made many connections in the course of writing this book and while looking for those who would be its readers. I thank *all* of those who welcomed it, and me openly—who offered friendship, advice, encouraging words, a place to hold readings, even just to read the manuscript! There are so many in the writing and publishing industry who freely share their knowledge, time, and resources—other writers and those who work with them are special beyond words!

And most of all, thank you to the *sages* who have encouraged me and shared their wisdom over a number of years, and more recently, as well. I truly couldn't have published this work without their strength and support.

Chapter 1

A Purely Mortal Being

‾‾‾‾‾‾‾‾‾‾

She floated in the Pacific, atop uncommonly gentle waves. Something beautiful and ethereal wavered in the air above her, its shape obscure—human, yet *not* human. She rose weightlessly to meld into it, leaving her physical body, now only a shell, floating on the surface of the water below. She—or they—looked upon that shell sorrowfully, pitying its vulnerability.

Together, they poised for flight into the open sky above, but where before the sky had been a cloudless, tranquil blue there were now gathering dark, threatening clouds.

Something black and winged swooped down toward them. Lark, and the spirit with whom she was one, shrank back, intimidated by the power of the huge winged creature. Its evil was as tangible as the darkness that closed in on them.

Their light and joy dimmed to a flicker. They intuited that this vision meant Lark would suffer, and that fact couldn't be altered. What was happening at this moment, and what would happen in the future, was beyond their control, maybe beyond the ability of the good in the world to fight against.

They were weak now, so tired. Suddenly, the spirit separated from Lark, and she fled back into her physical shell—her own body—purely mortal again. The beautiful, ethereal being hovered, gazing at her. She sensed its immeasurable sadness. She raised her hand, fingers reaching. It returned her gesture and was gone.

1

Chapter 2

Cracks in the Sidewalk

Before the Pacific, there were creeks. Before California, there was the South. Before adulthood and responsibility and commitment, Lark clung to the childish belief that she could control her world by simply avoiding cracks in the sidewalk.

If something bad happened—like she forgot her lunch money or a teacher reprimanded her for wiggling at her desk or she forgot to do her homework—it was her own fault. She had slipped up. If she did what she was supposed to do, these things wouldn't happen in the first place. She was a conscientious child by nature. Even so, she sometimes performed little rituals like most girls do at one time or another for those moments when she *did* slip up. She chanted, "Step on a cra-a-ack, break your mother's ba-a-ack!" as she hop-stepped along the sidewalk, trying to avoid any break in the concrete with a little thrill of fear for her mother's back.

But no matter how well she behaved or how carefully she hopped, she was only human, and sometimes her foot *would* accidentally land on a crack.

She was in elementary school when her father, Joe, died in a car accident, leaving three survivors—Lark, Wren, her older sister by a year and a half, and her mother, Pearline, who said in her sighing, Southern drawl, "This has been one more life-changin' day."

Through the remaining months of their junior year, the two of them grew so close that Pearline and Wren considered Hart a member of the family. But, by the fall of senior year, more than the season was turning. Lark first sensed the change one October day as red, gold, and brown leaves drifted down in front of the windshield of Hart's car when he pulled up beside a creek.

She remembered this place. After Sunday dinners of fried chicken, green peas from the backyard garden, mashed potatoes with gravy, and angel biscuits at the squeaky metal table in the kitchen, her father drove them here in the Ford Fairlane. She and Wren made their voices echo against the creek banks and waded in the cool water.

But that was a long time ago. On this day, too warm for early fall, she stood on the creek bank while Hart knelt in front of her and rolled her jeans' legs up to her calves so that she could wade in the cool water with him. With his baseball-roughened hand, he took hers and led her across stones slippery with green moss to a fallen tree that lay suspended between the two banks. They stepped along the trunk, with arms extended out to their sides, and sat down in the middle. In the water below, sunlight glinted off the scales of silvery fish.

Lark relaxed into this welcome break from filling out applications for university which, along with regular school work, had kept her so busy she'd had to turn down several dates with Hart. She noticed everything about him as he turned his face toward her—his dark brows and his eyes that changed color with the light. On rainy days they were gray-green, but today they were as green as the shady pools in the creek. She admired his pronounced jaw, shadowed by his cheekbone, and his full mouth that seemed always curved into a good-natured smile.

Though the beautiful day seemed to portend nothing except a promising future for them both, her insides quavered with a sense of the coming changes. Melancholy turned the day bittersweet and threatened to steal away her happiness.

And then a few months later, a scholarship—what she thought she wanted—offered her the exciting opportunity to go to a university in California. She'd been able to keep her grades up all through the years, despite her early loss. She had scored highly on standardized tests and qualified for a privately endowed scholarship that stipulated financial need, along with excellent grades.

Now that the opportunity was real, she wasn't sure whether she could do it—move so far away alone—but Pearline pushed her, as most mothers would.

"Lark, you just can't turn this down. It's the best thing that could happen for you." No one could be happier, or prouder than Pearline.

But Lark wondered—*how is Hart going to feel? What is he going to say?*

She told him as they walked under a bright moon and purple starlit sky. Try as she might, she wasn't able to hide her excitement.

"Hart, I got a letter today. I won a scholarship!" she said, breathless with anxiety. "Remember when I told you I had finished an application package for a university in California? The one I really, *really* wanted?"

"That one?"

"Yes, that one!" she said.

For some minutes they walked along in silence.

"So, are you really going out there then?"

Trying to sound more decided than she felt, she said, "It's the chance of a lifetime. I can't turn it down. It's the best thing that could happen … for me." She had relied on Pearline's words. From the corner of her eye she saw Hart study her face closely. She rushed to tell him of her plans to look for a roommate, decide on a major, and learn the details of the city she would live in.

"I'm happy for you Lark," he said, sounding defeated.

She couldn't believe he wasn't going to stand in her way. *At all.* He wasn't going to ask her to stay. In his strength—his *frustrating* strength—he was letting her go, gracefully.

Pearline's confidence in Lark's ability to adjust and do well out in California helped to get her on the plane. And so, she left those she loved behind in her small hometown.

Chapter 4
Finding Treasure

Lark avoided the cracks in the sidewalk for a long time. She became absorbed in academics then work, and never stopped long enough to think about the sacrifices she made. She lived and worked in California for more than twenty years with only infrequent visits back home to see Pearline and Wren. She was single-minded about work and dedicated every day of the week to it ... except for Sundays.

"So, ya' ready? By the way, Val's going with us."

It was not yet light outside and Duff was on the other end of the phone line, to tell Lark she was ready to go as usual. Sunday mornings weren't for sleeping late. Instead, they were fuel for Duff's creative work, and for Lark they were the hours when she freed her mind from the mental focus her work week demanded.

The nearness of Duff's condo and Lark's need for a substitute for Pearline and Wren in this big city of mostly strangers encouraged a friendship that was as long-standing as Lark's time in California.

"Duff! There's not gonna be room for stuff if we bring Val with us!" Lark said, thinking that they would be going in her own tiny car.

"Val's driving her gigantic SUV-e-e-e," Duff said.

They started from home before the sun fully rose, and made good time driving into the Bay Area, over the bridge into Oakland, and then to Alameda, arriving just as the flea market opened. Lark, relieved not to have to find a place to park, left Val and Duff to find their way while she studied Duff's blue hair from the back seat and enjoyed her cup of espresso-strength coffee. It looked as though today would be perfect for 'flea-ing'—the sun's light was just revealing the bay, the bridge, and the San Francisco skyline; the temperature would rise no higher than the 70s that afternoon; and the sky would stay cloudlessly blue.

Through long experience she and Duff knew to strike a trail toward the back to see as many of the booths as possible, and to wind up back at the entrance before the market closed in the middle of the afternoon. Duff pushed a rented grocery cart over the old airport runways for carrying their finds back to the parking lot.

As the sun rose higher in the sky, breaks in the aged pavement began to show, and Lark stepped over them—just as she would have stepped over cracks in the sidewalk as a child. She shook her head, huffed with derision, and turned her eyes away from the ground at her feet to find that Duff and Val were no longer walking beside her. Val was nowhere to be seen, but Duff's blue hair made her easy to find in the growing crowd. Lark drew near and heard her friend chatting, as if she hadn't realized Lark wasn't beside her all along, "Look at this li'l duck teapot! Isn't he cute? I'm gonna have to take him home with me."

Although Duff's taste was different from her own, Lark appreciated her friend's choices for what they were—*her* choices—so made no comment, only smiled because the teapot made Duff happy and helped situate it in the cart to prevent any new scratches on its vintage surface.

She turned her eyes to scan nearby booths for treasures to add to her own collections, but was frustrated in her search, until the sun began sliding downward from its noontime height, and they slowed their pace to enjoy the gyros they purchased from a food vendor.

Drawn by the glint of a gilt-covered frame that leaned against the leg of a rustic table, Lark knelt to inspect the oil painting within. It portrayed the head and shoulders of a girl who wore a thoughtful, melancholy expression. Her dark hair, raggedly chopped off at the chin, was blown by an invisible breeze, her lips were rose-red, her skin was pale pink, and her delicate blouse was white and sprinkled with blue flowers.

Although Lark had turned her back on many tempting items throughout the day, she found she couldn't do that with this portrait. She would take it home, and she would carry it under her arm, rather than risk damage to it in the grocery cart.

The bounce that the find gave to Lark's steps didn't last. The beautiful day, and its freedom from thoughts of work, passed far too quickly. More and more often on Sunday afternoons, her spirits sank as they neared the last booths. Val's excitement over her discovery of a table and chairs for her own tiny condo balcony barely lifted Lark's heart.

Duff hung a slightly rusty chair by one leg on the side of the cart, and said, "Val dear, thank goodness you found this so near the end." She lifted the second chair, hung it on the other side of the cart and then, careful not to damage the bongo drum she'd found, Duff upturned the small matching table and placed it precariously atop everything. They pointed the cart toward the parking lot, and awkwardly guided it toward the SUV with Duff pulling from the front, Val pushing from the back, and Lark walking alongside to keep a hand on the table and prevent it falling off. By the time they reached their destination, they were breathless with laughter over their efforts to control the overloaded, topsy-turvy cart. They arranged their treasures in the SUV, sighed tiredly as they climbed in, and drove over the Bay Bridge southward.

The day ended abruptly when they arrived home at dusk.

"Well, I think I'll take my teapot and my bongo and go home! Love ya' sweetie!" Duff said, and leaned toward Lark for a hug.

"Bye Duff. See you next weekend, if not before."

Still reluctant for Sunday to end, Lark lingered outside to admire the twilight sky and breathe in the night air. At last, she hoisted her finds into her arms and took them up the stairs to her own condo, closed her door, and exhaled.

At one time she, Duff, and any others who had come along for the day, would've collapsed onto the sofa or floor to watch television and play cards late into the night. But they were no longer of an age to do that and face work bright-eyed the next morning. She set down the backpack that held her smaller treasures and leaned the painting against the leg of a table. She stretched her arms over her head to relieve her aching back. Her movement, seen in the mirror over the table, drew her attention.

She studied her face. *Did it hold the answer as to why her moods were so low by Sunday evenings?* She didn't look any different. Her shoulder-length hair was the same dark brown, almost black it had always been, except for a few gray streaks that shone through here and there. The same dark eyes had returned her gaze when she was a small girl, except now fine wrinkles extended outward from the corners. Centered on her curious face was the same pointy nose. The same ears stuck out from her head at the top. Her skin was still so fair that a hint of blue showed beneath, despite living in sunny California for the last two decades.

Only her mouth gave her a start now when she noticed its unfamiliar grim outline. It was not as soft as it was once. *Well.*

There was no answer in the mirror. She left her image there, and wandered about her home listlessly. This took very little time, as her place was tiny and all she was willing to afford in the heart of San Francisco. She stopped her wandering at the table that was meant for dining, but whose entire surface was covered with beautifully bound books, bird statuettes, and old photographs.

Why did it seem she had begun to live only for her Sundays, Duff's easy company, and her collections? She lifted the backpack she had carried that day from the floor, carefully drew out the three bird statuettes she had found, and placed them beside the ones already there. She leaned over and tilted her head to look at them.

Her foot bumped the painting where it leaned against the table. She raised it to eye level and held it at arms' length to gaze at the girl's innocent face with its serious, dark-eyed expression, her eyes cast to the side, and at the way her body leaned into the wind that blew her hair.

Lark took the painting with her to lean it against the wall on her nightstand, where she would study it again and again.

Chapter 5
Living with Choices Made

At five a.m., like millions of other Americans, Lark woke to the music of a local radio station and resisted hitting the snooze button. Making her way around in the dark, she opened her eyes just wide enough to put on t-shirt, shorts, socks, and running shoes. Before stepping out the front door, she pulled on a jacket against the cool air breezing across the Bay Area.

Running was a necessity. She denied herself late-night work, television, or reading so that she could rise early for the flow of good chemicals and energy running provided and that got her through her commute, and a mentally demanding day of highly detailed technical work.

As she put one foot in front of the other, she stubbornly refused to open her eyes fully to the sun's early rays, and started slowly along one of several routes she varied day-to-day for safety and a change of scenery. With each step her blood flowed more strongly, her eyes opened wider, and her breathing and pace quickened. She shook out each leg to loosen her muscles and bounced on them just before she sped up to cruising speed. A thrill of appreciation rippled through her at the efficient way her body handled the demands of running, even after all these years.

The neighborhood was starting to buzz with activity as people left their homes and walked to their parked cars or to bus stops. She avoided the busiest areas by sticking to pathways around shops not yet open and older, well-kept row homes. The views were fantastic—the hills, the ornate architecture, rose-covered arbors, and green hedges.

She counted to the rhythm of her feet and fell into a meditative state. Endorphins flowed and her mind rose above thought, until she neared home again. Barely slowing, she darted up the outside stairs, pushed her door closed behind her, hung her hat on a hook by the door, and switched on the coffee pot.

After showering, she pulled on sober gray clothing in a style chosen to distract from the fact that there was a woman under them. Over the years, she'd found that this helped to make sure business stayed the focus of her relationships with men, who still held the majority at her workplace even in the 21st century.

She grabbed her commuter mug of coffee and headed out the door to her car—the smallest she could find in keeping with the increasingly popular philosophy of low impact on the environment, and the no-less-minor practicality of being able to zip in and out of traffic. Most of the time she didn't mind the commute to her workplace from her quirky, well-loved community—it was her time to daydream, fueled by the fun she'd had and the finds she'd made on Sunday.

But today she found her somber mood of the evening before returning.

Work … and men. She had centered her life around one, and left little time for the other. Loneliness grabbed at her as it had the evening before.

She didn't often question her lifestyle—she'd intentionally lived with single-mindedness. It simplified things. Long ago she'd chosen her career for the financial security and independence it would give her. And her choice had proven wise, hadn't it? It had cushioned her against the kind of hardships her family had experienced after her father died.

Yes, she felt lonely sometimes. She saw the commercials on television of women her age baking cookies, taking care of children. She sometimes watched romantic movies and, if she were to believe them, a nice-looking guy—a *good* one—might be handy to have around. But those movies showed another side to those relationships, too. They could be risky—all men weren't good ones. Romantic movies didn't always end happily.

And she didn't want to be dependent on a man, as her mother had been on her father. Pearline was crushed when they lost Joe—as were she and Wren, too.

She pulled into the parking lot at the end of her nearly hour long commute and sighed. *Why was she so off-center?* There was no time on a Monday morning for thoughts that were unproductive. And her life … well, *"it was what it was,"* she concluded in the phrase of the day.

She zoomed into the first parking space she found in front of a generic-looking office building, grabbed her bag, and slung it over her shoulder—glad that it wasn't heavy with folders of papers like the first briefcase she'd carried to work years ago.

Hurrying in to her Monday morning meeting, she entered a functionally-furnished room and squeezed in among her work associates who were putting down bags, getting out laptops, and setting down cups of coffee.

"Morning, Lark! Hope you had a good weekend ..." a coworker prompted. Still distracted, Lark only smiled and nodded in answer, made herself comfortable at the conference table, and slid her glasses onto her nose, which at one time she'd worn only in an effort to be taken seriously at work, but now she wore as a necessity.

She turned her focus to her supervisor, Edwin, who stood at the front of the room, droning about the status of her group's latest software development project. With an inward sigh she turned her chair more in his direction. The discussion circled the table as each developer updated the group on his or her program module. At last it was her turn.

"Lark—" Edwin prompted.

"Yes, I've finished the latest revision and I'm ready to turn it over to you," she said—now fully engaged in work mode ... until Sunday.

Chapter 6

Meetings ... sigh

At her desk by nine a.m., Lark settled in front of her computer. Before setting fingers to keyboard, she glanced out her office window at the beautiful view. It overlooked a park-like scene between her building and the others in the business complex, with a pond, trees, benches, and tables for having lunch. And there was a lengthy walking path for stretching the legs between long sessions sitting at a desk.

During her university years she'd daydreamed of an office with a view just like this, yet—

"Lark, Edwin says he needs you down in the conference room. Now. There are some configuration changes we're going to have to incorporate. Man, before we even got started! C'mon, almost everybody's down there already." Kieran barely finished his words before he breezed back down the hallway.

Thank goodness for team members like him who looked out for her interests. Issues often arose without warning and the various people who were responsible for parts and pieces of a project could be forgotten as impromptu meetings sprung up.

So much for looking at the view. When she'd envisioned a programmer's job she'd seen herself keying in code at a computer—fitting work for an introvert like herself. But the job involved far more human interaction than she had realized. And she couldn't remember the last time she'd walked through that park outside the window—it had been years.

After the spur-of-the-moment meeting broke up, Kieran followed her back to her office and made himself at home in the chair on the other side of her desk.

She sat down and sighed because of the changes that the team must now absorb into their already-heavy workload for the next several weeks. She forced herself to smile at Kieran. He was only a couple of years out of college, and she saw herself as his mentor. He often stopped by her office to chat and she felt it was her duty to cast their workplace in a positive light. Just because she'd been questioning her own choices of late, didn't mean she should crush his enthusiasm.

He said, "I shouldn't have spoken up to the customer like that … should I? But I just can't believe they want to make changes before we've even gotten started. They won't make any more, will they? I mean, we already have everything planned out—designed!"

Hmm, how to answer that? Should she say what she knew—yes, there'll be more changes before we start, and more after that, and more after that, until you're lucky if you have a good feeling about the product in the end. How did someone like her, who'd been around for so long, had seen so much, keep from dimming the light in those eyes that weren't far past boyhood?

"Our work brings rewards, Kieran. The software we develop is a help to the world. And that's worth all the effort we put into it." *So far so good, now for a dose of reality.*

"But you will sometimes—often even—have to give way to others' ideas—to their creativity. If you can accept that, and also learn through experience when to give in, and when to stand your ground, success will find you."

She sounded just like Edwin when *she'd* first started working here. He had seemed so wise to her, so *old*. Is that how Kieran saw her—*wise and old?* A smile tickled the edge of her mouth, but she didn't want Kieran to think she was laughing at him, so she sat up straighter and leveled a serious look across the desk.

"Just keep it together, Kieran," she said. "No matter what happens or how many changes we have to make, keep your cool. Remember this work is just taking a huge problem and breaking it down in parts. Those parts can get changed, but we have methods of keeping up with it all. I'm not saying it's gonna be easy, but I see potential in you. I think if you can keep your cool, you may be a project leader one day."

With this sort of work, one had to learn to be part of a team. A large part of her own success had been her ability to balance asserting her own ideas in a diplomatic way, while allowing others to shine as well. That's what Kieran was going to have to learn.

"Do you think so?"

His hopeful face and the cowlick at the top of his head again made her want to smile. She said, "I do think so. Now, scram!" She turned her mouth down in a frown, though laughter shone from her eyes, and said, "I need to get an email out with a recap of the changes, okay?" Kieran stood up, waved, and disappeared out the door before she could blink.

Aah, it was tiring, more so as time went by, for her to strike the balance she'd described to Kieran—giving in to others' creativity, her own having to fall by the wayside, unappreciated.

Sure, she had coped well over the years despite being a quiet, bookish short of person. She'd become a lead developer early on, had headed down the same road as Kieran, but it hadn't come naturally to her. She had to play a role, stretching her personality, to speak out assertively, more loudly, and to more people than she would wish to. Lately, she'd found it exhausting.

Bringing her thoughts back to the present, she focused on the task at hand. She placed her fingers on the 'a, s, d, f' and 'j, k, l, and sem' keys, as her typing teacher had called them long ago, and cast her eyes on the computer screen, sliding her glasses downward on her nose to glance at the papers at her side, yet see the computer screen over the top of them. She was going to have to give in and get bifocals.

Her eyes constantly made her think about her age nowadays. She sighed—yet again—and began to type out an email.

Her eyebrows lifted when she finished her task and glanced at the time on the screen. When she was intensely focused at her computer she was happiest. But if she wanted lunch, she needed to head down to the cafeteria as she had another meeting—a planned one this time—in less than an hour.

Lunch in the basement cafeteria, where people's voices rose to be heard over all the others, silverware clanged, and the cashier's computer beeped constantly, wasn't her idea of a peaceful break. She pulled a sensible salad and a bottle of water out of a cooler, paid, and turned to scurry back to her office, hoping for a few minutes of peace at her desk while she scarfed it down before scrambling to the next conference room in only thirty minutes.

Lost in thought, she ran into an obstacle as she walked out the cafeteria doorway, and found her face pressed against someone's chest. She pulled away from the man to regain her personal space, but his hands gripped her upper arms. The plastic container holding her salad skidded across the linoleum, snapped open, and left a trail of lettuce behind.

"I'm sorry!" the man said. She looked upward at his sheepish expression. He released her arms and they surveyed the mess and agreed it was beyond their ability to repair.

"I'll get someone to clean it up, and let me get you another one." He cupped her elbow with his hand, grabbed another salad from the cooler and placed it in her hand, then urged her into the checkout line. She felt powerless and self-conscious—as if everyone in the room stared at them, especially at his hand on her elbow, and could see her embarrassment—but she glanced around and was relieved to see that wasn't the case.

"I can at least introduce myself," he said, with an apologetic smile. "I'm Russert." He held his right hand out for her to shake. A stricken look passed over his face and he awkwardly jammed his other hand into his pocket. He cleared his throat and she watched his face distort, before he forced a smile.

She grasped his hand with her cool one, thinking he wasn't unattractive—he was probably in his mid-forties, his dark brown hair was graying at the temples, and he wore dark-rimmed glasses. She said, "I'm Lark. Nice … *um*—"

"It's okay if you don't want to say it's nice to meet me!"

She anxiously watched the clock and tapped her foot on the floor while they waited in line. She had only minutes now to get back to her desk, eat, and rush to her next meeting.

As soon as the money for her salad left his hand and disappeared into the cashier's drawer, she said, "I'm sorry, I've got to run, thanks!" and she left without looking back.

⁓

As she again scooted into a crowded conference room, her stomach grumbled, upset over her hurriedly eaten lunch. She sighed, *again,* over having to sit through another meeting, and turned her chair a little more toward the speaker.

Chapter 7

Questionable Behavior

The rest of Lark's week was routine, except instead of getting her lunch downstairs, she brought something from home. She told herself this had nothing to do with the salad incident, though she might be a little embarrassed still. But Friday came and she had nothing to bring from home, so she found herself in the cafeteria's check-out line again.

"Hi! Remember me?"

She knew it was him before she turned around. His smile reached all the way to his eyes, which were brown behind his dark-rimmed glasses.

"Hi … Russert, right?" she said.

"Yes. Have you forgiven me enough to have lunch with me today?"

She glanced at her phone to check the time, and said, "Yes, I guess I've forgiven you." His smile had been warm. She smiled to shore up her own lukewarm response.

"Great! You find us a table and I'll be there as soon as I can."

He joined the line to get something to eat, while she found a table as far from the hustle and bustle as possible. She wrinkled her forehead and wondered whether the action she was about to take would seem out of character to others. In the past when a man at work saw beyond her business-like demeanor and asked her to lunch or out for a date, she flatly said no—without an explanation, apology, or remorse. She'd surprised herself by agreeing to have lunch with Russert. But … it was her nature to be polite, and maybe he was still embarrassed and wished to make up to her for the salad incident. Still, she glanced at the tables around her. *Was anyone looking at her?* No—no one was paying her any attention, and there were several tables where men and women sat together. She was being ridiculous—this kind of thing was commonplace, and a small matter.

Nevertheless, she jiggled her foot nervously under the table while she waited for him to make his way to her.

At last he sat down, his eyes bright and his smile expectant. They talked about the weather, work, and other trivial matters people getting to know one another talk about, and lunch passed pleasantly enough. Even though their conversation was shallow of necessity, he listened politely when she spoke, and he smiled often. And it was nice to talk about something other than computer code during her workday.

Lunch was brief as usual. She collected her lunch wrappings and swung her legs around the side of her chair to stand.

He leaned forward, reached his hand toward her, and blurted, "Hey, would you want to come with me to a movie, maybe grab something to eat tomorrow evening?" The color of his face reddened while Lark considered her plans for the next day.

Her typical Saturday involved working from home and getting ready for the next week. And then on Sunday, she would flea with Duff. A pang twisted her insides again as she remembered her loneliness at the end of the day last Sunday. Besides, hadn't she just finished a nice lunch with this man? She could've eaten alone at her desk, could've gotten some work done, but—she let her shoulders fall— she was weary of her rigid life, of denying herself fun. One evening out did not imply a major life change … she said yes before she could wrestle any further with her decision.

"That's great! What time can I pick you up?" he asked, beaming.

She blushed—surprised that his interest pleased her. It felt … *nice*. She said, "Instead, why don't I meet you here, and leave my car while we're out?" He probably didn't realize she lived an hour away.

The corners of his mouth turned down and his gaze fell to the table. He said, "That'd be okay… I'll meet you then, say at six o'clock?"

She nodded her agreement.

Sitting behind the cars of other commuters in the darkening cityscape after work, their red taillights four lanes wide and extending into the distance as far she could see, she rolled her shoulders into the ease of tension that weekends brought her.

Her Saturdays didn't usually prompt any excitement as they were just another workday—only at home rather than the office. But while waiting for the cars ahead of her to move on this Friday evening commute, she had something other than work to look forward to.

Once home she went straight to her closet and pulled on her stay-at-home-Friday-evening sweat pants and t-shirt, while her eyes scanned the lacy, ruffled, and floral-patterned finds from fleaing Sundays with Duff. Her eyes stopped on a silk dress from the 1940s, its loose, flowing shape patterned with purple and turquoise feathers on a background of cream. Paired with low sandals and a light knit wrap, it would just suit her vision of a romantic evening out. Excitement rippled through her. Even though no one could see her in her closet, she covered her delighted smile with her hand. Occasions were rare when she could wear these things. Each time she added to this collection, she questioned her sanity—*when and where did she think she would wear them?* But she could never resist.

Having settled on what she would wear next day, her gaze landed on the gray drab of her conservative business clothes on the opposite side of her closet.

What had motivated her to accept Russert's invitation? What were these cracks appearing in her single-mindedness? And what would Duff say when she found out Lark wouldn't be able to spend tomorrow evening with her as she often did?

Goodness, did she only want to go out with Russert to wear something fun for a change?

Next morning, her run was easy. Returning home, she climbed the outside stairs and considered putting aside work for the day to visit the salon when Duff called to her.

"Hiya, Lark!"

She leaned over the railing to see Duff standing on the pavement below.

"Come with me for coffee, 'kay?" her friend invited.

She bounced back down the stairs, happy enough to be led away from work this morning, and matched her pace to Duff's slower, still sluggish one.

Except for Duff's wide and noisy yawns, they were silent on their walk down the hill toward a coffee shop at the corner of their street and the busier one leading to the freeway.

Without its weekday commuter business, the place was filled with Saturday-morning quiet and coffee-scented warmth. The décor—walls painted burnt orange, the ceiling dark brown—allowed customers to wake up gently, shielded from the sun's glare. They found a table for two beside a window with shades pulled halfway down.

Already wide awake with adrenalin pumping from her run, Lark jiggled her foot under the table and waited impatiently while Duff savored her first sips of hot coffee and became more alert. She wanted her friend fully awake before she told about her date.

"I have a date," she finally blurted.

"Wha-a-at"?

"I have a date," Lark repeated, sounding a bit defensive now.

"You do-o-o? With whom, may I ask?"

"A man from work. Russert is his name."

"*Hmm.*" Duff sipped her coffee and squeezed her eyes shut as if to form an image in her mind. "I'm seeing a button-down shirt, dark trousers—"

Lark completed the picture for her. "Yes, and dark-rimmed, nerdy glasses, v-neck pullover, conservative haircut. He's from *work*, I said."

"So where are you going on this date?" Duff raised one eyebrow, sat a little straighter, and primly took a sip of coffee with her pinky finger extended.

Lark gave the particulars, while her friend set her coffee cup down, thoughtfully brushed crumbs from the table, then looked out the window, all while avoiding Lark's eyes. She let a silence fall after Lark finished, seeming to consider carefully how to phrase her next words.

"We-e-ell, how long have you known this guy, Lark?"

"Oh … a few days."

"Are you turnin' over a new leaf—after all these years? Lettin' your guard down? Loosenin' up?"

Lark had to laugh. "Okay, enough with the clichés!" she said. Then, her voice became quiet, and serious-sounding. "I don't know Duff … I guess I'm tired of the same-old, same-old." She rolled her eyes. "Now you've got me doing it."

"Same-old, same-old—meanin' me?"

"Du-u-u-f-f-f!"

Duff smiled indulgently and tried to smooth Lark's ruffled feathers. "There's nothin' wrong with trying something new. It takes me by surprise that's all." Her voice took on a whiny note. "Maybe I'm jealous. What about us? *I* might've asked you to do something tonight."

"I know." Her friend was only teasing and was at least somewhat supportive. "But you have other friends, Duff. And we don't always do something together on Saturday night. And … and maybe I need to have some friends of my own."

"Okay, just take it slow, Lark. This is kind of new for you, ya' know."

Lark smiled, grateful really, that Duff was looking out for her. "Okay, finish your coffee," she said, "and let's go back up the hill. I have things to do today."

"Yeah, like what? Work?"

They rose and while Duff shambled toward the door, Lark bounced on her toes behind her.

"I don't know ... I might do something different today—"

"Lark, you don't know?! You work every Saturday!" Duff stopped and turned to look at her. She shook her head, bemusedly eying Lark. "The times, they are a'changin'!"

Again, Lark rolled her eyes, but a smile curved her lips.

Chapter 8
Seeing Russert

⎯⎯⎯⎯

The late afternoon sun warmed her arms when she stepped lightly to her car. She buckled the seat belt, arranged it so that it wouldn't crush her dress, and turned the radio to an indie rock station. She felt like a girl again—probably because she'd visited the salon for a massage, a facial, and to have her hair and nails done before returning home to dress for her date.

She steered her car southward and fifty minutes later pulled into the nearly empty parking lot of her office building. She hoped that if any of her coworkers saw her car, they would imagine she was working behind the closed door of her office. She didn't want to suffer curious looks or questions about Russert next week.

He pulled in just after her and opened her car door, holding out his hand to help her out. He wore a black t-shirt with a plastic image on front that suggested he was a science fiction enthusiast, along with faded jeans and sneakers. Her optimism slipped.

Dressed as a gentleman he might not be, but he behaved like one when they arrived at an out-of-the-way restaurant. After he spoke into the hostess's ear in a low tone, she led them to a table separated from the main part of the restaurant by a tall plant and a low wall. Lark supposed this was a romantic gesture, along with his insistence that he order for her.

Her mood lowered more with the ordinary food set before them by their waiter. Russert could have taken her to one of the excellent restaurants nearby. *Why had he chosen this one?* But she relented— he was *so* polite—deferring to her in conversation, listening intently when she spoke without taking his eyes off her. She had heard that was no small feat when it came to dating. In fact, there were times when he seemed too reserved when she asked questions, trying to get to know *him* more, and he turned the questions back to her again.

She couldn't expect perfection, could she? She was being far too judgmental. After all, they were just getting to know each other. Maybe he was one of those people who needed to get to know someone before they opened up. *'Just go with the flow,'* she muttered to herself.

"I'm sorry? Did you say something?" Russert asked, looking up at her from his plate.

"Oh, no. No. I … I'm wondering whether it's time to leave for the movie?"

She frowned when he turned his car toward an even more distant part of the city. Why go out of the way like this, when there were perfectly good restaurants and movie theaters not so very *far* from work? Could he be a serial murderer, taking her to some remote location? She shook her head. That was silly, *wasn't it?* She fidgeted.

Maybe he sensed her discomfort, because he said, "There's a science fiction movie showing at this theatre. It's a cult-classic. I know it's out-of-the-way, but … do you mind?"

"I guess not. I suppose it's reasonable to drive out of the way to see something … *unique*," she said.

Hours later, Russert pulled into the space beside her car back at the office.

"Here we are!" he said.

She didn't try to hide her yawn as she had throughout the movie and on the drive back too.

"*Oh!* Yes. Well," she said, "thank you, Russert. I've had a nice evening." To sound more enthusiastic, or to say it was great, or a blast, or something like that, would be a lie. But it had been nice to be out, and to see the city at night.

"I had a great time, Lark," he said in a low voice. With each centimeter he moved toward her, his eyes darkened a bit and she leaned more toward her own door.

She rushed to say, "Well. I'm gonna head on home now. I guess I'll see you this week. Good night!" She pulled the door handle and practically fell out the door, then jerked herself upright and stumbled to her car. When she pulled onto the 101, she didn't looking back through her rearview mirror.

Whew, that was a close one!

Once she'd merged into the flow of traffic, she made an effort to analyze her feelings about the date, but the long evening behind, together with the prospect of the drive ahead, weighed on her. Duff would want all the details tomorrow. She'd figure it out before then.

As expected, Duff's loud knock woke Lark next morning. She rose sleepily and opened the door without speaking.

"Wake *up*, woman!" Duff said when she walked through the door, set down the backpack she'd readied for the flea market, and headed to the kitchen to make strong coffee.

Lark shuffled back to the bedroom and groaned as she sat on the edge of the bed, not sure she had the energy for the market today. But she pushed her body to move and tried not to think about how tired getting in late last night had left her, pulled on jeans and a t-shirt, washed her face and brushed her teeth, ran her fingers through her hair, and shuffled toward the kitchen for her cup of coffee.

"You look terrible."

"Thanks, Duff."

"So, you got in late last night, huh?"

Duff's energy made her head spin. "Duff, I'm not ready for this. Where are we going today? By the way, I don't want to drive." It seemed it would be only the two of them today—no Val or anyone else along for the trip. She imagined Duff had fixed it that way.

Duff sighed, and said grudgingly, "Okay, we'll go in the Le Baron. Take your coffee. Let's hit the road."

"Thanks," Lark mumbled as she climbed into Duff's aged convertible and struggled to pull closed the heavy, squeaky door. Thankfully, Duff focused on driving while, behind her dark sunglasses, Lark's eyes adjusted to the weak sunlight and her coffee began to have an effect on her circulatory system.

Finally, Duff asked, "Well, are you gonna tell me about last night?"

"I have a much better time going out with you, Duff."

"That bad, huh?" Duff cackled then accelerated, causing Lark's head to hit the back of her seat as they pulled onto the freeway.

Duff didn't mention the date again until they had rented their grocery cart, and were making their way to the back of the market. "Okay, dear," she said. "You've kept me in suspense long enough!"

"Well, it was all right. I had a good enough time, Duff."

"That's all? Really?"

"I'm sorry to disappoint you!"

Duff touched her arm to stop her and turned to look into her eyes.

"All joking aside, Lark, I want you to be happy. You should have that kind of relationship. And, you know—it's time."

"Are you saying I'm getting old?" Lark asked.

"Well, you're like the rest of us—not gettin' any younger. Oh, loo-ook!" Duff was heading in the direction of her pointed finger ... toward the oversized head of an amusement park employee's costume.

Leaving the market for the return trip home, Duff gunned the LeBaron's engine, again slinging Lark's head against the seat behind her, and drove off over the Bay Bridge, as fingers pointed and smiles were hidden behind hands.

In the back seat of the convertible, silhouetted against the sunset, rode George Jetson—in the form of the head of an amusement park employee's costume—atop another bongo for Duff's collection.

Chapter 9
California's Sidewalks have Cracks Too

"Lark, how come you're still seein' this guy? I thought you weren't really interested?" Duff asked one Saturday afternoon after Lark turned down dinner with her because of a date with Russert.

In defense of her wishy-washy behavior, Lark listed excuses for both of them. "Because of his persistence, Duff. It's flattering that someone wants to see me so much that he can get past my indifference. He's so polite and … *unobjectionable*. I've been in a funk lately … sort of *dissatisfied* at work. He might be someone who can relate to how I feel about work because he works there too. And he's … you know … my age." *Ugh*. The more excuses she listed, the more lame they sounded.

Yet she continued her excuses, in a slightly whining and defensive internal voice. *So what if he wasn't exciting? She had been lonely before she met him. Maybe it was timing—could it be her biological clock was ticking, or could she be having a mid-life crisis? How humiliating.*

Out loud she said, "After all, Duff, who said—and I quote—'You deserve that kind of relationship. And, you know, it's time'? And then you went on to imply that I'm getting old!"

Duff looked only slightly ashamed. "Well, I did say that I'm not getting any younger either!"

Several companionable (if not romantic) months passed while Lark continued seeing Russert—weekend evenings when they strolled along the beach, in gardens, or at Fisherman's Wharf, then returned to her place to watch old movies. Dates centered on *her* wishes—ones most women would dream about.

All the while she hoped his personality would reveal itself or that they would find common ground on which a stronger relationship might take root and grow, yet neither happened.

Months passed while her efforts to get to know the *real* Russert were frustrated, and the lack of a solid connection between them continued. Their conversations always returned to trivial matters, even when she tested the waters of intimacy with him and tentatively shared what was near to her heart. He listened well, but he let her sharing fall into a still pond, the waves created by it left to dissipate against him, like a rocky shoreline.

Things didn't feel quite right.

Finally, exasperated with her ambivalence, with having to defend herself to Duff, with having to defend herself to herself, she began to turn down his invitations, wishing only to return to her former familiar and comfortable—albeit sometimes lonely—work-centered life.

Of course, this meant she now had to defend herself to *Russert*. When she tried to explain her lukewarm feelings for him, he insisted her feelings would grow over time. But she'd argued that point with herself and time had disproved it.

Hoping to avoid him and that being apart would make him see the absence of a connection between them, she stopped going to the cafeteria at work, and instead brought something from home or dashed out to grab something and hurry back to the office. She tried to slip inconspicuously down the hallways to avoid chance run-ins with him.

When she saw his number on her caller-id she didn't answer, nor did she respond to several pleading messages he left. At last, his calls stopped.

Other concerns—troubling ones—arose to take the place of thoughts of Russert. Even aside from her bored dissatisfaction at work, things weren't going well there and she couldn't quite put her finger on why.

People had begun behaving differently toward her. She'd tried blaming it on the down economy and the stress others might have over job futures, home foreclosures, or a hundred other things that went on in their private lives. But as time passed and evidence grew, she began to suspect it had to do with her personally.

Walking down the carpeted hallway toward her office one day, she passed several coworkers. Normally, she would smile and go by them with no thought as to the topic of their conversation. But as she neared them, she noticed one wave a hand agitatedly at the other.

"*Shh, shh, shh!*" Lark heard her hiss.

All three ladies' heads snapped toward her and then back toward each other, eyes widening. Their posture stiffened and they grew silent as she passed by. They were obviously talking about her and it made her uncomfortable. She wasn't used to others gossiping about her. With her air of cool professionalism and lack of emotion at work, she provoked no office drama, ruffled no feathers.

Others behaved even more rudely and took no care that she noticed them talking behind their hands to each other, eyes turned in her direction, giggling after she went by. She was astonished to find professionals behaving like schoolchildren.

And men! She noticed openly suggestive looks her way, making her blush with embarrassment. *Really?* How *dare* they?! And *why* did they? Even Kieran looked at her suspiciously, his usually smiling mouth clamped tightly shut when she encountered him at work.

Once she overheard a snippet of conversation just before she stepped into the office suite's kitchenette. "I can't believe she would do that!" And the response, "She brought it on herself—now she'll have to live with the consequences!"

An uncomfortable and stony silence fell when she entered the room. Lark's stomach felt as if a stone had settled to the bottom of it, too.

Confused and concerned, she walked straight to Edwin's office. The strange situation was affecting productivity—especially her own. How could it not? Some not only avoided her eyes, but seemed to avoid sitting beside her in meetings. Others hadn't stopped by her office to discuss their mutual projects with her as usual.

Edwin's administrative assistant said he was out of the office. Later that day, Lark stopped in again. This time his assistant said he was on the phone. Lark waited for fifteen minutes then gave up. She was usually escorted into Edwin's presence at his earliest availability. *Could he be avoiding her?* As her supervisor he was her most trusted confidant at work and had been for years past.

Weeks of rejection and turning away by others became a month. Every time she tried to confront others with their strange behavior—to find out if she had offended them in some way—she was met with their denial.

Her work came to a standstill. She began to fear the development project she was working on was being taken from under her as a colleague stepped in 'to assist.'

She had no recourse. Cracks were forming in the sidewalks of her world. Again. Her heart trembled as it had long ago. The control she'd regained after the childhood loss of her father and held over her life since then, was slipping from her grasp. Stolen from her. But this time, she didn't know why.

———————

She retreated into her own world at home. Sick with worry and unable to sleep, she soothed her heart and mind late into the night with food. Too tired and sluggish in the mornings to get up for her run, she gained pound after pound. Maybe if she layered fat around her, they wouldn't notice her—especially the 'they' who were men. If no one noticed her they wouldn't talk about her. She would be *invisible*.

To add to the rejection she'd been feeling at work, her car somehow acquired a scratch on the driver's side all the way from front to back as it sat in the parking lot at work. She received strange phone calls, both on her cell and her land line at home—heavy breathing or hang-ups late in the night.

She questioned her sanity. *Had she succumbed to paranoia?*

In desperation she reassured herself with common-sense explanations: the rejection from others and their secretive conversations had nothing to do with her; people dialed wrong numbers all the time; maybe someone didn't realize their key had dragged along the side of her car? Maybe Edwin truly was too busy to see her.

Then her thoughts made a leap—maybe her bored dissatisfaction at work had become noticeable and they were phasing her out … Edwin must be too ashamed of what was going on behind her back to see her!

She consulted a physician, who thought she might suffer from some sort of imbalance and prescribed vitamins, a tranquilizer to help her sleep, and something to help her with her social anxiety as well.

She was off-kilter, walking around in a daze, the situation was unhinging her. She couldn't remember a time like this, except of course after her father died. She had been all emotion then. She had hurried home at the end of her days then, and she had wished for invisibility then, too—like now.

Chapter 10

The Rain

Blessed understanding wasn't far away when she heard Russert's voice upon answering the phone.

"Lark? I want to see you. Please?" he said.

Holding the phone to her ear, she moved to the window and separated the curtains. She squinted through the raindrops and the fog her breath made on the glass to see him down there in his car, leaning forward and looking up at her through his front window.

She didn't want to see him. It wasn't that she wore an aged-to-gray t-shirt or that she'd rubbed off her makeup during a long day at work or that her place was littered with mail, thrown-off shoes, and take-out containers after a hectic week. No, it wasn't any of that.

She said, "Russert, I don't see—"

"I know things weren't what you wanted before," he interrupted, "but they're different now. Give me a chance to explain … *please.*"

His pleading compelled her to give in. He did sound different. After wondering what was going on in his head so often, she was interested in hearing what he had to say, especially with the emotion she heard in his voice. Something told her that this was important—as much to her as to him. She groaned inwardly, hoping that she wasn't making a mistake, and said, "Okay, come on up."

Though aware that he might make the mistake of imagining she was glad to see him, she opened the door before he reached the top of the stairs and stepped back to let him in.

He pulled her to him and kissed her as if giving in to long pent-up emotion. She pushed against his chest to free herself, and stepped backward, while he rushed to speak, his arms still reaching out to her.

He said, "I'm glad you agreed to see me. I can finally talk to you."

She watched his face twist as if he was distressed, and he shook his head as if to clear it, or as if disbelieving of the situation in which he found himself.

"Let's sit down," she said, and moved toward the sofa. She perched at one end, thinking he would sit in the chair opposite her. No such luck. He dropped down heavily right beside her. She could feel dampness emanate from his rain-wet clothes. She said, "What is it, Russert? We haven't seen each other for some time…"

He clasped and unclasped his hands while looking at them dumbly. He said, "I've been through so much lately. I've been hoping you'd get in touch with me, but you haven't. I think you must be angry with me."

"I don't understand. Why would I be angry with you?" Tension edged her words. His unusually high emotional state was causing a sympathetic response in her body. She took a calming breath.

With a slight whine he said, "You know … about my family—"

"No, I *don't* know," she said. She searched her memory for mention of his family—father, mother, siblings—earnestly trying to figure him out. Then her brows lifted and her mouth fell open as understanding glimmered through her denial.

"Lark!" Her name burst from his mouth like an expletive. "I came here to tell you it's ended." He exhaled, as if relieved. "My wife's agreed to a divorce. I may lose everything, but I'll be free and we can …" His eyes roamed over her face before he enunciated his next words, carefully, "My wife's moved out." His eyes probed hers. "And she's taken the kids. I'm probably going to lose my house. Forget that—I could even lose my job I've been such a wreck. All because of you … I mean because of *us.*"

She stared at him with wide-eyes and open-mouth. He must think her a dolt. His words had the effect of a physical blow. She shut her eyes against dizziness, and closed her mouth tight against nausea.

"Say something, Lark, I need you. You're all I have left now …" His fingers closed over her forearm.

She shook his hand off her arm and rose abruptly to turn and face him. Adrenaline added force to her words when she gasped out, "Russert, I had no idea you were married! We don't *have* a relationship anymore! And how could I have known? You never told me! *How* could you dispose of a wife and children based on what we had? *Russert?"* Her body shook as she stood over him, waiting for her words to have an effect.

His mouth opened and closed like a fish gasping for air. When he spoke his voice was quieter, halting.

"Lark, I thought my marriage was the reason you didn't want to see me anymore. I thought you'd found out. You know we have … we *had* something together." .

She determined not to feel anything. She would allow no weakness or pity to show and possibly spark hope in him. She watched his jaw tighten and his mouth straighten into a hard line. His eyes narrowed and he stood, angry now. She stepped backward.

His aggression collapsed as quickly as it arose. His shoulders slumped.

Was he going to admit defeat? She hadn't noticed earlier the dark circles under his eyes or his wrinkled, unclean shirt and unshaven jawline. A twinge of pity at last clutched at her heart.

"I … I *thought* we had something," he said. The burning intensity in his eyes was gone.

She needed a gap in which to think. "Excuse me for a moment," she said.

Breathing space was not easily found in her small condo. Around the corner from him in her kitchen, she leaned against the wall and inhaled deeply. She couldn't understand how her brief relationship with Russert had led to his belief an entire family was less important—and his assumption that she would agree! Had she given him the idea she felt more than she did? Was their rather shallow, emotionless relationship truly responsible for breaking apart a family? Or had there been trouble previously in Russert's marriage?

While pondering his mental stability, she moved to pull the cork from one of the several bottles of wine she kept on hand. With all that had gone wrong recently, she'd resorted to its numbing help, even though her mother had raised her to abstain. She reached for two glasses, but she set them down shakily and gripped the edge of the counter as the last shreds of fog in her mind burned away.

This was why her coworkers had turned their backs on her. Even in this day and age, to break up a marriage and family would be considered heinous by most—including her coworkers … and herself. This explained those long weeks of treatment as a pariah in the work community she and Russert shared. She bowed her head into her hands, remembering her confusion and sleepless nights.

Anger took hold of her. The changes that had been wrought in her life! She now avoided work whenever possible. It had become difficult, if not impossible, to get work done when others wouldn't communicate or cooperate with her. When she arrived for work she never knew what was in store—would someone block her moving forward in the parking lot, cut her off as she tried to pull into a parking space, or follow within mere feet of her car when she left for the day, making her fearful they would crash into her? All had happened more than once.

Nausea rolled through her, over those hurts and more. But ... an image of a wife and children standing alone flashed through her mind, making her concerns seem minor. Her concerns were minor in comparison, *weren't they?*

Still weighing her answer to that question, she poured wine into the long-stemmed glasses with trembling hands, sloshed the red liquid over the edge, and clanked the bottle against the delicate crystal. She returned to the living room and set Russert's glass on the table beside him. She avoided closeness and perched uneasily on a chair opposite him.

She sipped her wine and listened while he said his feelings for her had grown stronger since they'd been apart. Said that he'd missed her. Thought about her so often. He revealed the lack of feeling in his marriage for years and that his relationship with Lark had been the only one outside of it.

With as much kindness as she was able to muster, she explained her lack of feelings for him. Then she was silent. She'd said all she could to make him understand. She considered that Russert's mind and heart must have grabbed onto the lukewarm connection between them like a non-swimmer adrift in the ocean might grab onto any flimsy, floating object and cling to it for life.

He continued in a voice grown hoarse to try to persuade her that they could have a future together, and begged for another chance now he was 'free.' Met with Lark's stony expression, he at last grew silent. He looked exhausted and raised his hands into the air.

She asked him to leave then, and he did so, reluctantly.

She closed the door on him and the entire situation, lay down on her bed, and curled into a fetal position. At least now she knew she wasn't going crazy, although the situation certainly reminded her of life's unfairness. As she drifted off to sleep, the shape of a little girl faded in and out, her dark eyes filled with sorrow.

And she dreamt ...

Chapter 11

Retreat

She floated in the Pacific, atop uncommonly gentle waves

...

[and] raised her hand toward the spirit, her fingers reaching. It returned her gesture and then was gone. (excerpt from Chapter 1)

The bed shook with Lark's trembling and woke her. The sheets felt damp from sweat, tears, *or had the dream been real?* Had she been floating on water?

Dream or reality, it had reminded her how happiness can be stolen away and replaced by sadness, fear, and what seemed at times like real *danger.* Maybe she'd deluded herself all these years by believing that she controlled her world. Maybe pure evil did exist. And maybe it lurked, waiting for an opportunity to swoop down on us and gain control of our lives, despite our feeble human efforts to deny it.

Daylight can scatter the shadows of the night, leaving no darkness for anything frightful to hide within, and can reveal the things in our room to be the ordinary objects they were the day before. But the morning light edging its way into her room was dimmed by fog from last night's rain. And the hope trying to edge its way into her heart was dimmed likewise by foreboding that clung like black claws to the edges of her consciousness.

She gripped the edge of her covers with cold fingertips. *What is more real—the dark shadows and visions of the night, or the light—and possibly denial—that gets us through the day?*

The phone rang three times. The person on the other end hung up without leaving a message. It rang again three times, and then clicked over to the answering machine, *'Please leave a message after the tone.'*

"Lark, I know you're there. If you don't pick up, I'm coming over. And I have my key!" Silence. Click.

There was the sound of quick, light footsteps on the outside stairs. The door knob rattled as someone struggled with the unfamiliar lock. They entered quietly, the rustle of their full skirt made the only sound in the room.

Lark lay face-down on the sofa, left arm hanging off the side, mouth open, eyes staring into space. Duff placed her hand on Lark's back. It rose and fell with her breath. Duff huffed and said, "Lark, you've scared me half to death! *What* are you doing?"

Lark blinked her eyes. She hadn't seen Duff for days, she wasn't sure how many. Her friend had called and left messages, but Lark had not responded. She had retreated from the outside world as completely as possible—her only human contact the grocery delivery guy. She had known Duff would eventually intrude upon her self-imposed isolation.

Ashamedly, Lark touched her fingers to her eyes and felt their puffiness, likely they were bloodshot too. Sensing tenderness in her fingertips, she pulled them away from her face and examined them. Her nails were chewed down to the quick. She glanced surreptitiously toward the empty wine bottles and mood-altering medications on the table beside the sofa, reached toward them, but cringed—it was too late to hide them, or her dishevelment, from Duff.

Her concerned friend sat down beside her on the sofa. Her wordless sympathy teased away the small amount of control Lark had over her emotions, like a parent might gently tease a child's fingers away from a coveted object held in the hand. Lark's shame at being found in such a pitiable state eased. Maybe she wasn't so alone after all. She closed her eyes in a silent prayer of thankfulness for Duff. *Maybe every single person on this earth didn't hate her.*

Tears seeped from her eyes and made their way to her chin. From her gut sobs rose and racked upward through her chest. Duff edged closer and wrapped her arms around her shoulders. Her friend stayed silent, allowing her to weep and wash away the heavy burden she'd been carrying alone.

When her weeping subsided to sniffles, her body, drained of energy, was left leaning against Duff's side. Embarrassed, she grabbed Duff's sleeve and used it to wipe her tears. She rubbed at her face where loose threads from the quirky, up-cycled garment tickled her, and they laughed, restoring the light-hearted climate of their friendship.

As Duff reached for a tissue and handed it to Lark, her mouth twisted as if she was uncertain whether laughter was appropriate. She said, "Lark, dear, I don't know what's wrong, but I'm sorry for whatever it is. Your car hasn't moved for days. You haven't answered the phone. I've been so worried. Can you tell me what's going on?"

Lark took a ragged breath and closed her eyes again. *Could* she explain?

"Ah," she sighed, "it … it's terrible really." She didn't want to lose the lightheartedness they'd achieved and struggled to control her trembling voice.

Duff must have seen her struggle because she spoke, and gave Lark more time, saying, "I'm relieved to know you're safe, here at home. But it's unlike you to be so *dramatic*. You're usually so … *unemotional*. Here I find you with your hair sticking out all over, no makeup on, tissues and all sorts of bottles everywhere. It's a mess!" Duff was a woman who spoke the truth. Nevertheless she smiled mischievously to ease her criticism.

Lark sat up straighter and gasped, "Duff, I've lost my job." She wrapped her arms around her stomach to ease the pain caused by saying the words out loud.

Any hint of a smile left Duff's face. "Whaaaat?!" she said, and scooted toward Lark to look into her face. *"When* did you lose your job?"

"Last Friday."

"Why haven't you told me?! Never mind …" She shook her head and waved her hand. *"Why* did you lose your job, dear?"

"Oh, it's a long story! And I think it's more than one thing." Lark leaned over, still clutching her stomach, as she gathered words to explain.

Duff encouraged her. "Well, what do you *think* is the main reason you lost your job, Larky?" And she listened   just listened, like the best kind of friend would, as Lark told her all that happened.

Chapter 12

Lark Finds Words

On the previous Friday afternoon, Lark was surprised when Edwin appeared in her doorway. She hadn't talked with him one-on-one for weeks … though she'd certainly tried.

"Lark, I need to talk to you. Will you come down please?"

"Sure, Edwin." She reached to close her laptop and bring it along, her heart pounding.

"You won't need that," Edwin said about her laptop. She followed him down the hallway at a brisk pace and into his corner office. He turned his head to the side and said, "Close the door behind you, Lark, and have a seat." His leather chair creaked when he sat down heavily.

She perched on the edge of a chair across the desk from him and studied his profile while she respectfully, but anxiously, waited. He sighed, rested his head against the back of his chair, and seemed in no hurry to talk. His face looked haggard and older than on the last occasion when she'd sat in this chair. Though he wasn't in the corner office when she was just out of school and starting out, he'd been her mentor—just as she was Kieran's now. She and Edwin shared a mutual trust—at least they had in the past. She looked him straight in the eye when he finally spoke.

"Lark, you know the company's bottom line has taken a hit with the downturn in the economy."

She nodded, anxious to show she was listening—which she would do till he was finished—and then they could discuss *her* concerns.

He continued, "You've probably heard the rumors it might come to downsizing." He looked at her thoughtfully and pursed his lips. "No, perhaps you haven't heard. Well, I'm afraid that's the case. We've gotten word we have to reduce our software development workforce by twenty percent."

Mentally, she ran down a list of the employees in their group, thinking she might easily predict a few who would fall within that percentage. She felt a twinge of guilt, but was curious whether he would ask her to take on more work to make up for the loss of manpower. She started to volunteer, saying, "I'll do whatever—"

"No, wait," he said, holding his palm toward her to stop her words. "There's no easy way to say this, Lark ... I'm afraid ..." he sighed and shook his head as though beaten, his shoulders slumping. "Well, I'm sorry, but we have to let you go."

Dumbly she watched him push a pink piece of paper across the desktop toward her. He clasped his hands together and laid them atop the desk.

"Lark, your performance has slipped in the past six months or so. You've stayed away from work ... often. You've pushed your project timelines back not once, but three times." He tapped his desk with his hands for emphasis. "Others have noticed. Despite how *I* feel, despite your long history here, you're one of the ones they've chosen, Lark." He ran his hands over his face and sighed, his expression showed genuine sorrow, even despair.

She had no doubt he had fought for her. Head bowed, she pulled the pink paper toward her and held it between her trembling fingers. *How strange that they used such a gentle color for terminating employment.*

"Edwin, could this also have to do with ... Russert?" *Did he know?*

Edwin drew in his breath sharply, then pushed himself out of his chair and walked around his desk to lean against its edge, right beside her. He said, "Lark, that was a bad situation. And that kind of thing doesn't sit well—not with anyone who has a family."

"But Edwin ... I didn't know!" she protested.

"Didn't know?"

"I didn't know he was *married!* Not until very recently." Her voice was rising, threatening tears. She took a calming breath before she continued. "What I'm trying to say, Edwin, is that I didn't intentionally have a relationship with a married man. And, if you knew he was married, why didn't you tell me? I've tried to see you for weeks now! Have you been avoiding me?"

"I didn't feel it was my place to inform you of that, Lark. You're an intelligent adult. I thought being so, you would know what you were getting yourself into. Maybe I have avoided you to some extent—I've been uncomfortable with the knowledge."

"But I didn't *know* he was married, Edwin. I didn't *know.* I would've thought you knew me better than that, Edwin." She covered her face with her hands, hurt he hadn't given her the benefit of the doubt, hadn't come to her before this. Still, she wouldn't let herself give in to tears, not here. She clenched her jaw, took her hands away from her face, blinked away the water in her eyes, and straightened her posture.

"Yes, I can see now you might not have known, Lark. I've never delved into your personal life. I don't know what you're like away from here. But I should've realized—you're not in the loop as far as office gossip goes, are you? You don't talk about people, do you? That's part of why people around here never seek you out to go to happy hour—you're not like them, are you Lark?"

"No," she replied softly.

"Maybe you're right and I should have known. I am sorry, Lark."

When Lark finished telling of that Friday afternoon, Duff shook her head.

"Of all people, Lark! This shouldn't have happened to you."

"I don't know, Duff. I haven't been a very good employee for a while now."

"I know you've gone through some tough times lately. I mean, we have talked about it, but it seems to me, they should make some allowances after you've worked for them all these years."

"I suppose loyalty between a company and its employees isn't what it used to be—either way."

Duff nodded her head in reluctant agreement. "So what do you think is the *main* reason you lost your job?" she asked.

"Like I said, they needed to downsize, I *have* missed work, and was distracted while there, but I'm afraid the worst part was … the being talked about."

"The Russert affair. *Oh,*" Duff groaned, "sorry—no pun intended. But that only happened, what—weeks ago?"

"Well, it ended only weeks ago. But Duff, it's gone on for all the months I saw Russert, because people saw us going out, remember? Talked about us, maybe? That's why I was getting such a bad feeling at work. I *do* wonder if it's the main reason instead of the need to downsize. I'll always wonder. But, here's the thing …" Lark had to stop as her voice shook with emotion and she looked down at her hands, "I'm not sure I can get a job anywhere else here." She stood up to pace agitatedly, and continued. "My working community is pretty tight-knit. I mean people often switch back and forth from one job to another, work contracts are shared between companies, there is a network of relationships, and I have been getting the feeling the talk about me and Russert spread pretty far. And there is the internet, social networks … gossip spreads far and wide these days, whether it's true or false, fair or not. I'm not sure anyone will hire me!"

"But Lark, you didn't know he was married. *You* didn't seek *him* out!"

"I know, Duff, but people make assumptions. Sadly, it seems they assume the worst. It makes for more interesting conversation, and that's the way of the world these days, isn't it? All you have to do is turn on the television and it's all animosity and mean-spiritedness!" Her voice broke again.

Yes, she'd been naïve about her relationship with Russert. Maybe she should've questioned his marital status at the beginning. Now she'd had time to think about it, it would explain some things—the out-of the-way places; the way his eyes roamed crowds as if looking for someone he knew; the way he didn't dress to impress her, but as if he was going to the auto parts store.

But she'd been true to her trusting nature. She wondered if all of this would change how she thought of others, how she trusted them—or not—from now on.

Chapter 13

Broken

Though it temporarily eased her burden, Duff's visit couldn't fix Lark's problems. Even her efforts to entice Lark out to the flea markets hadn't worked. She'd given up eventually. In her last phone message Duff said, her voice discouraged and sad, "I'm here whenever you need me, Lark."

For over a month Lark wouldn't leave her nest. She listened to message after message left by others on her answering machine, too—Edwin, her mother, and Wren. Once in a while, she would answer and tell them everything was fine so they would leave her alone, and then collapse onto the sofa again, knowing everything wasn't. In time, all calls except her mother's stopped. Thankfully, Russert seemed to know to leave her alone at last.

She had stayed right where Duff left her. She didn't bother to move to her bedroom at night. Her living space only reached from the sofa to the kitchen or bathroom when necessity demanded. Much of the time she stayed in a food- and chemical-induced stupor—her mind and senses dulled to nearly every sensation. Around the sofa remained a litter of wine and medication bottles and balled-up tissues.

When numbness began to wear off, obsessive thoughts circled round and round in her mind—*I have no job. My reputation is ruined. I don't have any friends. Well maybe a few, but not many. I don't have a husband to take care of me. I'll never have children. Why can't I just disappear? Why work so hard for so long—what was it all for? How could this happen? What did I do wrong?*

Then, she would pour another glass of wine or pop another capsule into her mouth and sink below the surface again, where her thoughts

44

couldn't reach her. Blessedly, a still-present sliver of self-preservation kept her from foolishly taking more than the doctor prescribed or from concocting a lethal combination.

One afternoon, out of necessity she pulled herself off the sofa, her floppy-socked feet dragging. As she passed the doorway of her bedroom, a flash of color caught the corner of her eye. She stopped, heart fluttering, and turned. It took her a moment to focus her bleary eyes on the object beside her bed where she'd leaned it against the wall on a better day.

As she moved closer, her eyes scanned rapidly over its surface, drawn again by the vivid colors; the texture of the thickly layered paint; the dark eyes fringed with lashes, blue-shadowed and tense; the pinkish blue fair skin; red lips; pointy nose; and flushed cheeks; the innocence of the blue flowers on her white sweater; and finally the black, chin-length hair, wind-blown and ragged. Sympathy for the frightened-looking little girl swelled inside Lark.

Overpowered by all that was out of her control—by her longings and dissatisfaction with her life—she sank to her knees and gave in to emotion. Something snapped inside … something had broken … *what was it?*

She wept until exhausted and fell asleep, right there on the floor.

Chapter 14
A New Path

When Lark woke, it was dark outside.

Feeling a need to comfort that broken place, she made her way to the kitchen and placed her teapot under the tap. Water splashed into the metal pot with a clear ringing sound. The layer of cotton that medication created between her mind and the sounds the world made was gone. She pulled a bag of sleep-encouraging tea from its box while waiting for the pot to whistle. The tea bag was so silken in her fingers, the loose tea leaves so beautiful. There were green grass-shaped pieces, dried crumbles of brown leaves, even golden bits of dried fruit. Holding the tea bag to her nose, she breathed in the aroma of a summer day frozen in time. Scent was heavenly.

Deep darkness was still visible through the opaque bathroom curtain. There was still time for restful, dreamless sleep before morning.

She sipped her cup of tea while perched on the side of the tub and watched steam rise from the hot water flowing from the tap. She poured in drops of lavender oil and sprinkled therapeutic herbs over the surface. She let her clothes fall to the floor, stepped in, and sank gratefully down into the water. The muscles from her neck to her toes let go of their tension and soreness.

Although a higher, stronger part of her had control now, as thoughts will do, hers stubbornly tried to fall back into the grooves they'd worn so well in her mind these last weeks. She determinedly pulled them back out, inhaled, released her breath slowly, and tried not to think at all. Again, willful thoughts slipped in to fill her with hopelessness. Yet again, she pulled them back.

The effort reminded her of an old suitcase record player she'd had as a child. Red and white with a latch on the front, it played 45s. Sometimes its needle would get stuck in a scratch on a record and repeat the same song snippet over and over. She would thump the needle arm with a finger so the needle would hop out and ride smoothly over the surface again.

Memories of all the bad things that had happened recently seemed like scratches on the record of her life. She would use the help of something outside her thoughts, outside her mind, to 'thump' the needle out of those grooves, thump her mind away from repeating to itself events of the past, trying to get her stuck again. What was past was past. There was a future. Maybe a different kind of future.

She was *sick* of feeling sick. *Tired* of feeling tired. Worst of all, she'd allowed it to happen … she'd seen herself sinking and hadn't stopped her descent. She had fed herself with bad food, too much medication, too much alcohol, had wallowed in lack of movement and grubbiness for weeks.

Stop! Her body had tensed again. She lay back, took a deep breath and just let go. She just *let go*.

Her body relaxed.

When the water had cooled, she slipped into a long nightgown, covered her bed with fresh sheets, and slid between them with a contented sigh. She didn't turn on the television and welcomed the silence instead. She reached for the dictionary she kept beside her bed for help when reading, and turned to the V's. Her finger followed the columns, down, up, over: '*vic-tim—someone destroyed, sacrificed.*' She frowned, and her finger drifted of its own will down the column and stopped, '*vic-tor—a winner or conqueror.*' A dichotomy of words, of paths, and of choices.

She closed the book, yawning. The torn, broken place inside her felt warm and soothed. Resting her head on her pillow, she fell easily into the sleep of the weary, but peace-filled.

When she woke she noticed that her thoughts weren't of her troubles. Instead, she felt a rush of gladness when she saw the sunshine striking the wall of her bedroom. This was a sign it would be a glorious California day—the best kind, with a sky so blue and clear it could make a heart ache … with gladness, this time.

She sat up in bed, placed one foot on the floor, followed by the other, ready today to follow a new path. A tree damaged by a twister could go on living—even broken could form new growth.

She carried a strong cup of coffee to the seat in her bay window with its lofty and private, three-sided view of the city. There, she pulled the curtains all the way back, propped pillows up for her back, and curled her legs under her.

Below people rushed to their cars or to public transit throughout the bustling city. Unlike them, she had nowhere to go today. She allowed herself to feel glad about that, rather than regretful.

Her gaze stopped on the horizon to the west, where lie the Pacific. Although she couldn't see the water, she sensed its presence. When the wind blew just right, it brought with it the ocean's salty air and she imagined she could hear waves crashing. Anytime she stood at its edge, gentle waves lapping at her feet, or lie floating in its vastness given over to its power, she felt calm. She closed her eyes now, imagining the warmth of the sun, the grittiness of sand under her feet, the soothing rhythm of the waves. That its tides rose and fell predictably with the moon's phases was reassuring to her. Its rhythms had been constant since an awe-inspiring hand set them in motion long ago.

So unlike a short, chaotic human life—jerked around and changed by events. She groaned and leaned forward agitatedly.

Yet, that awe-inspiring hand had also created forces that brought change to nature, as well as to a human life—to challenge and then clear away the detritus, leaving behind a stronger form. All of nature was subject to winds, storms, and quakes—a painful reality. Didn't every human life have its good times and its bad times—its crests and troughs, like the ocean; its waxing and waning, like the moon?

She closed her eyes and imagined herself floating in the Pacific. She saw a huge wave headed for her, and knew that if she fought to control it, fought with fear against drowning, she would sink. But if she relaxed, if she sought peace, she would float instead, and would survive—*if* she *released control to its power.*

Her eyes snapped open. She had to relinquish control.

She had a choice between two alternatives—to despair of controlling the uncontrollable, and drown—what she'd been doing of late, by escaping through chemical aids and retreating into her cocoon—or she could seek peace. And that meant accepting what had happened to her, and moving on.

How she would move on?

She had lived frugally for the last two decades, as much as one could in this city. She had denied herself, and now had the means to survive even if she didn't bring anything in for a while—especially if she lived in a place with a lower cost of living. And she knew of one place like that—back home, of course.

Home? It hadn't been that to her for a long time. Serious thoughts of moving back there hadn't occurred to her since she'd moved to sunny, exciting California. Low cost was the only thing that might draw her there—except the only people (save Duff) who would love her no matter what, even when she felt the rest of the world turned against her.

If she had floated, she was now sinking below the surface with that thought. *Relax and ride the waves.* She floated again and lost herself to time …

And her next step became clear. Her eyes popped open in astonishment. It had been so easy.

She moved about with purpose. Threw away empty bottles, take-out boxes, and tissues. Cleaned everything to a fare-thee-well as her Mama used to say. All that remained was her closet. If anything illustrated the diverging paths of her life, it was the contrast between its two sides: the left, where she kept her drab business suits, ordered by workday; and the cluttered right side, where she kept her collection of vintage dresses, whimsical shoes, bags of every shape and size, and colorful costume jewelry—the things she loved.

Without pausing to ponder or regret, she tossed all the business clothing onto the bed in a pile to take to a donation center for women who could use it to find a needed job.

She felt tired, but everything looked different now.

———

At the end of the day, her last step along that new path was on her way to the phone beside her bed. She dialed, and was amazed she remembered the number after not calling it for so long. She waited for an answer, her eyes glued to the girl's portrait on the bedside table where it leaned against the wall.

"Lark! Honey, how are you? I've been worried about you. You haven't called, or answered my emails sometimes … have you been sick?"

"I know, Mama. I'm sorry. And no, I'm not sick …" *At least, not anymore.*

"Well, what is it?" Panic edged its way into Pearline's voice.

"No, no, it's okay." Lark paused thoughtfully. "Everything is just fine. I wondered whether—are you sitting down?" She laughed and swallowed before she said, "Can I come for a visit? A rather long visit?"

Chapter 15

Homemade Quilts and Breakfasts

Plans for her trip had been made quickly. Now here she lay, in the high four-poster bed she'd slept in growing up that made the ceiling seem so near, covered by a quilt stitched by the hands of a long-gone ancestor. From the kitchen wafted the aroma of sausage, biscuits, and strong coffee. She hoped her mother had made peppery country gravy too. She shuffled sleepily from the bedroom and straight to the coffee pot.

"Good morning, honey. Sit down and have some breakfast," Pearline said, and patted Lark's forearm with her time-worn hand—knobby from arthritis and years of fingering and pinning fabric as a seamstress. She poured Lark a glass of juice and set it beside an empty plate.

Lark bumped into the metal table when she sat down, and it protested with a metallic, squeaky bounce. Juice splashed over the rim of her glass onto the imitation wood grained tabletop. The table was so not-feng-shui, but comforting in its familiarity.

Pearline still lived in the modest rancher Lark had grown up in—low-ceilinged, with the same knotty pine paneling on the walls and the same linoleum on the floor. *Some* things didn't change, thank goodness.

Along with the sausage and biscuits Lark expected, there were scrambled eggs, and cantaloupe and tomatoes from the garden. Pearline's biscuits—the like of which Lark had never found anywhere else—were slightly dry and held their texture under a smothering of the gravy she hoped for. Comforted that her mother remembered her favorite breakfast, she savored every bite, one foot curled up in her chair, one swinging above the floor, while Pearline sat beside her drinking coffee.

Lark patted her mouth with her napkin and sighed. She understood Pearline's curiosity and her tendency to worry. She'd kept her in suspense long enough. "Mama, I know you're wondering why I wanted to come here," she said.

"Well, I'm tryin' not to wonder too much and to just enjoy you bein' here, Lark." Pearline's uncertain smile betrayed her worry.

Lark smiled back—she hoped reassuringly—but then she had to tell her, "I'm afraid I don't have a job anymore."

"I'm sure sorry about that!" Pearline looked into her eyes, tilting her head slightly. "But that's not all, is it? Somethin' tells me, you didn't come here just because you're in between jobs, Lark. There's more isn't there?"

Pearline had the heightened sensitivity about her children many mothers have. Lark always found it uncanny. Whether she or Wren had been bullied by another child at school or had forgotten to take her lunch one day or hadn't done her homework, Pearline always knew.

"So much has changed out there. I must be getting bored with California. Maybe I'm having a mid-life crisis." Lark could see her efforts to reassure her mother were failing by Pearline's doubtful gaze, and by her lips, tightly clamped together—always a sign that she was losing patience. So Lark gave up and told her—about the relationship with Russert and its end, how she felt it was partly to blame for the loss of her job, and about the troubling dissatisfaction she'd felt with her life there before she'd even met him.

"So Mama," she said at last, "I don't know what I'm going to do now."

As if unfazed by everything Lark told her, Pearline said, "Well, you don't have to know what's next, Lark. Maybe you should just rest for a while. I'd love to have you here with me, you know."

Of course, that possibility had entered Lark's mind already. "I'll think about it," she said.

"Good," Pearline said, placing her palms on the table to push herself up out of the chair. "Now I'm going to get ready to go to the beauty parlor with Wren. I need my roots touched up. Do you want to come?"

"No thanks, not this time," Lark said.

Pearline didn't pressure Lark to go and left to get ready, while Wren took her place at the table and gave the sisters a chance to catch up on their separate lives.

"Not much seems to have changed here at home, Wren. How've you been?" She eyed Wren while waiting for an answer. Her sister had a wan sort of beauty—fair skin and a delicately boned face, framed by the paleness of prematurely graying hair. Wren still lived here, because it was natural for her to do so—she and Pearline had always been close, and Wren, who had never been lucky in love, or perhaps had never found the right man, was still single.

Wren said, "I'm pretty much the same as always ... good really."

Reticent Wren. "How is Mama enjoying retirement?" Lark asked.

"Oh, she's comfortable enough with her pension and savings, and I've gotten a raise, too. Even though the factory had changed to a production line, the work was taking a toll on her. It was time for her to retire."

"Remember just after Daddy died ... when she had to look for work?"

Wren smiled and continued where Lark left off, "And she found that secretarial job, but got fired when she forgot to tell her boss about a phone call? And then, that job as a cook, when she was too slow and couldn't keep up with the orders?" Wren covered her mouth with her hand to quiet her laughter.

Their laughter was affectionate though, rather than scornful. They grew quiet, remembering. At the time, just after their father's death, there hadn't been so much merriment—only discouragement when Pearline lost those jobs. Their family had needed the income, even the girls, young as they were, understood that. Pearline was barely able to scrape by without Joe's modest but dependable earnings.

While the girls caught up in the kitchen, Pearline puttered about her bedroom with a tired expression on her face and worried about Lark. *Things never changed.*

Despite having a life that ran smoothly now that her girls were raised and stood on their own two feet, she was a woman who knew from her many friendships, and from living in a small town, that challenges would never cease—there would always be mountains to climb for those who walked the earth.

But Pearline was a generally positive person, who had climbed her own mountains and stood at the top victorious. She sighed and pulled her shoulders back, knowing in her heart that Lark would come through. She headed to her closet to find something to wear to town. In her sixties, she wouldn't be considered elderly by most in this day and age. But like her hands, her posture showed the effects of years bent over a sewing machine.

She pulled out some of her stretchy knit pants, a matching top, and a longish vest to hide her hips. If it weren't for Wren keeping her stylish, she would probably look like an old lady. She glanced one last time in the mirror to be sure she hadn't overdone her makeup—which would make her look like a floozy—and picked up her pocketbook. Her generous hips were visible despite the long vest that she hoped would hide them, and they swayed from side to side as she left the room.

Lark and Wren's chatter in the kitchen reminded her of the closeness they'd shared as children. She smiled to see them with their heads together at the table. Wren was always so interested in Lark's California life. Pearline suspected she envied Lark a little, as sisters will do. As she entered the kitchen, she said, "You sound like two little birds chirpin' in here."

"Mama, we've been talking about how you had to find a job after Daddy died," Lark said.

Pearline poured the remaining coffee from the pot into her cup. "Oh yes, I remember." She nodded her head toward the tabletop. "Right there ... bills piled up, week after week. An' I couldn't pay them. Even our survivor checks let me do away with only a couple of them. I was *so* worried." She leaned against the counter and sipped her coffee. Right after Joe died she'd grown more and more discouraged with every week that passed while the refrigerator and cupboards grew emptier.

She could still see her girls' small faces, their spoons hovering in the air above their bowls, while they absentmindedly chewed their cereal. Their big, dark eyes had watched her so carefully. She could just see them peeking over the edges of their bowls when they held the rims to their lips and drained the last drops of milk. All while she looked through that pile of envelopes and grew more and more discouraged.

But then had come the Sunday morning when she circled an ad for a seamstress in the newspaper, and hope had tiptoed into her heart. She knew how to sew ... she had stitched all her girls' clothes on her own sewing machine. She'd gotten that much-needed job, and it stuck—thank the Lord. She was finally able to buy the things they needed, with a little left over even.

Her girls' dark eyes looked at her expectantly now, just like they'd done back then—time to leave the past in the past. She said, "Lark, we always go out to eat after getting our hair and nails done. But there's some sandwich things in the refrigerator, so help yourself. I'll make meatloaf tomorrow night so you'll have a good, home-cooked meal then."

"I'll be fine, Mama. I'm just going to rest, you know." Lark smiled, reminding her mother of the conversation they'd had earlier.

With the two of them gone and the house quiet, Lark pulled out her laptop for company. Following up on the idea that began forming in her mind before she left California, and that she intended to keep to herself for the time being, she searched the internet for property listings and a place where she could nurture the creative side of herself that had been neglected for so long. She scrolled down page after page. The homes she found looked as if they would house a family—a father, mother, two children, and two pets, with a swing set in the backyard. She had none of those things. Ranch homes like this one had been what they were for too long and seemed too set in their ways.

Disappointed with her findings, she eliminated some of the restrictions she had placed on her search and explored other types of properties, opening her mind to surrounding areas outside the little town she had been born in, even scanning the announcements for auctions. Her eyes stopped when she saw the words, 'waterfront property consisting of a 1970s-era house with acreage and smaller structures included.'

Memories of long-ago Sunday drives with her family entered her mind—when she sat in the backseat of the Fairlane with the wind blowing through her hair, a happy smile on her face. Her father's protective presence still with them. Wading in creeks.

She emailed the auctioneer to get all the details about the property. The auction would be held in October.

The idea of making such a huge change in her life after all she'd been through lately made her feel weak as a kitten.

Chapter 16

Pearline, at the Beauty Parlor

Pearline's favorite place in town was the beauty parlor that belonged to her friend, Betty. She felt kindly toward the regulars, who she counted among her friends.

She loved the smell of the place—nail polish, perm solution, and shampoo. She loved the rickety old town house, in Betty's family since the 1800s, with wooden floors that creaked with every footstep. She probably should've chosen hair dressing as her occupation instead of sewing, because she loved that place so much.

She and her tidy little Wren settled into their usual chairs—Pearline in Betty's chair in front of the mirror that stopped at her waist thankfully, so she wasn't reminded of how large her lower half was, and Wren across the small table from Florence who did her nails every week.

Pearline and Betty caught up on the week's news—Betty's husband had to visit the doctor earlier in the week for vertigo, and Betty was worried that the doctor hadn't been able to figure out the cause yet. They grew quiet, each thinking about their own doings during the week, but returned to the present when the intermingled conversations around them intruded on their thoughts—"And she said …," and, "Weeelll, that's a shame!" and, "I told him …!"

Pearline and Betty decided they'd better pay attention or they would miss something! There were two other hairdressers, another nail lady besides Florence, and Cricket who shampooed hair, not to mention several other ladies in various stages of perms, colorings, and haircuts. Adding to the ladies' chatter were hairdryers buzzing, the front door beeping, the phone ringing, and water spraying at the sink where Cricket rinsed out a perm. A person had to really pay attention to hear the news!

Betty's comb paused in midair and she tilted her head so that her ear could pick out the ladies' words, while Pearline kept her eyes glued to Betty's face to get her reaction … but it was a false alarm. The ladies behind them had settled down and had come to their senses, their ruffled feathers smoothed back down. Now, they were smiling and nodding, having moved on to a gentler subject.

Betty grabbed some foils in one hand to hold between her fingers, as she held up a section of Pearline's reddish toned hair with the other hand. Her good humor seemed to be leaving—maybe she was worried about her husband's vertigo or felt tired from standing. That was one thing Pearline wasn't sure she could do—stand on her feet all day. Her ankles would swell and she bet her arms would ache too. She looked forward to this time with Betty—time she'd spent with her every week for years now. Not wanting to lose the opportunity for a good chat, Pearline decided to tell of her own good news, but she sure had to speak loud over the whir and buzz of that old hood hair dryer!

"The *best* part of my week, Betty, is that Lark came for a visit and is at my house right now!"

"*Noooo*—but that's wonderful, Pearline! How is she?" Betty asked. She'd listened to Pearline's worries in past weeks about Lark not calling or emailing.

Pearline trusted Betty, so she told her of the troubles Lark had been going through.

"Things haven't gone well for her out in California lately." With all the indignation a mother feels about a child of her own done wrong by the world, she went on, "Why, Lark's lost her job because she had a relationship with a married man, and she just doesn't know what to do now!"

And then, Pearline realized after she completed her sentence and looked up at Betty's face in the mirror to get her reaction, expecting a sympathetic "tsk, tsk" or "tut, tut," that instead, Betty's mouth hung open, her eyes glued to Pearline's. They were right in the middle of one of those odd silences that fall in a beauty parlor when it happens that everything is turned off at once and takes whoever is immersed in conversation by surprise. Unnoticed by she and Betty—who had been having what they thought was a relatively private chat—all the dryers had switched off, chatter had stopped, the perm was no longer being rinsed, and now Pearline's last words hung in the air, still echoing in everyone's ears, "LARK's LOST HER JOB … HAD A RELATIONSHIP WITH A MARRIED MAN …"

Pearline stood up and turned, the plastic cape rustling around her legs as she faced the roomful of ladies, all looking at her open-mouthed, suspended in time.

"Now, y'all have to realize Lark didn't *know* that man was married!"

"Of course, Pearline."

"Mmmm-hmmm."

"We know, we know, Pearline."

But Pearline had a sick feeling in her stomach as she turned back to Betty's chair. The ladies' faces looked a little too smug, their mouths a little too drooly, and in their eyes glittered something a little too near delight, rather than sympathy. She sat back down, a frown on her face, and harrumphed. Mad at herself and at everyone else now too.

Betty pretended as if nothing had happened and changed the subject.

As Pearline lay in bed that night, worrying about what had happened that day at the beauty parlor, she had a bad feeling that telling of Lark's troubles might come back to haunt her. Why did she even have to tell anyone about what had happened to Lark?! It wasn't their business. She knew that wasn't the way to be! She'd just meant to lean on Betty's sympathetic ear to ease her own worried heart a little. Was that so bad? She groaned and restlessly turned on her side.

"Oooooh, Lordy!"

Yes, Pearline meant well, always. She had a good heart. But by the time she lay in bed bemoaning the events of the day, the town's network, called the grapevine in the past, had been in action for hours—phone lines busy, emails darting back and forth, posts made on blogs and social networks. News of Lark's 'transgression,' as it was interpreted, her 'relationship with a married man,' and the resulting loss of her job—news that intentionally left out Pearline's last assertion that Lark didn't know the man was married, because that would've taken all the steam out of the whole thing—was known by most in town, no matter whether they even knew Pearline, or Lark.

To give credit where it is due, some kind words were said that night, and some carried the benefit of the doubt—the realization that the whole story might not be known.

But there were words spoken by the mouths of those in whose lives hurt dwelt and colored their actions, who did know Lark and were jealous of her success out there in California or who took the news and cast upon Lark their own stories—the betrayals and infidelities they had experienced in their own marriages, or their parents', their own children's, their sister's, brother's, friend's, neighbor's. And their words were cruel, their judgment of Lark harsh, and their subsequent actions … well, we'll let One who is wiser be the judge.

The day after Pearline 'had her roots touched up,' Lark puttered in her old bedroom in the late afternoon. It looked as though she would be staying for a while, so she rearranged the furniture to suit herself. She placed an old photograph on the bedside table of their family, taken while Joe was still with them. The savory aroma of meatloaf and rolls pulled her attention away.

Comforting occurrences that she'd taken for granted as a child, stopped Lark in her tracks with their meaningfulness now. Her mother's cooking reminded her how nice it was to be cared for in that simple way. Yes, Duff cared for her out in California, but this struck her to the core—this was mother-care—there was nothing else like it, and healing no matter the child's age.

"Come on into the kitchen, Lark! Supper's ready!" Pearline called out.

She minded her mother and headed for the kitchen, bracing herself for a talkative evening on her way. Pearline and Wren seemed to want to know every detail of her life!

Thankfully, though, talk centered on the others' lives that evening.

Wren spoke of her work at the local library. Always the bookish type, she was well-suited for a librarian's quiet job. Still, as in all jobs, there were some difficulties. Wren talked of her concern about the lending of physical books, evermore threatened by digital ones. Lark admired Wren's positive attitude when she said these were challenges and not defeats, and even ventured that the library might become a special place—maybe the only place—where people could hold and borrow books made of paper pages bound between two covers. She didn't intend to stop trying to discover ways for the library to remain useful. It was a place beloved to the family, where they had visited often during the girls' growing up years.

"Mama, I don't know when I last had fried okra—it's so good!" Lark said. It was one of Pearline's specialties and a childhood favorite of Lark's.

The okra had been harvested from Pearline's garden at the peak of its goodness.

Pearline's eyes remained on her plate. She looked a little tired when she answered distractedly, "I'm glad you like it, dear."

"You haven't overdone it in the garden, have you?" asked Lark.

"Oh … no, I'm fine."

"How was Betty yesterday? Did you have a nice visit at the beauty parlor?" Lark asked.

A frown shadowed Pearline's face, and she distractedly responded, "Oh, yes. I always enjoy talking to Betty …"

Dissatisfied with her mother's response, Lark mentioned something that might perk her up. "If it's okay with y'all, I think I'll stay a while, at least a few weeks into October." *Y'all?*—it seemed fragments of Southern dialect she'd dropped to fit in out west had already worked their way back into her conversation!

Her news had the desired effect on Pearline. "Lark, that'd be wonderful!" she said. And Wren smiled her approval of the idea.

"Would it be okay if I invite Duff here to stay with us for the second weekend in October? She was the only family I had in California. She'll bring *lots* of fun with her!"

They caught Lark's enthusiasm about a visit from Duff and talked over where to have her sleep, deciding she would use Lark's single bed, while Lark moved in and shared her mother's double bed for a few days.

They spent the rest of the evening nibbling homemade cookies and watching a romantic movie. The images on the screen captivated Lark, especially the emotions playing on the man's face as he discovered he was in love. As the credits began to roll, her mother's voice brought Lark back to reality and she reluctantly pulled herself away from the world to which she had escaped.

"It's bedtime girls!" Pearline said.

They groaned, but dutifully minded their mother and left to brush their teeth and put on their pajamas. It was as if the clock had been turned back in time.

———————

As Lark lay waiting for sleep, her mother came into her room and sat on the edge of the bed.

"Mama, I feel guilty for not visiting for such a long time, and now for asking you to let me stay for a while."

"Honey-y-y, don't you waste your time on that. Bein' here when you need us is what family is for in my mind. I raised you and then I set you free. You grew up and left the nest! That's what children are meant to do. It lets them be what God made them to be, and to fulfill His purpose for them.

"Of course, Wren and I missed you. But I guess that held a hidden blessin' too. You learned independence, and to stand on your own two feet. But when a child needs help, really needs it, no matter how old they are ... well, that's what family is for." Her voice caught in her throat and she shook her head. "*I love you Lark*, just like I did when you were little." Pearline rose, leaned over Lark, and kissed her forehead tenderly.

The torn and broken place inside Lark glowed warmly.

Chapter 17

Gardens, Mahjongg, and Blue Eyes

Lark and Pearline gazed along the bedraggled garden rows and talked about planting cool-weather greens.

"I think we'll wait till next week to plant them. Maybe it'll be less humid then." Pearline took off her gloves and clapped them together to rid them of dirt and leaves. She'd been including Lark in all talk of the future.

They had harvested the last offerings of the summer season from the weary-looking plants, whose stalks were bent and turning brown. Lark carried the loaded basket as they walked toward the shed to put away their tools.

"Tonight is my Mahjongg night," Pearline said. "My group has a game once a month. Do you want to come? We'd love to have you ..."

"Um, no thanks, Mama. I think I'll stay here and do some work on the computer, maybe watch television."

"Well, Lark, you can't stay in the house all the time, dear. You've been here a week and I don't think you've gone anywhere!" Lark's mouth opened to say something in her own defense, but Pearline patted her arm and said, "Well, that's okay ... anyway, how about going out to eat with me and Wren tomorrow night? She wants to go to Latour's in Forestlee. They have Cajun food—you know, like jambalaya and gumbo—and their bread puddin's out of this world!"

"That sounds good, Mama. Let's do that." Maybe accepting the invitation for tomorrow night would ease her guilt. She *had* avoided her mother's invitations out all week. Her mother loved people and found a way to be among them every day it seemed. Whereas she was perfectly happy to be on her own. But her mother was right, she should probably get out, and now the weather had cooled in the mornings and evenings, spicy Cajun food sounded like just the thing.

Lark was about to hang up when Duff picked up the phone.

"It's about time you called me!" Duff fussed immediately.

"Hi, Duff!" A few melancholy tears gathered along the rims of Lark's eyes at the sound of her friend's voice. Without knowing Duff's hair color this week, she couldn't form a picture of her in her mind.

"How are you doin' way out there?" Duff asked.

"Pretty good, Duff. How about you?"

"Missin' you. I still haven't found anybody who'll go fleaing with me on Sunday. I need help to get bongos and teapots ... and cartoon characters back to the LeBaron."

"I know ... I'm sorry Duff. I've got an idea though—will you come and visit us? Soon?"

"What? Me come out there?"

"Yes. I need your opinion about something and ... will you?"

"Well, when exactly, Larky?"

"You could fly out and stay for a long weekend in October."

"Well, I s'pose I can. And, just what do you need help with dear?"

"I want you to come with me to an auction for your point of view. And ... there's something I need you to bring from my condo."

That evening while Wren drove Pearline and Lark to Latour's in her sensible car, Lark told them that Duff had accepted the invitation for a visit in October, and that set the stage for a cheery evening. They arrived at the restaurant at dusk, the sunset visible behind the row of downtown buildings that stood shoulder-to-shoulder on the square. The sky was clear and starlit, and the early-Autumn air was cool and soft. Lark looked up and saw the star she and Wren as children called the wishing star. She closed her eyes, remembering to keep her wish a secret so it would come true.

Through the large front window, she glimpsed people moving about inside, silhouetted against warm yellow light. Though not musically inclined, Lark recognized the accordion and fiddle when Wren opened the door and Zydeco music tumbled cheerily out. While Wren squeezed through the crowd to ask for a table, Lark thought she might have to wrap her arms around Pearline to wait in the only tiny remaining spot amongst the noisy crowd clustered around the door. She craned her head to look past them.

The walls were aged brick, and darkly stained wooden beams stretched across the ceiling. Oyster-shell pendants suspended between the beams cast soft light over everything and, together with lit candles on the tables, made the room cozy rather than somber. More light glinted off stainless steel from the open kitchen in back. Black wooden chairs were scattered around tables for four, and black leatherette booths lined the walls. In contrast to the relaxing look of the place, the music pulsated loudly, making her heart pound in rhythm with the beat. Preoccupied as she was with watching the people, it didn't seem they had waited long when they were shown to a booth far away from the crush at the door.

In the background, Lark was conscious of Pearline recounting her Mahjongg game the night before, but she was distracted by the social event taking place all around their table. Customers moved from table to table to chat, and even rearranged tables and chairs to regroup and visit with someone new. A man in a baseball cap took his lady-friend by the hand and danced a jig in between the tables. Others seemed focused mostly on the food—stews, potato salad, hush puppies, and bread pudding—served by white-aproned waiters who barely avoided collisions as they darted to and from the open kitchen upon hearing the call, *'Cuit!'*

Because of all the goings-on around them, a waiter's baritone took the ladies by surprise. At once all three of them turned his way. Lark's heart skipped a beat.

His smile was heart-melting, his hair dark, almost black, and wavy nearly to a curl.

"Can I get you ladies some wine?"

"No, honey, we're teeee-totallers!" Pearline blurted.

Lark blushed guiltily, embarrassed in her mother's presence by her recent indulgences.

"Iced tea then?" he asked, gracing them with that rather devastating smile again. They collectively took in a breath. Wren recovered first.

"Yes, I'll have tea ... sweet, please."

"Me too," said Pearline.

Lark couldn't help looking into the blue eyes that returned her gaze intently. Was it her imagination? Somehow his smile seemed different when directed at her. She blushed before quickly looking down at her menu and, and denying her real feelings, flatly ordered her drink. "Water with lemon," she said. A long pause. *What was he waiting for?* She determinedly kept her gaze on her menu.

"Okay, I'll get those drinks for you and come right back."

Pearline, determined that her girls hear her over the crowd, raised her voice a decibel or two and continued her story, having finally arrived at a description of the apple pie dessert at Mahjongg night.

Still discomposed, Lark hoped her reaction to the waiter had gone unnoticed. She braced herself to again avoid looking at him when he returned with their drinks, but when he held her water glass out and she reached across Pearline to take it, he turned the glass so that their fingers intertwined, and he wouldn't let go until she looked up! The effect of his touch and burning blue gaze combined to first electrify her and then leave her as weak as the water in her glass.

A smile twitched at the corners of his mouth, turning his expression a little triumphant as he turned his focus to taking their food orders. She felt irritation raise the fine hairs on the back of her neck. He seemed *too* self-assured. She sat up straighter, determined to show she could be as hard and cool as ice. She did *not* like to be played with. And she did not like his type—so sure of himself and his efforts to manipulate her—*hmmphf!*

She still refused to look at him when she placed her own order by pretending to check her phone, and he went away.

When a different waiter set her gumbo in front of her, she was finally able to relax. Pearline told her to sprinkle some ground sassafras leaves and some of the freshly chopped green onions over the top of her gumbo to finish it off. Her eyes closed with its comforting warmth and its spiciness tickled her nose. It was perfect—the chicken was tender, the Andouille sausage mouthwatering, and the roux dark and savory. She turned her full attention to it, and forgot all about the waiter.

Lying in her bed at Pearline's that night, the memory of blue eyes and dark hair returned to make Lark toss and turn, relive every nuance of his expressions, words, and movements … and wonder why she was *still* thinking about him.

Chapter 18

Pearline 'Stews'

―――⁓⁓⁓⁓⁓―――

While Lark tossed restlessly in her bed down the hallway, Pearline lay in her own bed, a worried expression turning down the corners of her usually smiling mouth.

The Mahjongg game hadn't gone well the night before. Discussing it over supper had reminded Pearline of that. Usually, she enjoyed the ladies' lighthearted ribbing each other over bad luck during the game and, though she kept herself from puttin' in her own two-cents-worth, she didn't mind too much the Pressfield news she heard. People could be like quicksilver—so changeable and unpredictable—and if she knew some of the goings-on around town, she could understand them better. So when she saw someone who behaved differently than she might expect, she knew the reason why. They might be unfriendly because they were sad a marriage was goin' bad or maybe extra friendly because a new grandbaby had arrived.

Oh, she knew that she wasn't supposed to even listen to gossip. But if she didn't, how on earth would she know who among her friends needed a helping hand? Of course, she always tried to keep in mind that what she heard might not be totally reliable. For instance, she would never be mean to anyone based on the talk she heard. Now, it never hurt to be nice to someone, but treatin' a person cruelly, based on what you heard, well … that wouldn't be right.

The girls had been unusually quiet and polite last night, though. Talk had begun of a marriage in trouble, but hushed up quickly and mysteriously when Pearline looked up from her Mahjongg tiles to see what was goin' on. She'd caught the eyes of a couple of the ladies studying her, who looked away when she noticed them, and when she walked into the kitchen for a second helping of apple pie, she surprised two of them, who hushed their conversation right up.

Knowin' this town and how news travelled, she suspected she knew what was going on—talk of Lark. And it was all *her* fault, she despaired.

Chapter 19

Discretion, in Duff's Point of View

With a mix of apprehension and excitement, Duff boarded a plane with its headings set for very different parts, on a Thursday in October when Lark expected her Down South for a long weekend. She looked forward to spending time with Lark and her family, but how would she seem to others in a traditionally-leaning part of the country? She hoped she could contain herself and behave discreetly!

Nearing its destination, the plane descended over one of the most beautiful landscapes Duff had ever seen from a plane, with stretches of fall-colored trees winding through pastures and farmland. Rivers and creeks glinted in the sunlight. Cotton, yet-to-be-harvested, did indeed look like dustings of snow, as Lark said it might.

And there stood Lark, waiting for her in the airport lobby.

"Hi ya' honey!" she called out as soon as she spotted her friend. *Oops!* She clapped her hand over her mouth, but her smile broke through the edges. She abruptly dropped her huge, Mexican-serape-covered bag, and more carefully, leaned the rectangular brown-paper-wrapped parcel against it, then hurried toward her friend in hopping steps, as fast as her tiny feet would carry her. She clasped her hand over her crumply, coral felted-wool hat, which had slipped to the back of her head. She felt her matching coral coat slipping off one shoulder. She tugged her short olive-green skirt down a bit over her black ankle-length leggings. At last she stood on tiptoe in her back high-top sneakers and Lark enveloped her in a hug. Together they laughed and squealed in delight. *So much for discretion!*

"Where are your mom and sister?" she asked, peeking over Lark's shoulder.

"They're waiting at home," Lark said. "Mama has baked lasagna for you, I hope you're hungry!" Neither of them could stop smiling as they walked to the car Lark said she borrowed from her sister Wren.

At Lark's mom's house Pearline and Wren greeted her with hugs like she was a member of the family. She raved over Pearline's lasagna, so welcome after her journey across the country, when she had only packs of nuts and dry airport food. The fresh sourdough bread she'd brought—cushioned by wads of brown paper in her bag—was a perfect accompaniment, they said, and she told them she might become addicted to Pearline's sugary-sweet tea.

She regaled them with the stories she'd mulled over and stored up while she flew across the country—of her fashion design work in San Francisco, her circle of friends, her latest finds at the flea market, including a robot made of rusty old cookware and a twelve-inch-tall figure of an alien. And she'd brought photographs of her home and favorite places to bring to life her own and Lark's existence out there.

By the time dinner was over, she felt as if she'd always been a part of the family. They had lingered over the table till they were too tired to sit there any longer. Pearline and Wren went to bed while she and Lark settled in to watch an old movie in the living room. Mostly, though, they discussed plans for the next day when Lark would give her a tour of her hometown, ending the day with a visit to a restaurant called Latour's. When they exchanged wide yawns, and could hardly keep their eyes open, they walked to the door of Lark's childhood bedroom.

"Duff, the picture?" Lark said.

She stepped into the bedroom and returned with the brown paper wrapped parcel. "Here it is, safe and sound," she said, and handed it over to Lark, who tried to quietly free it from its wrapping so as not to wake the others. She watched her friend hold it at arm's length and study it as she walked down the hallway to her mother's room for the night. *Why was Lark so taken with that painting of a little girl?*

She hadn't even said 'goodnight!'

Chapter 20

Pressfield

F riday dawned clear and beautiful, one of those perfect fall days with low humidity and temperatures just right for being outside. If the bright sunshine beaming through the curtains in their rooms hadn't woken the younger women, the aroma of Pearline's cooking would have.

Over another of her mother's breakfasts, Lark looked down at her waist, where a roll of fat spilled over the top of her now-tight jeans. *She couldn't keep eating like this.* Pearline's wonderful cooking was only adding to the weight she'd already put on!

But her willpower wasn't strong that morning and she ate two biscuits with real butter and honey from the local orchard market. She glanced over at Duff who apparently had no concerns whatsoever about tight jeans, destined as she was to stay thin, no matter how much, or what, she ate. Lark watched as her friend vigorously shook the honey bottle, then squeezed out the last drop.

"Would y'all stop at the orchard today and get me some more honey while you're out?" Pearline asked. "I'll make you a list."

Lidded cups of coffee and a list in hand of pantry items to pick up for Pearline, Lark and Duff—who were borrowing her car for the day—left quite early to carry Wren to work. From the sidewalk in front of the Victorian house that served as the library, Wren turned to wave goodbye with a rueful expression. Wren loved her job, but Lark thought her sister looked as though she would much rather go along with them instead.

The scent of ripened apples wafted through the open car windows as they neared the orchard. The air felt cool, but the rays of the morning sun and the sight of autumn daisies at the entrance warmed them. They strolled among the tables of squashes, sweet potatoes, small pumpkins, and apples. It took both of them to carry everything Pearline had written on her list, including the honey, back to the car.

While waiting for her favorite local shops to open, Lark drove past the county's historic plantations, telling Duff of the lore and history surrounding the stately homes, with their smaller outbuildings that once housed servants and their stories of ghosts, famous people who had lived there, and books written within the walls. Their route carried them by her old high school, where she remarked how the oak trees in front had grown tall over the years. She drove slowly past the baseball fields in back where she'd watched her boyfriend play for the school team. She told Duff how she'd felt proud to be the girlfriend of a baseball player, about sharing hotdogs with Pearline and Wren as they watched the team win and lose—in the cold wind, the hot sun, and sometimes the rain.

"Was he just a high school flame? What was his name?" Duff asked.

Was he? Just a high school flame? Lark supposed so … she'd left him back in high school and hadn't seen him since.

"His name was Hart," she said. "And yes, he was a high school boyfriend." 'Flame' didn't seem to accurately describe what they'd had. That word implied something that burned intensely and guttered as it slowly went out—and that wasn't what had happened. "It went on … maybe a little longer than most high school relationships." Her cryptic answer would have to do for now, as they had pulled up at her favorite bookstore on the town square.

They pushed open the tall, heavy door of the narrow brick building. Before they stepped inside, their noses filled with the scents of aged book leather and yellowed pages. As a child Lark would get lost for hours amongst the leaning shelves that overflowed with books from a few weeks to centuries old. She would sit and read at the antique tables or in one of the overstuffed chairs tucked into corners here and there, where a floor lamp cast a circle of light around her and created her own little world. She would stay there until old Mr. Watkins found her and shooed her home. The shop was much the same, except Mr. Watkins was gone now, and replaced by a granddaughter.

She and Duff lost one another amongst the shelves until, an indefinite time later, Lark found Duff at the register paying for a picture book of fashion design history dating up until the 1970s, and thrilled because she could reference it in her work.

They had lingered until lunchtime and Duff's stomach was rumbling— how Lark didn't know, considering the huge breakfast the tiny woman had eaten. They walked along the sidewalk to the Pressfield General Store on the corner.

"Duff, you have to save room for a fried pie," Lark said as she reached for the door handle. "Lynelle makes them. We went to school together for twelve years!"

They walked through the quaint front of the store and the aromas of freshly ground coffee and roasting peanuts and cashews, past shelves overflowing with grocery items, to the café counter in the back.

Lark waited for Duff to order, and her mouth watered as she pictured the sandwiches made here for as long as she could remember. Her father often brought the girls here on Saturdays for a sandwich followed by a fried pie when he brought them along 'to town' for shopping at the hardware store. The sandwiches were made of soft, freshly baked rolls, piled high with tender, juicy chicken 'roasted on the premises,' and barbecue sauce made from a secret recipe that oozed out the sides. Lark picked up a stack of paper napkins to carry to their table.

She thought she'd seen Lynelle's head through the window to the kitchen, and that Lynelle had seen her too, but the woman's net-covered hair ducked quickly down again, and dashed Lark's hope of introducing her to Duff.

They sat at one of the wooden tables, its dark surface scratched and wobbly from years of use. When their sandwiches were brought to them, Lark noticed with disappointment they were much thinner than of former days, the chicken not piled high like before, the roll dry, the sauce ... *was there any sauce on there?* Lark didn't remark on this to Duff, not wanting to dampen the spirit of the day.

They labored through their sandwiches, while Lark hoped the fried pies wouldn't disappoint. She walked back to the counter to order them, and caught Lynelle behind the baked goods case this time. Did she just imagine Lynelle ducking out of sight and sort of ... lurking behind the counter?

"Lynelle!" she said. Lynelle looked up, frowned, and blushed bright red, obviously embarrassed.

"Oh. Hello, Lark," she said flatly. Lark felt her heart sink. Why did Lynelle behave so strangely? Usually, her old friend would've come around the case and given her a hug, and would probably sit at her table and catch up with her life in California.

"How are you?" Lark asked tentatively, the corners of her mouth turning downward.

"Oh, *I'm* fine. How are *you*, Lark?" She said the words snidely, even angrily. Lark shook her head confusedly.

"I'm good ... visiting Mama for a few weeks."

"Is that *right*?" Lynelle responded.

"I … I'd like to order two chocolate pies," Lark said, feeling she might cry. It was the last days in California all over again.

"We'll bring 'em out to you." Lynelle said flatly again, turning away.

Lark sat down, while Duff studied her with concern. "What is it?" she asked.

"Nothing … it's nothing." Lark sighed. She'd have to put it down to a long time between visits, because she couldn't think of anything she'd done to make Lynelle behave so. Maybe she heard of the long time that had passed since Lark visited her mother and was judging Lark, thinking her neglectful or selfish? Or, could somehow … somehow … the word about the mess in California have gotten around here?! Lark shook her head in disbelief. Could that happen? The cities were over 2,000 miles apart!

When the pies arrived, they were cold, and heavy with grease.

"*Ugh*. Sorry Duff. Things sure seem to have changed here."

"It's okay, Lark. They're pretty good." Lark knew Duff was only trying to make her feel better. She felt embarrassed that one of the few people who remembered her in her hometown, treated her so … badly. She couldn't finish her pie, stomach sick with uncertainty and rejection. The torn place inside that she thought well on its way to healing began to ache.

In early afternoon the two friends returned to Pearline's, going their separate ways to nap and freshen up for dinner at Latour's. Lark paid extra attention to her hair and makeup, and her spirits lifted despite the let-down at lunch. She pulled on skinny jeans, a creamy white blouse, and one of her flea market finds—a moss green sweater, quirkily knitted with uneven lapels and edges. She was unaware that it made the most of a charming, elfin quality that was special to her, and made her eyes snap darkly. She tinted her lips in a muted shade. Lipstick always made her feel better.

The four of them filled a booth at Latour's and Lark's heart glowed. She sighed in contentment, and felt silly when her eyes watered over having the people she cared about most sitting all together right here with her. She shook off the melancholy that tried to dampen her good mood, and let her eyes discreetly wander around the room. *He* didn't seem to be there. She told herself she felt relieved—now she wouldn't have to be on her guard to behave coolly toward him. She remembered his flirting last time. So sure of himself! She turned her attention to the menu.

"Hello, ladies!"

His pleasant voice startled her just as it had the time before. Her hand reached for her throat to prevent a gasp escaping. Did he sneak up on ladies on purpose?! She looked up into his smiling blue eyes, and could've kicked herself when she smiled back at him. His smile widened.

"Let's see … all of you will have tea, right?" His eyes touched on everyone around the table, and then stopped when they rested on Lark, "Except, water with lemon for you, yes?"

She blushed, astonished he remembered seeing her … *them*, and that he remembered what she … *they*, drank. "Yes," she replied.

"Extra sweet for me!" Duff blurted.

He disappeared and others delivered their drinks. Others took their order too, and placed their food in front of each of them when it was ready.

Because their lunch at the Pressfield General Store had been unsatisfying, Lark wasted no time putting a forkful of the potato salad that was served alongside the gumbo into her mouth—not a lady-like, one-potato-chunk kind of a bite, but a can't-quite-close-your-mouth kind of a bite. She looked up, hungrily chewing, and caught the blue-eyed water's look from where he stood in the open kitchen. He leaned over, his hands on the counter, arms extended, triceps flexed, holding her eyes with those intense blue ones, and wiped his mouth across his shirt sleeve. Lark's stomach lurched. He held her gaze for noticeable ticks of the clock, then she gulped, potato salad sucked into her windpipe, and she bent over into a coughing fit.

Pearline thumped her on the back … hard. "Lark, you okay, honey?"

Lark was terribly inexperienced at flirting, and was now so flustered she would not let her eyes leave their table for the rest of their meal. She was *not* looking for whatever he was looking for! *Was she?*

"Can I get you all anything else?" he asked, as he took up their mostly empty plates, with mischievous laughter in his eyes.

Pearline replied, "No, we're headed out the door, we've been here way too long anyway!"

Lark purposely looked away to get her things while the others, quicker than she, left her behind fumbling for her bag. She craned her neck to see around the waiter of the blue eyes, leaning into the booth on the other side of the table as he cleared away the plates and glasses. She saw the back of Duff already scooting toward the door behind Pearline and Wren.

She dared to glance at him as she worked her way out of the booth.

"Are you out with your family tonight?" he asked.

She paused, breathless from her scooting. "Yes." And seeing he was still curious, she said, "My Mama, sister, and a good friend."

"Ah. Did you enjoy your meal? You had the gumbo?"

"Yes, it was fine." *Really, it was more than fine.*

"You should come in sometime and try our chicory coffee. We grind our beans fresh around ten in the morning and our beignets are gettin' powdered sugar about that time too. If you let me know sometime when you might come, I'd like to have a cup with you."

His smile disarmed her. It seemed … genuine. She closed her open mouth. As her hesitation lengthened, his smile fell a little.

"Maybe … sometime," she offered lamely.

She hurried her efforts to get out of the booth in her too tight jeans, trying to suck in her tummy so he wouldn't see the roll above her waistband—because he was *still* looking at her!

'*A beignet—that's about the last thing I need!*' was her thought, as she hurried along after the others who had disappeared through the door.

Chapter 21

The Auction

Goosebumps rose on Lark's skin when she stepped out the door to judge the weather and to decide how to dress for the auction. She yawned and rolled her head on her shoulders to loosen the tension in her neck.

Sleep had seemed impossible the night before. Excitement about the auction, combined with worry over the vague feeling something wasn't quite right with Lynelle, kept her tossing and turning, and sleep eluded her for hours. She had gotten up to have a cup of her sleep-encouraging tea, and at last drifted off around midnight.

Her excitement made keeping her plans secret from Pearline and Wren difficult. She didn't want to raise Pearline's hopes about the possibility of her moving back here permanently, not when she hadn't yet seen the property.

Her heart beat erratically as she leaned over to tuck the legs of her khakis into suede boots and stood up to buckle a belt around the waist of her long sweater for extra warmth.

Duff appeared in her usual leggings with ankle boots this time, her coral coat draped over her shoulders, and purple hair curling around the brim of her coral hat. Purple. Feeling as if she and a cartoon character were going for an outing, Lark hid her amused smile from Duff and wondered what the locals would think.

Once again borrowing Wren's car, they drove in the direction of Echo Creek which divided Pressfield from Forestlee, on its way to join the larger river about a mile downstream. Their drive took about thirty minutes, giving Duff time to ask questions.

"I know we're going to an auction today, Lark. But fully inform me, dear, what you're thinking of doing."

"Well, I'm not sure California's the place for me anymore, Duff. I'm loving Mama and Wren's company. And I'm *happy* now you're here."

Duff nodded in encouragement, but her face wore an anxious expression. "Go on …"

"I don't want to live with Mama—I've been independent for too long. *Way* too long. So, I started looking online for something—a place of my own—and I ran across this place we're going to see today." She handed Duff a description of the property from the auctioneer's website, and Duff read without speaking for several moments.

"You don't think you're biting off more than you can chew, Lark? I mean, going from a tiny, one-bedroom condo to a ten-acre property with a house four or five times as big, and two other buildings besides!"

"I know, I've been thinking about all that too, Duff. But my life has changed. I might as well change with it. I'm going to need something of an income. I'm too young to retire, and with the two extra buildings— they're actually cottages, by the way—I thought I could rent them out and have something coming in. And … it's all a long term investment."

"Are you sure you're not jumping into this as a knee-jerk reaction to the bad time you've gone through out west? And, in regard to my own interests, Lark—" Duff paused, and Lark could feel her sideways glance, "you're my best friend and favorite neighbor—if you're seriously considering staying here, it's going to mean a big change in my life too!" Duff's voice trembled with her words, her normally indomitable spirit sounding as if it was standing on shaky ground.

Lark took her eyes off the road a moment and looked over at the profile of her friend, feeling sorry that she was causing her hurt. She said, "We'll talk more about this, okay? For now, will you keep an open mind, and try to give me the most objective advice you possibly can, while we have a look?"

Duff nodded, but her expression was understandably conflicted. "I'll try," she said, grudgingly.

Truthfully, Lark had her own doubts. In fact, if Duff hadn't flown all the way here for this, she might've backed out. This experience felt like an emotional wringer. It would take relying on gut feeling, wisdom, willpower to stay inside her budget, and plain old luck to end up a winner at the end of this day.

"First things first, I have to have a look around, see whether it might work. And I really do want your honest opinion. I mean you're not excited about me moving here. Mama and Wren might see it with more enthusiasm than the property is due, in hopes of me staying here. Right?"

"You know I'll tell you what I *really* think!" Duff looked over at her, and her face broke into a mischievous grin.

At the entrance to the property, Lark turned off the main road and passed an uninspiring black and white auction sign. With a deep breath to shore up her resolve, she looked at the road ahead. Gravel stretched in two lines in front of the car with grass in between. They entered a stand of trees, and drove … and drove, until it seemed they'd entered another world, surrounded by nature on all sides, finally arriving at a knoll upon which several cars were parked.

Having never taken part in an auction, and knowing this was a fairly large property, she expected the other bidders to be much more able than she, and to put her likely lower bids to shame, but the ordinary cars parked here eased her nervousness and she felt a swell of optimism. They had arrived quite early to give themselves plenty of time to tour the property before the auction.

Following a path toward a gray structure they glimpsed through the trees, Lark gasped as they stepped out of the shade onto a grassy slope, and the house appeared before them like a vision from a fairy tale. Clad with weathered and aged-to-gray cedar siding and roofed with wooden shingles of the same material, its length stretched from their left to their right. In its middle was a screened front porch whose double-doored entrance centered under a high gable. Gingerbread trim curved in each corner of the porch framing. Except for the plain, long windows, it was a gothic cottage. The quirky mix of architectural styles gave the house a cobbled-together air. The overall effect was no less than enchanting to Lark.

They walked around small groups of people who talked quietly together, to the back of the house, where they found displayed upon a table a plat of the land, a list of everything included in the auction, and a fan of paddles with numbers on them. The auctioneers were friendly and courteous, reassuring Lark that they would take her seriously as a bidder, and that all would be handled professionally. She signed the necessary papers, and received a paddle with the number '14' printed on it in black.

She and Duff took in the view behind the table. The property jutted out into the creek on a short peninsula. The house, situated on a ridge above the water, had an eagle's-eye view of the creek and cottages belonging to others, way on the other side.

Turning to face the back of the house, Lark took in a wall of windows that rose to a point in the shape of an 'A,' and through them could see a tall, sloped and beamed ceiling. A deck ran from one side of the house to the other, with a pergola over one end. Trying not to show how pleased she was with the place, she hid a shiver of excitement, and motioned for Duff to follow her up onto the deck.

A gray kitten meowed and twined itself around the square railing posts. Lark gasped and reached down, but it darted off before her fingers touched it, and stepped onto the low branch of a tree extending out over the water from the 20-foot high ridge, placing one paw assuredly in front of the other. Lark turned away from watching, fearing it would fall. She hoped it wouldn't—it would seem a bad sign—not to mention what it would do to the kitten!

Leaving the kitten to its brave adventure, they entered the house through the doorway off the deck and stepped into the living room.

"Wow!" Duff said, when she saw its impressive openness. Although ordinary-sized for this part of the country, it was huge in comparison to her living space in San Francisco.

To their left a stone fireplace reached all the way to the sloped ceiling, where dark wooden beams stretched from the highest point and extended downward to the upper wall of the second story. Two second-story catwalks ran along each side of the room with doorways to rooms along them, the one on the left accessed by a spiral staircase. Intrigued, Lark motioned for Duff to follow her up.

At the top was the master bedroom. Like downstairs, lots of light came through tall windows. There was an adjoining bath with a pink marble tub and picture window with a view to the northern end of the property and the creek beyond. The room was disappointingly outdated. She would have to make friends with the pink marble.

Descending a stairway at the opposite end of the catwalk from the spiral one, they crossed the main living area, wended their way around other possible bidders, and climbed stairs from the foyer up to the catwalk extending along the other side. At the top, there were two bedrooms sharing a bath in between of the same pink-marbled era as the master.

Lark glimpsed her expression in the mirror. Their tour of the inside had dampened her spirits. The place needed many things—paint, new flooring, a good cleaning ... She forced the muscles around her mouth into a half-smile. She *wanted* this to work out more than she'd realized. There were possibilities here despite the work involved. She *could* make it her own. She needed this place, these projects. She pulled her shoulders back, took a deep breath, and returned downstairs, followed by an unusually quiet Duff.

Their tour of the inside finished with the kitchen, with its dark, ornate cabinetry, then another bedroom below the master, and a room that was both laundry and mud room with an entrance to the north side of the house. More than enough house for one person.

As Lark exited from the front door on the side of the house opposite the creek, she paused and looked up at its height, feeling her excitement return. Yes, the inside needed a lot of work, but the outside felt so right—a storybook cottage in the forest, with the sound of water rippling against the shoreline below. Her head swiveled to take in the tall tops of the trees, and down the long trunks to the mossy understory. Wildlife probably watched her right now.

But the house wasn't the only consideration. Curious to see the body of water that edged the property, she led the way down a gently sloping path alongside the house with Duff still following dutifully behind. Noticing an open doorway as they passed the lower level, they peeked into a chilly, junk-filled basement, then continued down the leaf-carpeted path to the water, and stepped out onto a weathered gray dock. Walking to the end, Duff seized the opportunity while they were alone.

"So, what are your thoughts, Lark?" she asked in a subdued voice.

"It's quite large, isn't it? I mean, could it be too much for me?"

"Think—you'd be out here all alone in that big house. At least, until you had renters for the cottages, right?"

"Yes." Lark tried to imagine living there. *Would* she feel too isolated here? She looked out over the water and saw a fisherman guiding his boat along the creek, could see someone on a dock at a cabin across the way. Her thoughts took a hopeful turn. "But Duff, think how much fun it would be to make it my own! I mean, I could do whatever I wanted to. Make it whatever I wanted it to be."

"Yes, there's that. But it needs *tons* of work. Not to mention the cost. Could you do it?"

"You know me, Duff, I've saved and made good investments for years, plus I did get a severance package. Let's have a look at the two cottages and see whether they could be rented out. That will help me decide. If they're not *too* far from habitable, then I might have something coming in before long." They climbed back up the slope toward the cottage whose shape they could just see peeking through the trees, on the side of the property facing an inlet, rather than the main channel. Entering through a squeaky door onto a screened porch, Lark felt the structure was solid enough, but older than the main house. It was covered with board and batten wood weathered to gray, while the inside was paneled with knotty pine just like Pearline's.

"Duff, I think this could make a nice home for someone. And I would have company—a neighbor. I think I wouldn't be alone here for long—" Lark's words stopped abruptly with a look toward her friend who wouldn't be her neighbor much longer. She shook off that spirit-dampening thought, and checked her watch to see that the time for the auction was not far off. At a quicker pace they passed the main house and the growing crowd of people, to the cottage on the other side and up the ridge, overlooking the main channel of the creek. Similar to the first, without the screened porch, it looked as if likely built by the same builder and during the same era, probably the 1960s.

Little time remained before the auction for apprehension or doubt to overwhelm her. They joined the crowd gathering in front of the auctioneer's table as the auctioneer began to speak.

"This property consists of one 2,600 square foot home and two separate 900 square foot dwellings, on ten acres of land, with 1,700 feet of waterfront. There is a minimum that must be reached in order for the property to be sold today—so don't start the bids too low!" A wave of nervous laughter rippled through the group of bidders. The auctioneer shuffled some papers in front of him and, before any of the bidders saw it coming, quickly raised his head and barked loudly, "Who will start the bidding?"

Someone else made an offer. *Whew!* The starting bid was well within her limit. Lark held her paddle high, along with many others. As the auctioneer advanced through one raised bid after another, some fell out, leaving their paddles by their sides. But Lark's paddle smartly snapped up with each bid.

Lark stopped her tentative smile that threatened to give away the thrill of victory when she looked around to find the only remaining bidders were she and a slick-looking man who was alone. His expression—jaw firmly set in determination—made her stand up straight, her mouth turned serious again. He looked angry, as if he realized he was not going to get the property as cheaply as he had hoped and that he couldn't believe this chick was continuing to bid against him. His face grew stormier as the bid rose higher. Finally, his hand remained at his side at what Lark hoped would be the auctioneer's last call.

"Going once, going twice … *SOLD* to number 14!" She closed her eyes and opened them again to see the opposing bidder smack his thigh and angrily stride off. A soft smattering of applause rose from the few remaining bidders. And that show of good will brought a smile of gratitude mixed with relief to her face.

The auctioneer's grin showed he was pleased with the level the bids had reached. He came over to Lark where she stood with her head spinning dizzily, grabbed her hand, and shook it vigorously. "Congratulations, little lady! You got yourself quite a property!"

Her eyes were large and her mouth formed an "o" as she disbelievingly returned his handshake.

Chapter 22

Breaking the News

Still, Lark put off telling Pearline and Wren until Duff returned to San Francisco, this time in consideration of *Duff*, whose spirits were low enough already about leaving Lark behind. She and Duff had a long talk Saturday night, again seated on the sofa side-by-side, Lark's body turned toward her friend, her legs folded underneath her.

"So, you're not comin' back to San Fran," Duff stated as if trying to convince herself.

"No." Lark shook her head, feeling a mix of regret and relief.

"Things are going to be different without you. It's good for me you've been sort of ... out of it for a while." Duff looked sheepishly from the corners of her eyes at Lark. "I mean, I'm forcing myself to get used to being without you on weekends, especially Sundays. I know I've already said it ... but I'm sorry for the way things turned out in San Fran, Lark. It wasn't fair to you, and now it feels like it's unfair to me, too. But I do have a good feeling about this for you. You seem different here. Happier. Kind of glowing or something."

"I *do* have a good feeling about this," Lark said. She didn't want to say she knew it would work out, because she didn't know whether it would. And if it didn't, well ... She said, "Duff, thanks for understanding." She knew what being gracious might be costing her friend.

"Will you come visit me sometimes?" Duff asked wistfully.

"Without a doubt! Now, I need to ask a big favor—I need your help selling my place and my car out there and overseeing the packing and moving of my stuff."

"Must I?" Duff whined, collapsing backward on the sofa.

All of them went to the airport next day to see Duff off. The tiny purple-haired woman hugged Pearline tightly. They had become fast friends. She and Wren clasped hands and smiled at one another. Then Pearline and Wren stepped aside to allow Lark to say goodbye.

She hugged Duff, who patted her tenderly on the back in return.

Duff said, "Take care of yourself, now. Call me anytime." The two of them dropped their arms to their sides and stepped apart. With her gaze fixed on the ground at her feet, Duff continued, "I'll take care of your things out there—you don't have to worry about that."

"Let's just say goodbye for *now*—we'll see each other again before long and we'll keep in touch by phone and online." Her friend's face was still downturned. Lark reached her hand out, and gently touched Duff's arm. "Duff?"

"Okay," Duff said tearfully, and nodded her agreement while she fumbled in her coat pocket for a tissue. She turned toward her terminal and blew her nose loudly, her body language as droopy as her coral-felt hat, and waved goodbye before she turned the corner and was gone.

Back at home, Pearline took some Brunswick stew out of the freezer to have with the last of the sourdough bread Duff had brought. The three women sat around the table drawing comfort from their soup. The absence of Duff's loving spirit was perceptible. Lark thought her news might be just the thing to cheer them up. "I have something to tell you two," she said.

The other women looked up, Pearline with a worried expression on her face.

"It looks like I'm going to stay here for a while."

In a cautiously hopeful voice, Pearline asked, "How long a while, Lark?"

"A long, long while. I've bought a house!" Like a child, she clapped her hands together and wiggled her feet under her chair, so that she bounced up and down.

Her voice breaking with happy emotion, Pearline exclaimed, "What?! Honey, that's wonderful!" and pushed herself out of her chair to shuffle over and hug Lark.

Practical Wren pressed for more details, "Where?" she asked.

"It's at Echo Creek. Waterfront. A house and two cottages." She filled them in on all the details as well as her plans.

Duff was sending a fully loaded moving truck across the country to the gray house, and it should arrive on the first Monday in November. The gray house belonged to Lark on paper—all that remained was to physically claim it by moving in. She felt pressured to have it ready before all her belongings arrived.

One week remained. She would need help.

Chapter 23

Shared Troubles

Help arrived in the form of Pearline, Wren, during her time off from the library, and anyone else Pearline could muster together, which included Cricket Dumas.

She came with her own arsenal of cleaning supplies in the back of her car—ammonia, vinegar, lemon and orange oils, a bolt of soft flannel fabric to tear into cleaning rags as needed, scrub brushes, and mops. She swept in straw-hatted and work-booted and announced she was here 'to do a little job of work.'

Lark began, "I think we'll start with the kitchen. It—"

"Uh-unh," Cricket replied firmly. "We're goin' to start at the top! Just like you're s'posed to clean a house!"

The rest of them could tell this woman knew more about how to go about this than they, so … they started at the top. Even they understood that all the dirt and dust from up high would float right down. It made sense to do things Cricket's way. They started with the ceiling on the second floor in the master bedroom. Cricket insisted they throw open all the upstairs windows first. Lark shivered when the chilly early-November air blew in from the northwest side of the house.

"It's going to be too cold. Isn't it?"

"No, no!" said Cricket. "Soon as y'all start workin' y'all will love that fresh air!" And they did, as Cricket set them to washing the ceiling and walls with a solution she concocted herself.

Together they cleaned each upstairs room, lighting on it like a swarm of busy bees. Pearline worked down low in short bursts, with frequent rests to massage her arthritic hands. Wren worked quietly, with efficient movements, and tidied up after them, throwing away used cloths and refilling spray bottles. Lark worked in an inexperienced, and she felt, clumsy manner, but she watched carefully the way the others worked, and learned. Cricket—energetic, her movements quick and sudden— worked harder than any of them, though that didn't stop her breathlessly chattering away, keeping them entertained.

"Y'all know my real name is Catherine. But my Mama saw how I jumped and hopped about, and gave me the nickname, Cricket. You know how you named your girls after birds, Pearline? Well, my Mama nicknamed *her* chil'uns after bugs! There was me, Cricket, and Grasshopper, and Doodlebug."

"Those were happy nicknames, Cricket," said Lark, and she couldn't hide or help her laughter.

"Oh, we were happy. Yes indeed, poor as church mice, but happy." They all became quiet and thoughtful, each thinking of people they knew who were indeed happy, even under the various and unfortunate circumstances life dealt them.

The company of each other and their talk made the morning fly and work get done. They took down light fixtures and washed them before hanging them back up to sparkle in the sunlight. They wiped the richly stained wooden door and window frames with lemon oil until they shone. They cleaned and then polished the windows with old newspapers from Cricket's car trunk. And the fresh autumn air flowed through, doing its part.

By lunchtime they had cleaned every square inch of the master bedroom and bath. Lark was disgusted by the well-used carpet though, and frustrated that, despite all their hard work, the house still smelled musty because of it. So, while the others thought about lunch, she called around to find a crew to rip out all the carpet and take it away. She wanted the whole house clean now she saw how everything shone and the clean scent of lemon oil floated through the air—above floor-level at least. She found a crew to come next day, who promised they would have all the carpet out before the sun set.

She told everyone as they drank hot coffee and munched on sandwiches on the back deck in the fresh air. Dry late-autumn leaves blew around them, and sunlight sparkled on the surface of the creek below.

They perched—two in an old swing suspended from the wooden pergola that sheltered part of the deck, two at a nearby table made of rusty metal and weathered wood left by the former occupants—and chattered about inconsequential matters for a while. But, as talk amongst women will, their chatter turned to matters close to their hearts. And then, to talk about talk.

Cricket mentioned how people *might* say what they shouldn't, how they *might* talk about everybody else's business. She said in her opinion it was "okay to talk, long as you're not sayin' somethin' that'll hurt somebody." She paused while she slowly chewed a bite of sandwich and watched Lark carefully.

Lark became self-conscious and shifted in the swing uncomfortably. But she felt forgiving of Cricket's bringing that subject up, because her affection for the lively, truthfully-spoken woman had grown by the minute. Lark loved truth-speakers, they seemed the most trustworthy people she had ever found—even when the truth they spoke hurt—with the intent to right a wrong, of course.

"Lark, now don't you worry 'bout what people been sayin'. It's a case of what *we've* been talkin' about. People don't know you. Don't know your story." Cricket shook her head.

Lark looked at her perplexedly. Cricket seemed to think Lark knew exactly what she meant. But she didn't. "I'm sorry, I don't—" she said, face blushing hotly, not knowing what to say or ask, to gain more understanding. Her confusion was interrupted when Pearline spluttered, sat forward agitatedly, and scooted her unfinished sandwich onto the table. Her mother stood up and began to pace, wringing her hands.

"Oh, Lark! It's all *my* fault!" she said, placing one hand on her stomach and the other on her hot forehead.

"Mama, what is it?"

"Pearline, you mean she doesn't know?" Cricket asked.

"I guess not!" So Pearline explained all about that unpleasant episode at the beauty parlor. About how she had told about Lark's troubles in California, and that her words had been overheard and taken wrongly by the ladies there, even after she'd tried to make clear the true situation.

"Mama! It's okay. You didn't mean for that to happen, I know. This is not something that's new to me anyway. I've dealt with rejection for a while now. I'm getting used to it." She snorted—though it sounded rather grim.

Cricket told what she'd heard at the beauty parlor as she washed hair at the shampoo sinks.

"Listen. People are gonna go and talk, for better or worse. There's nothin' you can do about that. That's just what people do. Yes, Lawdy! They're takin' it the wrong way and makin' it a big deal. Just like they shouldn't. Just like you *know* people will go and do!" She shook her head. "They're sayin' you broke up a marriage and lost your job over it. And you had no choice but to move back here. When I hear 'em, I try to set 'em straight. Betty and Pearline told me you didn't even know that man was married! An' I believe that."

Lark sighed heavily—her excitement and joy over her new home extinguished with this new knowledge. Well, it explained the déjà vu she'd felt as she went about her business around town. She remembered Lynelle's treatment of her the day she'd taken Duff to the General Store for lunch—her snide way of responding to Lark and that she seemed angry about something. The treatment that bordered on hostility at stores around town, the ignoring, the way people wouldn't meet her eyes.

Pearline sighed heavily. Cricket sighed heavily. Wren's only reaction was to look down at the wood floor of the deck. She never seemed surprised, disappointed, or even particularly pleased at the behavior of others. In fact, she simply didn't discuss other people, unless she found it unavoidable, and then only carefully with as much kindness and grace in her words as possible.

"Oh! I think we might as well get back to work and get our minds off this for now. Let's see what we can do with the rest of the upstairs," Cricket said, throwing her hands in the air.

They didn't mention their lunchtime discussion again, it was too unpleasant, too troubling—no one wanted to deal with it. And although they moved more slowly that afternoon, they cleaned two more bedrooms and a bathroom to sparkling too. As their last little job of work, as Cricket called it, they vacuumed all the carpets in the house, so next day when the work crew removed them, less dirt and dust would fly through the air.

Next morning, Lark opened all the windows before the others arrived, grateful that the day dawned with a clear sky and cool air again. The group of ladies included Betty today, Pearline's hairdresser and owner of the beauty parlor. Betty, like Cricket, was wise in the ways of the world, having heard many a story from her position behind the beauty shop chair, and brought a soothing, matter-of-fact and unflappable vibe to the day. The others needed it, somewhat depressed as they were with the realization of Lark's damaged reputation roundabouts.

As promised, the carpet-removal crew arrived early then worked busily, and noisily. Their stomping boots, carpet ripping, chatter, and lively Latin music drowned out any conversation the ladies attempted. Staying away from the carpeted areas and the dust the guys stirred up, the girls scrubbed the kitchen. Lark kept her feelings about the dark-wooded, ornate cabinetry to herself, knowing if she mentioned wanting to rip out the cabinetry, she would get different opinions on the wisdom of doing that, and how to go about it, besides refusal to clean them if she planned to rip them out later. A plan grew in her mind to do that work herself, and save the good, flat pieces of wood to build some bookshelves around the windows in the living room for her books. She pictured a library for herself with a table and chairs, maybe a window seat.

As she wiped down cabinets, her thoughts were on the ladies' conversation yesterday, and threatened to overwhelm her with worry about the environment she had moved to. But she remembered the new way of thinking which occurred to her before she left San Francisco. She could struggle to control the uncontrollable and drown, which is what she'd done when she retreated from the world in California and tried to escape the inescapable through chemical aids.

Or she could seek peace. She reminded herself that her only *control* over her circumstances lie in her *response* to them—in the *choices* she made with what she was left with. So she would *choose* positive action, positive friendships, and positive places to do business if need be. The key was accepting and moving on. She moved other thoughts to the forefront of her mind—of the many things she needed to do, rather than the things she could do little about.

Again, lunchtime arrived quickly. To blow away the dust created by the carpet removal crew that covered them from head to foot, Wren, Betty, and Pearline rolled the car windows down and took off to find some lunch for them all and bring it back. Cricket and Lark stayed behind to rest and collapsed side by side into the wooden swing beneath the pergola. Their conversation began effortlessly and flowed forth—Cricket was a good talker and Lark was a good listener—their spirits were kindred. It took only one question.

"Cricket, I hope you won't feel this question is rude, because it really isn't any of my business, but I'm curious ... I can tell you're an educated woman. Intelligence and thoughtfulness comes out in your conversation. Your way of speaking changes from time to time, and becomes very refined. It's made me wonder why you aren't doing something other than cleaning houses and shampooing hair."

Cricket looked at Lark from the corners of her eyes, smiling beatifically, with an impish twist, as if caught in some misbehavior. "An' what else exac'ly do you think I *should* be doin'?"

"I don't know ... maybe teaching? You seem knowledgeable about many things."

Cricket took on that refined tone. "Well I am an avid reader, and yes, I am educated—I have a Master's in Social Work. As for my speech, I weeded out colloquialisms to present myself professionally, but I s'pose, nowadays I do tend to go back and forth."

Lark nodded understandingly. "I had to change the way I spoke when I moved to California to be taken seriously in my career. My accent often threw people for a loop, especially men it seemed. I think they expected me to bat my eyelashes and call them Rhett when they complimented me on it! But Cricket, if I'm not being *too* impertinent again, why aren't you practicing?"

"I did for many years."

"But why stop, you're not so old … oh, I'm sorry!" Lark sheepishly ducked her head and covered her mouth with her hand, shocked and embarrassed that her curiosity won out over good manners. "You don't have to answer, of course!"

"No it's all right, Lark. Discernin' these things about me, judgin' I'm not what I might appear to be, is fine. We all must make judgments, discernments. However, if you *disrespected* me or condemned me for the type of jobs I do or for the way I talk or for the age-old reason—for the way I look—then that would rankle with me.

"No, it's not the act of judgment that doesn't set well with me, but the practice of some who judge and then *condemn* without ever allowin' the one they condemn a voice, without gettin' to know them, or tryin' to understand them." She sighed heavily, realizing she had strayed from the subject because of her passionate feelings. "Now it's my turn to apologize," Cricket continued. "As you can see, you've touched on a subject I feel strongly about. To answer your last question, I stopped because I lost my optimism and my motivation."

"*Ah,* I see." Lark identified with the loss of drive for a career certainly, and finding someone with a similar experience made her want to hear more.

Cricket gave a wise half-smile, as if she could see into Lark's mind, and continued her explanation. "To understand, you have to put yourself in the shoes of someone who, as a counselor for many years, listened to or in some way tried to help alleviate other people's problems, five days a week. And then sometimes volunteered on evenings or Saturdays to listen to people who didn't have insurance or who didn't speak English, maybe like those guys inside tryin' to do an honest day's work for an honest day's pay, legally of course." Cricket turned to glance toward the house, and then went on.

"I listened to life's problems and tried to help with them for a long, long time, and I did help. I saw people improve in the way they handled themselves or in their outlook—their way of seein' their problems. But others …" Cricket paused and shook her head. "Others lived in situations they had little control over. I could tell they suffered in between the times when they could come and see me. I was a professional like my colleagues an' left it at the office, so to speak, but over time the ones I couldn't help stayed with me. I lost my ability to distance myself mentally and emotionally. In some ways I think that made me a more compassionate therapist, able to see their problems more clearly, but ... it took me down. It became a heavier and heavier burden. I'd lay awake worryin' about the people I was tryin' to help. Hopin' I was giving them the right advice. *Hmmph*, just hopin' sometimes they'd *take* my advice!"

She paused, as if remembering. Then pushed against the wood of the deck floor with her foot to get the swing going again, sighed, and lay her head against the back of the swing. "The last straw, so to speak, was a woman I'd tried to help for some years. She was mentally fine, but almost too nice for this world. Other people's misjudgment of her life, their gossip about her, and mostly the actions they took based on their misjudgment and gossip, affected her life in a very negative way. It all combined to the effect she was rejected by her community, family, friends, workplace ... *everyone*, and then the proliferation of freely-shared opinions on the internet and the quick spread of information—sometimes sorely inaccurate information—left her without an escape or recourse. She couldn't make a new life ... move to a new place as people could in the old days.

"She was too gentle a person, dealt with too harshly by society. I don't know what happens to good people these days. Respect for simple human dignity, for people's stories, for what made them who they are seems to have gone out the window. There's so little compassion." Cricket's light brown skin had taken on a grayish tint.

"I didn't know how to help, except to tell her to rise above it. And sometimes that advice doesn't help. It takes a long, long time to rise above it. *Hmmph*—a lifetime. Sometimes that doesn't save a person, and it's only after they're gone, if then that people realize who they *really* were.

"She sought escape through drugs and alcohol, spiraled downward into addiction, and eventually overdosed. I'd tried hard to help her. I was angry for a while. Took a downward spiral myself, but over time, I came to realize I'd done the best I could."

Lark, struck unable to speak by the story, was so *very* self-conscious. Her face felt hot and she knew that she was blushing to her hairline. She set her gaze straight ahead and swallowed. Tried to calm her breathing. It all hit so close to home. *The woman had fallen into ultimate invisibility.*

Meanwhile, Cricket continued. "So, I left it all behind. Withdrew from practice, went home, tried to figure out what to do afterward. Dropped my professional speak and went back to the way I talked when I was jes' a lil chile! Nothin' wrong with that. It's an honest thing. And it's truer to who I am at heart. I try not to take myself, or life, too seriously these days. As for the jobs I do, they're good honest work, I like to be around people, and sometimes I can still make a difference in the lives of others."

"Yes, I see that you can." Lark was recovered from her embarrassment and reached for Cricket's hand to pat it warmly, feeling surely she'd found a new friend, someone with compassion and deep understanding. "I like the way you speak. It makes me smile." Cricket's way of speaking didn't diminish her, but made her an individual.

That evening Lark pulled on pajamas and thankfully crawled into her bed at Pearline's, tired after another day working at the gray house. She considered what to do until Monday—her move-in day. She could hardly wait. She would sleep at Pearline's over one more weekend and had three more days for some last minute readying. The house was clean now and, with the carpet out, smelled practically brand new.

The next step would be to paint. She would start tomorrow on her own. She didn't want to impose any longer on help from others. They'd given her enough of their time. Besides some time alone— in short supply at Pearline's— would be welcome. She longed to reflect on her state of mind since moving south and before that last huge step when the moving truck would head toward the gray house from California.

She had found little time to ponder the troubling revelations Pearline and Cricket had made about the town's culture. She needed to try and come to terms with that knowledge—more waves to ride, more responses to control. *Sigh.*

She glanced at the painting of the girl beside her bed and then closed her eyes, falling into deep sleep like an innocent child, and a bone-weary one at that.

Chapter 24

Turning to the Wind, Pine, Water, and the Moment

Lark pulled on comfortable old clothes that Wren had given her, as she'd done all week. She hadn't looked very appealing—never wearing makeup, cleaning house till she was grubby every day, only to shower, and collapse exhausted into bed each night. Unappealing and tired she might be, but she stayed true to the plans she'd made the night before and headed out to get paint, right after she grabbed a cup of coffee.

She pulled away from Pearline's satisfied with the new car she had bought locally. Small and useful, with a squarish back compartment, it could easily handle the loads she needed to carry for the work ahead.

She shivered, then ran her hand down her tingly, goose-bump-covered arm and realized the hair on the back of her neck stood out too. Knowing the symptoms weren't from cold weather, but instead were a result of the anxiety she felt every time she had business in Pressfield, especially now she'd learned her suspicion others talked about her was true. And not only that, but that public opinion about her wasn't … favorable. She felt the outside of her skin might even *look* prickly to others. The lack of confidence and the trembling she experienced in California those last months had returned.

The staff of two at the paint store turned out to be … not especially friendly. One of them gave her cursory attention, waving a hand in the general direction of the paint sample cards, and then they both disappeared. After she selected her paint samples, she waited patiently at the counter for minutes on end, wondering where they had gone, and then had to step to the open doorway to the back and call out.

"Hello?"

At last one of the guys reappeared and she was able to order her paint. From among the hundreds of choices there, she chose a pale, creamy shade of gray for the walls, reminding her of rain and cloudy skies, which she loved every bit as much as blue skies. She chose a darker shade of the same color for the ceilings, which were so high she wanted to bring them down and make the rooms seem cozier.

Her slight irritation with the service at the paint store changed to dismay as the salesman rang up her purchases unsmilingly, snapped out only necessary words to her, and behaved all the while as if doing her a favor. If this weren't the only paint store in town, she would have taken her business elsewhere. But she had wasted time waiting, so she asked with resignation when her paint would be ready, saying she would run errands and return to pick up the cans after lunch. She would give them plenty of time.

Though she brooded over his behavior, she decided to give him the benefit of the doubt. After all, anyone could have a bad day. And maybe she did seem prickly—through her body language, her expression, maybe the tone of her voice. She would try to be conscious of this with the next person she encountered in town.

She stopped by the library for a card, relieved to be treated kindly. Of course that could be because Wren who was back at work that day helped her. Lark found a book to read at night, if she could stay awake long enough, and a lengthy audio book to listen to while she painted. She patted Wren on the back before she left, noticing that her sister kept clutching the back of her neck and rolling her shoulders. She was probably sore and stiff from all the work she'd been doing at the gray house.

She picked up a lunch and drove to a town park. She sat at a picnic table beside the pond to eat, and watched a mother hold her toddler's hand to keep him from falling in the water, while he leaned away from her and tried to grab the ducks, the water, a stick from the ground. The little boy's antics amused her and lightened her mood. She looked at her watch … time to return to the paint store.

Ten gallons for the entire interior of her house sat inside the doorway of the store. She knew they belonged to her as the clerk motioned with his hand toward them. Again dismayed, she realized he had no intention of helping her load them into the back of her car.

"*Hmmph!*" she said under her breath, as she picked up the first two cans then pushed the door open by backing out of it. Considering her large purchase, the staff could have treated her with a little … *a lot*, more courtesy! She refused though, to expend her energy fuming. Instead she would put the incident out of her mind and focus on the work ahead.

Back at the gray house, she stayed true to her experience as a programmer, methodically tackling the task of painting her entire house by breaking up the job into parts, so that she wouldn't be overwhelmed by the amount of work ahead. She began in the bedroom that would be her own. This room would be important for rest, and its comfort would restore her energy for other work in the coming days, weeks, and months. When finished, she could move on to other rooms. *One step at a time, and only the present moment to think about.*

She attached a roller to a long handle and knelt to open the can of lovely, creamy gray paint. *Wait.* This was taupe … not gray. She rose to find her paint card to compare, knelt beside the paint can again, held the card beside the liquid inside—yes, it was the wrong color! She plopped backwards onto her bottom, the corners of her mouth turned downward, and she groaned. She was tired and sore, and with a task ahead that might overwhelm her if she let it. It was already well into the afternoon, and she had hoped to get this room painted today!

She would have to return to the store and ask them to correct their mistake. First, she would need to check the other paint. Thankfully, she hadn't brought the other cans inside but had left them in the back of her car. Her exasperation grew with every can she opened—all the wrong color.

She tiredly threw her bag across to the passenger seat, collapsed behind the steering wheel, took a steadying breath, and drove back to the store where she tried—despite her appearance in raggedy jeans and t-shirt, a face free of makeup, and stringy hair—to seem as if she was still a professional, making a stand to defend her input to a computer program at work. She pulled her shoulders back, tried to suck her puffy stomach in, and looked the clerk levelly in the eye. But she couldn't stop gritting her teeth.

"You have given me the wrong paint color," she said, making an effort to assert herself by calmly and truthfully stating the facts. She pried open two cans and slid them across the counter toward the clerk. At first he looked confused, but when he glanced upward from under his brows and smiled slightly at the other clerk, Lark realized with a sinking heart that this situation might be more than just an honest mistake.

"Let's see what we have here. *We* don't usually mess up on the paint colors," he said condescendingly, as if she must, of course, be the one who messed up. "Let's see, this is 'light taupe,'" he said about the first can, and then about the other, he said, "and this is 'medium taupe.'"

"I didn't ask for those colors," Lark said, holding out the paint card she had shown him earlier in the day.

"*Hm.* I don't see how that could have happened." He shook his head, stubbornly standing his ground.

"I never even knew paint colors existed by those names. I asked for 'mystic rain' and 'cloudy skies,' the ones on *this* card," Lark protested, holding out the paint card she had shown him that morning—the only one in her possession, because it was the one from which she'd chosen her colors. She was losing her cool. Her voice, uttered from a chest tight with frustration, trembled when she protested, "I wanted grays, not browns!"

A smirk twisted the corners of his mouth as he said, "Well, we can mix up some more paint for you, but I can't give you your money back on those ten cans of paint. I have a receipt here, with *your* signature that lists the colors we gave you and shows you knowingly walked out of the store with those colors this morning." He placed the lid on an open can, tapped it down loudly with a hammer and pushed it across the counter toward her.

Lark fumed. She hadn't looked at the colors listed on the receipt before she signed it. She had assumed they would treat her right. Her brow furrowed then her eyes narrowed. There was something very odd going on here. Both clerks stood across from her, obviously both firmly set on giving her a hard time. *Why?* Wasn't the customer always right? She took a steadying breath.

"No thank you," she said. "Because I'm going elsewhere and I will take this paint—all of it—and give it to a charity. At least something good will come from this!" And she pulled her two paint cans off the counter, turned on her heel, marched to the door, backed out, plopped the cans alongside the eight others in the back of the car, and climbed in behind the steering wheel, her heart pounding hard and fast. She felt as if she would hyperventilate. Her stomach churned sickeningly. *What was going on here?*

And then she realized. Not only were others possibly shunning her in this town, but her life would be made difficult—maybe not by everyone, but by some. Stress would be added to her life, making her sick if she let it. As punishment? To get her to correct her 'erring' ways? She shook her head confusedly, glancing through the store window. She could see the two clerks snickering at her. Her posture slumped and her head sunk down between her shoulders.

Wait a minute ... she'd done nothing wrong! She pulled her head up and shoulders back, and looked each clerk directly in the eye for a certain moment. Then, she calmly backed up and pulled out, heading her car toward Forestlee. She would have to drive further out to get some things done it seemed. Despite the strength she'd determinedly displayed, her face burned and her eyes watered. Her insides felt torn, aching.

Half her day had been wasted, but she tried to make the best of her trip to Forestlee. She focused on the beauty of the landscape as she drove—the fall colors that always comforted her, the beautiful blue of the sky, the sparkling water in the creeks flowing underneath the bridges she crossed. She stopped at a home supply re-use center and left the ten cans of paint, feeling encouraged with the thought of helping someone else with a contribution.

Even so, when she arrived at the Forestlee paint store and stood before the clerks, she shook in her shoes until she realized they would treat her kindly and with respect, as any customer should be. The guys gave her a cup of coffee and, this time, she puttered around the store while waiting for her paint. On her way back home, despite refusing to even glance in its direction, her breathing became shallow when she passed the Pressfield paint store.

Her control lay only in her response. She had to *refuse* to let petty meanness do that to her or to make her afraid. She had nothing to fear. She wasn't a little girl anymore—she was an adult now. Had learned how to be strong. She was loved by a few people; she tried to do the right things in life; she had made herself secure through her own hard work.

She remembered the conversation she and Cricket had shared. It would be easy to give up like that poor woman who lost her life to addiction and an overdose. It might be especially easy after doing the hard work of coming back once and finding it necessary to do it again.

As she stopped her car in front of the gray house, she bowed her head and closed her eyes. Her resolve was there, at her center. She gave herself over to something bigger than herself, bigger than this situation. Although she didn't speak out loud, she asked for help from above, to lift her, and keep her from descending. She pictured herself cradled in God's hand.

Opening her car door, she heard the wind blowing through the trees, smelled pine and water. Her heart slowed, and her breathing deepened. Her mind cleared. Strength and resolve returned. Peace had returned.

Back in her room, she poured the lovely gray paint she'd wanted into a tray and began to roll it onto the ceiling. She sighed contentedly. While it might seem odd to like the color and mood of a rainy day, it was Lark. Rainy days at home were the ones she enjoyed the most. There had been many a work day in California when she'd looked out her office window at the rain coming down in sheets, dripping off the eaves of the buildings and the leaves on the trees, splashing on the ground. At those times, she had longed to be at home, reading a book, and having a cup of tea.

The sky was darkening into evening through the windows when she'd begun rolling the ceiling, and it was late into the night before she stopped. She leaned backward to stretch and relax her tired and sore back. Although this week had been hard physically, she did feel she carried less weight. She'd been so busy, the thought of food and eating had been secondary, and Pearline, who had helped her most of the week, hadn't had time to cook.

After cleaning her paintbrush, she turned off the lights and closed the door behind her, and headed back to Pearline's to sleep for only three more nights.

Chapter 25
Moving Day

Lark looked outside every few minutes while she munched an apple and waited for the moving truck. She'd turned down Pearline's breakfast earlier—might as well get used to it. She would miss Pearline's cooking, but would probably be a smaller person for it.

The phone rang. She swallowed a mouthful of apple. "Hello?"

"Have they arrived?" It was just Duff.

"No, where are they, Duff?" Lark whined.

"I'm sure they"ll arrive soon. Did you finish everything you wanted to?"

"Yes but … can I call you back once they get here? They're supposed to call because the GPS won't get them all the way …"

"Oh sure. But don't forget to call me sweetie!"

"Okay." She hung up before Duff could say another word.

The phone rang again right away, and it was the movers at last. Pacing outside with her cell phone clamped to her ear, Lark guided them from the highway into the surrounding countryside, and finally to the entrance to her property. She hung up when they said they had entered her drive and went outside to stand on the front porch to listen for the sound of the truck's engine.

The burly guys sat in a row in the cab when it came into sight. The driver expertly swung the truck around, backed it up to the porch, and they wasted no time unloading her furniture—her bedroom things first, in reverse order to how they'd put everything on when loading up her condo under Duff's direction. It took some doing to get everything upstairs, and she didn't envy them their job. They moved on to boxes filled with her collections of bird statuettes, seashells, candlesticks, and vintage clothing. Then were her sparse living room items, and boxes of her books she told them to stack in the back of the room, where she hoped to make her library. Last were her boxes of mismatched dinnerware in a variety of eye-catching patterns—collected from flea markets, of course.

She closed the door behind them after thanking them profusely, and gasped as it occurred to her she'd forgotten to call Duff, who picked up on her cell at work.

"Well, it's about time!"

"I'm sorry, I got busy."

"Of course you did! Well, how does it feel? Tell me how it looks."

"Well, I painted, and the walls and ceiling look wonderful, but my furniture is tiny and there's not enough of it in these rooms. I'm going to need some things ... lots and lots of things! I wonder whether there are flea markets here."

"You may have to find an urban area for the kind of things we have out here. Otherwise, you'll have to go to the retail stores."

This conversation brought Lark's thoughts around to wonder whether she would have to go to an urban area for her every need, if she was to be treated as she had been at the Pressfield paint store a few days ago, and her wish Duff was here to go with her and look out for her.

Before she lay down to sleep that night, her first in her new home, she softly padded down the stairs in her pajamas. She stopped before the fireplace. Stepping up onto the stone hearth, she lifted the picture, draped the wire on back over a hook, let it settle into place against the stone. She stepped down and backed away.

Was it her imagination or did the girl look as if curiosity was getting the best of her, and as if she just *might* turn her head and have a look around?

Chapter 26
Karma

─────〜〜〜─────

Lark felt connected with her friend over the many miles separating them when she looked inside the box boldly labeled, 'OPEN FIRST.'

Understanding her love of coffee, Duff had wedged Lark's professional-grade maker onto the moving truck last, so it would be one of the first things she unpacked and, just like back in California, her coffee would be ready at the flip of a switch on her first morning in her new home. From the same box she pulled a clay cup, slanted as if the potter accidentally bumped the form and knocked the clay sideways. A whimsy, it brought a smile to her face and reminded her of the many Sundays she and Duff spent flea-marketing together. She poured extra strong coffee into the cup atop cocoa and sugar, poured in a bit of cream, settled the cup's matching clay lid on top, and stepped out her front door, warmly dressed against the chilly morning air.

Taking care not to slip on the dew-wet leaves on her way down the path toward the dock, she inhaled deeply. The ever-present scents of pine from the needles she crushed underfoot and of wood smoke from the fireplaces of other homes along the creek, made up for the hint of dead fish and damp mustiness.

On a recent outing with Wren, she had spotted alongside the road a cast-off Adirondack-style chair, and though it boggled her sister's mind, Lark begged her to stop the car and together they lifted it into the trunk. The chair only needed a stabilizing penny-nail or two to make it good and sturdy again, and it now waited for her at the end of the wooden walkway. She loved its wide arms, perfect for setting her cup of coffee on. She settled into the chair, knees higher than her bottom, and pulled her woolen sweater close around her.

Fog hung low over the creek and the sun's first rays were just peeking out behind her. She could feel their warmth like a friendly hand on her shoulder. A bird called out and she turned to look behind her toward its source on the bank, but saw nothing except a slight movement on the surface of the dock. She turned a little more in her seat, bringing her feet up underneath her and saw a large … no, a *huge* spider. It crept slowly toward her on only six legs, making her glad she had raised her feet. *Ugh.*

Just behind it another movement caught her eye. A lizard darted its head over the edge of the dock to eye the spider. It had the poor spider's two missing legs sticking out of the sides of its mouth. Lark tensed in her seat, uncertain what to do. Help the spider or the lizard? The spider was stalked, its life in danger. But the lizard might be her friend if he would get rid of big, furry spiders for her.

Again, she heard the bird. This time she saw movement in the light fog along the bank. Squinting, she tried to make it out.

"*Mew!*"

She pressed her hand to her smiling mouth to keep her laughter inside. It wasn't a bird at all, but the gray kitten she tried to befriend on the day when she first toured the house. Not quite as small as before, it was long-legged now, though still skinny.

Lark remained quiet and still, watching and wondering what would happen next.

The kitten hesitated before stepping onto the first weathered board of the dock then, spying the lizard, hunkered down on all fours, head low to the ground. Even from where Lark sat she could see the kitten's pupils grow larger and darker as it focused on its prey. Wiggling its hind legs into pouncing position, it leapt—its feet hitting the ground only once before it reached the lizard, which elusively slithered underneath the dock. The kitten peaked over the edge, ears pointed forward. Not seeing any signs of the lizard, it sat down on its bottom and nonchalantly licked a paw.

Lark shook her head sorrowfully at the spider's hopeless situation. It had eluded its stalker and moved, perhaps seeking a safer spot, but in so doing drew the kitten's attention and, with a quick pounce and a flick of the kitten's paw, was sent flying out into the water.

She dipped a finger into the cream atop her coffee and stretched it toward the kitten. It stretched out its neck, sniffed, and then stuck a tiny pink tongue to the cream. It allowed her to touch the soft fur between its ears for an instant. Then as quickly as it appeared, it darted back down the dock and disappeared into the fog again.

She remembered that among Duff's friends she had heard that animals could be protective spirits—she could sure use one of those. *Maybe she wasn't so alone here after all.*

She turned back to face the water. Her laughter over the drama, or comedy—depending on how one looked at it—that had just played out broke the silence and echoed over the creek. Crows cawed and scattered from the trees above. She cupped her coffee in her hands to warm them, and gave thanks that nature had taken its course, allowing her to only observe and not intervene—or play God—in the situation.

She pushed those thoughts away before they brought her round to her troubles, and instead laughed again. Laughter made her feel warm inside, helping to push troubling thoughts away. This morning, it felt as if good karma was in the air.

Good karma. Lark's spiritual beliefs developed from exposure to different religions and cultures out in California. Duff's friends introduced her to the idea that a person's actions created something akin to a force around them—if their actions were evil, they would generate evil for themselves and others with whom they came in contact. On the other hand, if a person's actions were good, a force for good in their own life and in the lives of others would be created. Maybe if she projected goodness, that would create good karma for her here—sort of battle evil in an indirect way.

Well, she really had no choice in the matter. She had never spent her time trying to hurt others. Scheming or devising ways to do so would go against her natural inclinations, and she would have to become a different person in order to do it. She relaxed her head back against her chair. The sun's rays were growing stronger. She let her sweater fall from her shoulders a little.

She didn't want to spend her time thinking about battling evil, even defensively. She'd once read that when people knowingly do something that hurts others, they usually believe they are doing right, but what they've done is taken the evil into themselves (Kushner 2002 Third Printing). And that was what *made* it evil—*knowingly* doing something to hurt others. No, she did not want to take evil into herself.

She wished to let it go. She laid the backs of her hands on her chair, opened her palms, and imagined releasing … *yes, letting go* … as the water lapped against the bank and the sun's warmth lifted the fog around her.

Chapter 27

The Way to Her Heart?

"Lark, now you're living here and not way out in California, Wren and I think it's time to have some new family traditions," Pearline informed her during a phone call, just two days after she had moved from her house to the gray one. Pearline went on, "We're feelin' a little let-down over here. You kept us company for weeks, and there was Duff's visit, then we were all busy helping you to get your house ready. And now, it's just the two of us again. So we've decided we should come to your place for Thanksgiving! What do you think?"

Her question took Lark by surprise. She hadn't thought about the coming holiday season. She looked around. Her house was far from ready for company, with unpacked boxes in every room, but celebrating a holiday here could only make good memories. And the prospect would give her reason to fill up some empty spaces. She said, "I think that's a wonderful idea, Mama."

The three put together a menu and grocery list while brainstorming at Pearline's at the squeaky kitchen table over a meal of course, and on Saturday afternoon before the holiday, they drove all the way to Forestlee to the new grocery store there to find the very best ingredients. The modern store was stocked with unexpected things, all grown without pesticides and made without preservatives. Lark—who had eaten mostly organically when she lived in California and was used to beautiful fresh fruits and vegetables year round—insisted they visit the store.

"But Lark, look at the prices of these groceries! They are dollars more than the kind I usually buy," Pearline said.

"I know, but listen, Mama, I want you to try them. It will be my treat. You will be amazed, I promise, at the difference in how everything tastes. Please?"

Pearline gave in to her daughter's 'hippie' sensibilities.

This outing reminded Lark of the three of them shopping together when she was a child. Their biggest, most fun shopping trips were on the first of the month after their government survivor's assistance check arrived in the mail. Shopping trips during the rest of the month were done with much thought and angst, while her mother kept a running total in her head as they put each item into the cart, with Lark or Wren having to return items to the shelves if the total got too close to Pearline's carefully budgeted limit. Now thankfully, none of them needed to worry about affording groceries, and they could enjoy this trip—even putting a few extravagant items for their holiday into the shopping cart.

Lark browsed the aisles more slowly than her mother and sister, who knew just what they wanted, and darted here and there after it. She glanced at them every so often, smiling at Pearline's slightly stooped waddle in tight, stretchy pants, and admiring Wren's upright and slim figure. Watching their happy anticipation was worth the trouble and fuss.

An uncanny feeling she was being watched made her pause. Her smile fell and she looked behind her, then cast a glance to her left and right, but saw no one who seemed to be paying any attention to her. *Odd*. She stopped near Pearline and Wren as they talked over how many Brussels sprouts to buy, when her eyes stopped cold on a startlingly good-looking man ... *gasp* ... that waiter from Latour's!

Thank goodness he hadn't seen her. She quickly looked away and pushed the cart closer to her mother and Wren, determinedly keeping her head turned. She didn't mention seeing him to the others, but walked stiffly behind them, wishing they would speed things up and get out of there. *So far, so good*.

They stopped in front of a cold case of frozen turkeys. She saw her mother turning over the same brand of turkey she had purchased all her life.

Lark sighed. "Mama, *look*," she bent over the case and found a smaller bird. "Farmers raised these turkeys in pastures with green grass out in California. See? On the label, it tells how they fed them only nuts and berries—no antibiotics or hormones. They're delicious. I used to—"

"She's right."

Gulp. Yep, it was him. As always, he got the attention of all three of them at the same time.

He smiled in his charming and disarming way, and walked down his side of the cold case, round the end, and down their side, while their eyes stayed glued to him the whole way. He said, "This one is even better, though. It's a Cajun deep-fried turkey." He grinned, and held out a frozen turkey.

"I … I don't think we want a Cajun Thanksgiving. Thanks all the same." Lark tried to sound gracious, and made an effort to return his smile. After all, there was no reason to be rude.

Pearline said, "You're a waiter at Latour's, aren't you?"

"Yes ma'am, and you've hurt my feelings a little bit. Cajun Thanksgivings are more fun than you know," he said, with a mock-hurt look at Lark. "You could make up for hurting my feelings by coming to Latour's with me for coffee. You haven't taken me up on my invitation?"

Lark felt her mother and sister's eyes turn to her as she hesitated, trying to decide how to respond.

"That's probably because she's been busy moving and working on her house." Pearline seemed to feel the need to step in for her, even though she could have no idea what the waiter was talking about.

"Oh?" He turned from Pearline to Lark. "You've moved nearer or further away?"

"*Um*, I've just moved *here*."

"*Ah* … so, if you're not doing anything when you're finished here, how about coming back to Latour's with me for that coffee?" His eyes were warm, his expression no longer teasing but open, and … hopeful?

"I … I don't have a car with me—I rode with them," she said, pointing her finger unnecessarily at Pearline and Wren.

"That's okay, I can take you home."

"But I live at Echo Creek."

"Not a problem."

"Go ahead Lark, we'll be fine, and we're almost finished shopping," Wren said, nodding her head at Lark, and cutting her eyes in a meaningful way at her.

They were conspiring against her!

"Good," said the waiter, whose name Lark still didn't know! "I'm finished now myself, so I'll check out and wait for you at the front of the store."

"Okay," Lark responded, feeling defeated. She turned to frown at Wren in her own meaningful way. *She* certainly hadn't been any help! Feeling mean-spirited and ill-tempered, she imagined how they would react if they found out they'd sent her off with … well … with the bogeyman. She continued to frown at them as they stood there smiling indulgently at her without a worry in their heads!

A few minutes later they found that 'good-looking waiter from Latour's' waiting beside his cart at the front of the store as he promised.

Lark paid for their groceries and glanced one last time toward her mother and sister who were pushing their cart toward Wren's car, and were also looking back all the while to watch Lark walk away with … with a *stranger*. Lark pulled her sweater closer against the chilly evening air and *'hmmphed'* under her breath in their direction.

As she and … the *waiter* … crossed the parking lot, she peeked at him. He looked masculine and carelessly handsome with a day's growth of beard shadowing his jaw. He held the door of a black sports car open for her and waited for her to slide in, before closing it solidly and pushing his cart to the back to unload his groceries. His close physical presence after he slid in beside her caused her to lean with shyness toward her door.

Really, he projected nothing but a friendly, companionable vibe. *Oh, she might as well make the best of this.* She decided to meet his determined efforts to get to know her and broke the silence herself. "You aren't working on a Saturday night?" she asked.

He turned to look at her with his eyebrows raised, a slow smile curving his lips.

"I have every other Saturday night off, so I can have something of a social life."

She caught herself staring at him, became embarrassed, and forced her gaze to the view in front of the car.

"My name is Charles Latour, by the way." He held out his hand, palm up.

"I'm Lark." She took his hand into her icy cold one.

"It's nice to finally know your name," he said.

They soon arrived at Latour's where he took her hand and led her through the crowd toward the back of the restaurant, then through a narrow hallway, and into a small office. Lark's quick, assessing glance took in a desk with a table butted up against its side, two chairs, a couple of filing cabinets, and a coat rack.

He pulled out a chair for her. Then stepped outside the doorway and turned back toward the room.

"I'll be right back with some coffee! Don't go anywhere!"

He'd brought her to the office and his last name was Latour, maybe he was more than a waiter. *Interesting …*

She sighed. *What was she doing?* She hadn't prepared for this! She'd come to Forestlee today to spend time with her mother and sister—no thought of romance in her head! She fidgeted with her makeup, clothes, and posture while she waited. Then, disgusted with her preoccupation with how she would look to him, she turned her attention to the details of the room for clues about this person who so persistently tried to get to know her.

The walls were deep red. There stood an aged wooden desk, with a hutch rising up the wall behind it holding stacks of paper. Some papers hung over the edge of shelves as if placed there in a hurry. A warmly glowing lamp stood at the far corner of the desk. There was another stack of papers on the desktop, with a laptop settled atop them. Black-framed photographs of motorcycles were arrayed on the wall beside her.

Charles returned with two cups of coffee, and she had no more time to decide what the room said about him. "Here you go," he said, and slid a brimming cup on a saucer toward her. He pulled off his sweater and threw it over the coat rack, before he sat down at the desk across the table from her. She couldn't help noticing his shirt stretched tight across his chest when he raised his arms and clasped his hands behind his head, his chair squeaking as he leaned back.

"I'm glad you decided to have coffee with me," he said, showing that disarming smile again, his blue eyes looking directly into hers.

She tried to return his smile, but feared it came across weak. She felt nowhere near as confident as he seemed. Instead she just felt shy. Determined not to nervously chatter away, she waited for him to continue. Pretending to be cool and calm, she sipped her coffee even though it was too hot, and singed her tongue to tastelessness right before Thanksgiving. She supposed that served her right for behaving disingenuously.

But the coffee was delicious and disarmed her … just like Charles's smile.

"*Mm*," she said, before she could stop herself. It was strong and fragrant, tasted of cream, and was there chocolate … cinnamon? He had so quickly found the way to her heart! "Great coffee!" She was determined now to be her true self.

"You should taste it in the morning, right after its ground—like I asked you." He looked at her from under his brows with mock sternness.

"I'm sorry about that. As my mother told you, I have been moving and very busy."

"So you moved to Echo Creek?"

"I bought a house there."

"You're lucky, that's a beautiful area."

"Yes, I am fortunate," she said. *Was she? Fortunate again? Maybe. Maybe not. After all, he didn't know her whole story, did he?* How much did she want to reveal about herself at this point?

There was no ready answer to that question, so she prompted him instead.

"Latour's is the name of the restaurant ..."

"This is my restaurant. Well ... mine and my Pop's."

"Night Charles!" three young waitresses called out and giggled as they took their jackets and scarves from the hooks on the wall directly across the hallway from the office. They peeked slyly into the room through the open doorway, possibly curious about the woman Charles had troubled to bring back here.

Charles smiled slightly and dismissed them with a wave.

Lark could hear other stirrings outside the open doorway—sounds of pans clanging together, a broom brushing across the floor, and low, tired-sounding talk from the kitchen. Though some employees had departed, they weren't alone yet, and she still felt safe with this person she didn't know well. But he *was* a business owner, and she knew from Pearline that this restaurant had been here for years—he wasn't likely a bogeyman. Besides, she and Cricket had talked so recently about taking care not to prejudge people. She was finding herself hypocritical—she'd been closing the door on Charles before she really knew him.

The silence lengthened. She became lost in the musical notes playing in the background, so beautiful, tears smarted in her eyes—alternative acoustic guitar, soft vocal tones—different from what she was used to, like the man who sat across from her.

He was gazing into his coffee, lost in thought, turning and turning his cup on its saucer.

She said, "It must be getting pretty late. It looks like your employees have finished for the evening."

"Yeah, we close at ten. You don't have to go yet, do you?"

Maybe she was looking for escape out of nervousness, but she had no real reason to leave, and her curiosity had been piqued now that she knew a bit more about him. "I can stay a while. So, are you a chef as well? I noticed you in the kitchen ... once."

"You noticed me, eh?" His grin, devilish this time, gave her no doubt he also remembered the intense look they'd exchanged when she was first here back in October. Unable to meet his eyes now, she had to look away. Heat rushed to her face as she blushed.

"I cook when things get really busy. I do everything and anything that needs doing. My Pop keeps the financial side of the business going, and I keep the people and food side going."

Now they could hear cupboard doors closing, the brush of fabric as coats were pulled on. Someone called out, "Charles, you want me to turn off the lights out here?"

"Yeah, go ahead. I'll lock the back when we leave. See you Monday."

With everyone else gone, the place was very quiet and dark, the small lamp on Charles' desk cast the only remaining light.

Lark said, "It sounds like yours would be the more difficult work, I mean between yours and your … 'Pop's.' "

"I love it—wouldn't do it otherwise. So now you know what I do, what about you? What do you do during the week?"

Lark carefully thought about how to word her answer. She hadn't yet had to explain her reasons for moving here to anyone other than family and Duff.

"I worked in a high-tech industry in California for about twenty years, but wanted to make a life change … I bought the property at Echo Creek as an investment."

"Good for you!" He raised his eyebrows as if impressed, and paused to sip his coffee. "But, what do you *do?* You look like a person who wouldn't sit still for long."

"You're right!" she said, and laughed lightly. "I'm working on my house, and I have two cottages on the creek that I hope to rent out after I've redone them. I expect I'll stay busy, bruised, and my muscles will ache for some time to come!" She showed him her hands, nails broken off, with paint still here and there where she'd been unable to wash it off.

His eyes tilted up at the corners when he laughed. "You don't do the work all by yourself, I hope?!"

"No, I have help sometimes."

"What are you working on right now?"

"As soon as things settle down after Thanksgiving, my plan is to rip out my too-dark and overly-ornate kitchen cabinets so that I can have new ones installed."

"Ha! I'd love to see you doing that! You must be tougher than you look."

She grinned. "I can be tough when I have to be!" Saying that, gave her pause. She hadn't been feeling so tough emotionally …

Their conversation flowed easily until near midnight when she could no longer hide her yawns. It was late for her. She usually went to bed early, physically exhausted. "I'm sorry, I'm a little tired," she said.

"Let's get our coats, and you can tell me how to get you home."

They climbed into his black car again. Although Lark's personal vehicle choices were driven by economy and usefulness, she could appreciate the looks of Charles's sleek, comfortable, and expensive car.

As he drove Charles posed more questions, leading her to describe in more detail her life in San Francisco, and explain more about why she'd ended up back here. She delicately avoided revealing too much about things she wasn't ready to share.

He had been asking personal questions, and turn-about was fair play so, before she had time to control her impulse, she asked one that was important to her.

"You're not married, are you?" she asked.

"No, of course not!" He took his eyes off the road and turned to look at her. "Why?" He sounded surprised by her question.

"Maybe I'll tell you sometime," she said, too tired to go into it all now.

At the gray house she waited for him to walk around the car and open her door. She stepped out, taking his extended hand. When she stood up, his body was within inches of hers and she swayed dizzily, but resisted the flow of energy that pulled her toward his chest.

"I'd like to see you again," he said.

She slipped her hand from his grasp and searched for her cell phone to cover her awkwardness. "I'd like to see you again too," she said.

They exchanged phone numbers, keying them into their phones right then. Only the taillights of his black car were visible in the dark when she paused at her front door to watch him leave.

"Mew!"

She looked down at her feet. She hadn't seen the gray kitten since their adventure on the dock. More friendly now, it brushed against her ankle. She bent over to run one finger along its back, thinking the wild thing would allow no more than that. And it did allow her a moment's touch. Remembering it was night and how very alone she was out here, she cast a quick glance out into the blackness where she could no longer see Charles' taillights, then stepped into the house, leaving the door open to see what the kitten would do. It hesitated, tail curled in the air like a question mark.

"Come in, you can stay with me," she coaxed. It stepped forward— one paw, two paws, and then trotted in as if right at home. She closed the door. *What would the night ahead hold for her with a wild kitten loose inside?*

In the kitchen she set out water and tuna fish, but her thoughts were on the time she'd spent with Charles. She had no plans for a romantic relationship. In fact she'd planned to avoid such, after her experience with Russert. So why had she entertained the possibility of seeing Charles again? She supposed it was chemistry. She certainly wasn't attracted to every man she saw. In fact, she didn't understand her lack of interest in perfectly attractive men, with whom Duff or her friends fixed her up in the past. At times she'd wondered whether something was wrong with her, as it seemed every woman who was single except her suffered from some degree of preoccupation with men.

But this … this *thing* with Charles was spontaneous, making it all the more powerful. There had been no plan or intention to attract. It had just happened. Maybe that made it more right. But memories of Russert quickly returned. That had seemed spontaneous also, and certainly was not meant to be.

She felt sure that Charles was not married, as he said. But there was something that made her hesitate … *was it his looks?* She'd never been very attracted to men who were *too* good-looking. She supposed she thought they couldn't help but be 'players,' using the strong attraction they held for women for all it was worth. She suspected she was being exceptionally naïve to think he felt any kind of unique attraction to her. If she found him strongly attractive, there were many other women who would also. Maybe he started relationships often with women who came into his restaurant!

Wait a minute! What was she doing? Casting those judgments she so despised! What a hypocrite she was becoming. For now, she would let her head rule her heart … and the rest of her, and forget about him … and his coffee.

<hr />

She glanced at the painting over the fireplace as she passed on her way up to bed. Where was that look she noticed on the girl's face recently—as if she might turn her head and have a look around the room? Now, her eyes seemed stubbornly turned away, hair blowing in the wind …

Chapter 28

Thanksgiving

Lark turned her thoughts fully to the holiday and found a substitute for her flea markets in the shops in Forestlee. She searched for a table for the library in the back of her living room, and found just the right one—antique birds-eye maple, with collapsible ends that she could fold out for special times like Thanksgiving, and fold down again when not needed into a smaller size to use as a reading table. Its worn surface and slightly warped planks didn't discourage her ... a few flaws added character and interest—kind of like in people.

Peeking in the window of a shop, she noticed her reflection in the glass. Her nose and cheeks were rosy from the cold. She looked warm in her long knit coat that extended to the top of her boots, with a colorful knit scarf round her neck. And she looked healthy and ... *happy*.

The colorful displays inside drew her eye away from her reflection, and lured her into the folk art gallery, where she found a hand-made glass bowl to hold a centerpiece for the holiday. Gleaming in the warm light cast downward from railroad pendants, were four Windsor-style chairs, two with arms, two without, to go around her new table. Someone had built them by hand, rubbed the surface till smooth as butter, and then put the parts together with wooden pegs—all done so that they would last several lifetimes. She lifted the price tag and cringed, looking around her to see whether anyone might see how much she was about to spend, and glad she'd come alone so no one would know how much she liked them. These special chairs hadn't been created with perfection in mind—the lines were curvy not straight, and no two were exactly alike—each was a work of art, unique and different from the others.

Before Thanksgiving arrived, several of the chairs received added character from the gray kitten, who used the legs as scratching posts and then arched its back, fur standing on end, and darted away with a sideways scoot when Lark fussed.

On Thanksgiving morning the family of three gathered in Lark's kitchen, none of them fully awake yet. Of course they had to have coffee. Wren found the recipes they used in a cookbook written by a chef who believed in casual entertaining. Pearline assigned duties.

"Lark you do the rolls—bread can be so temperamental, and you know your own oven. And maybe you should do the turkey too, since you've roasted this fancy kind before! I'll make the cornbread dressing and apple pie … and Wren … you make the cranberry relish and roast the Brussels sprouts—I'm so glad I taught you girls to like your vegetables!"

As Pearline cut shortening into flour for the pie crust and Wren washed the Brussels sprouts, Lark slipped the turkey into the oven and left the roll dough to rise, then headed to the main room to turn on music. She put in a mellow jazz cd whose drifting notes reminded her of fall leaves tumbling out of the sky. She spent some time polishing her new antique table, and set out three white ironstone plates with gold linen napkins alongside. She set the new glass bowl in the center, with brown-shelled walnuts and pecans, fall leaves, and pinecones arranged inside, flanked by newly polished silver candlesticks.

When she returned to the kitchen, she paused at the sight of Pearline busily rolling pie dough, saying to Wren who busily chopped celery, "remember when …". The gray kitten, 'Karma'—she had to keep reminding herself—had positioned herself to the side of the room, already having learned food often fell to the floor, and quick kittens were rewarded with tasty morsels to cart off like hunted-down mice.

The sight filled Lark—who was learning to love being in the center of a family again—with contentment.

The phone rang.

"Hello?"

"Happy Thanksgiving!"

"Happy Thanksgiving to you too, Duff! Who are you having dinner with today?"

"Oh, Val and her soon-to-be husband. I think we may just go out for Chinese, though."

"Sorry I'm not there to fix turkey and dressing for you." She'd done just that for many years for the two of them, with the same small pasture-fed turkey she was roasting for Pearline and Wren today.

"Me too. Anyway Chinese will be festive, don't you think? And more importantly, I have news for you—someone offered the full asking price for your condo!"

"No! Oh, but that's great! So, it's all but sold—"

"I'm sure you'll get a call soon from your attorney. And you're gonna have to come out here to finalize everything, so plan on staying with me. Give me a call when you know the date. We'll have fun and make it special, okay?"

"Sure, Duff. Enjoy the holiday today," Lark said, with some longing in her voice. She stood at the windows that overlooked the creek and turned her gaze westward, thinking of Duff beyond all the states in between them.

"I will, sweetie, you too. Are you having dinner with Pearline and Wren?"

"Yes, we're cooking now. I wish you could be here. Maybe next year?"

"Maybe. Tell them I said hello and Happy Thanksgiving!"

Lark lay down the phone, her mood dampened. This was the worst part about moving, leaving Duff. Sometimes she wished Duff could, or would, move out here too. But the news that her condo had a likely buyer was good. It meant less worry over the cost of improving her new property—something to be thankful for today.

———

When the day neared late afternoon and all the preparations were made, Lark lit the candles and stirred the fire so that they would feel its warmth across the room.

At the table they joined hands and Pearline made a request.

"I want each of us to say a little something, you know ... what we're thankful for. I'll start. I'm thankful for this time with you girls. There couldn't be a more special day for me. I ask blessings for you, Lark, for your new home and life here. And for you, Wren, for whatever your gentle heart desires. Wren?"

"I am thankful for my family—the two of you. And the caring we have for each other. May we always have caring and kindness, love and understanding, in our hearts for one another. I hope we can always be like we are at this moment. Lark?" the two of them turned to look at her.

She took a deep breath.

"I am … *so* thankful to be here. To be home again. And for the two of you, and for Duff, and Karma … and for so very, very *many* things …"

Then, they each closed their eyes and said their own silent prayers.

Chapter 29

A Tangled Ball of Twine

As Duff predicted, Lark received a call next day from her attorney in San Francisco, saying her condo had indeed sold. He said her presence would be needed at the closing.

On the plane to San Francisco, Lark wondered whether she'd forgotten something. Her thoughts were wrapped around one another like a tangled ball of twine. The quickly changing events of the last weeks were overwhelming—meeting new friends, feeling rejected by old ones, the auction, moving and leaving her best friend behind, trying to settle into a new home, a holiday, selling her old home, throwing things into an overnight bag, and flying westward to sign papers and say goodbye to that part of her life. She looked forward to some time when she came back home to think about and absorb it all. For the next couple of nights, she would sleep on Duff's pull-out sofa—another reason to rest when she got back home.

She felt she'd barely set her feet on the sun-warmed California soil when she met next morning with her attorney and the new owner of her condo to sign the papers and turn over the key. Afterward for a small amount, she gave away the key to her tiny car to Val's husband-to-be.

Next evening, as the sun began its descent over the buildings to the west and the Pacific beyond them, Lark and Duff walked up the hill and over one street to their favorite restaurant. City lights came on all around them, and Lark felt both excitement over an evening out with her friend in the city, and melancholy she wouldn't have another for a long time.

They entered the restaurant's black-painted door, and were enveloped by its atmosphere—happy chatter and mellow piano jazz, the sensation of warmth, and the aroma of good food.

Following a hostess who threaded through closely clustered tables to the opposite side of the restaurant, they neared a cheerful group seated at a long table. Lark felt surprised that they were led toward them rather than to a table for two. Drawing closer, she saw they were those she and Duff spent time with in the past at the flea market or at Duff's get-togethers. There were Val and her fiancé and, as Duff led her to the far end of the table, Lark was further surprised to see her young protégé, Kieran, and ... Edwin! She had seen neither of them since her last day at work. She hugged Kieran and hoped her quiet sobs went unnoticed.

"Lark!" Edwin exclaimed, and that seemed all he could say before he hugged her tightly.

"Edwin, I'm *so* glad you're here. I've missed you, and we didn't really—"

"I know." He smiled a tender, watery smile. "Let's sit down. We'll catch up and have dinner." A gentleman, he pulled out a chair for her so she could sit beside him. Kieran sat on the other side of her, blushing to his hairline and seemingly incapable of speech. She patted his hand and gave him a motherly smile. Her gaze stopped at Duff beside him, and she smiled wryly because of her friend's trickery in getting her there, and making her believe just the two of them would have a going-away dinner together. But it changed to a genuine smile of gratitude when she remembered Duff's thoughtfulness in inviting Edwin and Kieran.

The group chattered and laughed through several courses. Lark joined in the broader conversation only a few times, mostly observing the quirky urban style and behavior of the people around her and contrasting them with the small-town people she was getting used to again. But people were the same everywhere. The ones here might have more knowledge of the wider world, might have had more varied influences on their lives, and might be interesting to talk to, but when all that was taken away, deep down they were as simple as the ones back home. Their conversations, while they began with talk of current world or national events, eventually narrowed down to events in San Francisco, their own neighborhoods, their workplaces, their homes and families.

She and Edwin didn't need many words to communicate. She knew he was sorry for the way their working relationship ended. He knew she felt hurt for the same reasons. And they both knew life was unfair.

"The world has changed since we first started out, hasn't it Lark?" Edwin asked.

She nodded and returned his sorrowful look, knowing he didn't mean for the better. She wanted to ease the worry for her she saw in his eyes. She didn't plan to feel hopeless about her future, and she didn't want to leave him feeling that way either so, as she was learning to do when her thoughts took that downward turn, she simply turned her back on the negative and turned instead to the positive.

"Edwin, I'm doing okay. I have bought a house of my own—I'm a property owner now! And I'm with my mother and sister. I'm making some new friends. I'm making a new life there. And it's okay." As she patted his hand where it rested on the table, his brow smoothed and his eyes took on a sparkle.

"I do know you're okay. Change can be good. It can open doors you never even knew were there … can be quite wonderful, really. Maybe you'll inspire me to make my own change. I am thinking of retiring." They discussed the possibilities retirement might open up for him, and Lark's own brow eased. Seeing Edwin might be the best part of this trip. To close the door on that life of many years with a smile. To know the person who looked out for her back then could look forward to the future, too.

They stayed for hours, moving on to coffee and intricately created and ridiculously small desserts, until yawns began bouncing around the table and some remembered they had children to get home to, and babysitters to send home.

Lark walked with Kieran toward the door and gave him encouraging career advice, telling him he could call her anytime, knowing he would miss her mothering presence at work. She hugged Edwin before they parted, content that all was well between them, and grateful that after tonight they would be able to carry a mutual peace into their new lives.

She and Duff were the last to leave. They bundled themselves into their capes and scarves and stepped out into the windy, chilly night. They walked slowly, neither in a hurry for it to end, not knowing when they would meet again after tomorrow.

Duff said, "Lark," as if to get her attention before saying more, while hooking her arm through Lark's and pulling her closer to her side. "Tomorrow after you leave …" Duff stopped, and pulled Lark's arm to stop her, too. She leaned toward Lark to look into her face, as if her meaning would be more likely to be understood if Lark could see her. Then she continued, saying, "… *promise me that you'll remember something you learned from us here … a soul that has freed itself from the bondage others try to impose, that can express itself freely, be true to itself, is safer to be friends with, to trust, than a soul that is in torture, captive to the labels others—that the world—tries to place on it, or even to the ones it tries to place on itself."*

Lark was taken aback by Duff's seriousness. *Was her friend trying to protect her?* Duff had been somewhat protective toward her in times past. After all, she had no children, no family of her own, only her friends. Of those, Lark was the closest. Duff continued with more heavy words.

"Lark, I think, despite your forty years and your experience living in a big city and fending for yourself, you have a tender heart. Remember the hard lesson you've learned lately. You can't return to a state of naiveté about relationships, you know." She hooked her arm back through Lark's and pulled to make her walk beside her again.

Duff's words frightened Lark. As Duff meant for them to do, they reminded her how she'd trusted and suffered heavy loss because of it. She frowned. *Duff was certainly darkening the mood, wasn't she?* But when she looked into her friend's eyes, she forgave her. Duff was trying to help and had given her something to think deeply about.

She recalled Russert's holding back, the way she never felt he gave away his true self, that she never really knew him.

And then she thought of the people she'd shared dinner with tonight. The open faces, the willingness to talk freely, the lack of confusion when talking with them. They were all creative people who lived their lives being true to their hearts—no matter what others thought.

All that would require deeper thought. And she felt tired, so tired. *Tangled twine ...*

"Okay, Duff. I'll try to be careful," she said, and with that, she yawned widely and loudly.

"Lark, whatever comes your way, and I hope it's all good, just remember you're loved, and you can always come back to San Fran," Duff said, with a catch in her voice. She turned away quickly, picking up the pace of her steps and Lark could no longer see her face.

Chapter 30

Untangling the Twine

Lark woke several mornings after she returned from San Francisco feeling unrested. She'd hardly slept last night … again. What was causing this restlessness at night and lack of motivation and energy during the day?

For one thing, she hadn't been working on the house. For another she'd been eating anything and everything she wanted. She felt no pleasurable expectation … about anything. Thanksgiving had passed. It was gray outside. It would be some time before her new home was finished to her liking. Her old home was gone. It felt cold and damp here … always. And, if she went anywhere to try to cheer herself up, she would probably be treated rudely or ignored or even feel threatened, unless she went to Forestlee or beyond.

She recognized this mode of thinking from when she hit a turning point in San Francisco, when she became so sick she knew she *had to* pull herself out of her escape from life. Her thoughts and feelings had been similar, and she had to thump them, like the needle on an old record player. *So*, she'd do it again, and she'd catch herself *before* she became stuck this time.

She sat up and groaned. She had to face the fact that moving her body, drinking less caffeine—*hmmph*, maybe she'd switch to decaf—eating fruits and vegetables and *not* eating *everything* she wanted, were the first steps to feeling good again—to sleeping well, thinking well. And it would have to begin soon, wouldn't it? Well, *sigh* … this morning. She'd just have to put one foot in front of the other. *A path—wasn't there a path?*

She stepped out the door dressed in toboggan, gloves, and running clothes that felt unfamiliar now. She could run along her gravel road which had alongside it a fairly clear path carpeted with grass and leaves for her running feet. Her body objected with every footfall. Joints creaked, even felt like bone grinding against bone. *Was that sinew tearing?* She could take only baby steps, shuffling her feet along. It wasn't exactly running, rather sort of stumbling. At the end of her road, she calculated she'd run about three-fourths of a mile. She would need a longer route eventually. A cross-country run around the perimeter of her acreage would be perfect, but trees, fallen branches, rocks and all kinds of seed pods and other things fallen from trees, stood in her way right now.

She limited her run to only one trip down the drive and back. Slow and easy was the way to go, for now.

Back inside she flipped the switch on the coffeemaker to brew decaf, then showered and made her bed for the first time that week.

With her cup of coffee in hand, she stepped out to the deck, letting the kitten out the door with her. The trees were nearly barren of leaves now, except for a few strong ones still clinging with everything they had to the branches, fluttering dark brown, against a background of clouds in varying shades of gray.

She propped her elbows on the deck railing and gazed outward over the creek. Birds swooped low over the water, searching for tiny fish beneath its cold surface. Duck-like birds bobbed on the surface, leaning forward now and then to submerge their heads and search underwater for their meal.

She had promised herself some time to think when she returned from San Francisco. She took a deep breath before allowing her thoughts to probe the tender places that hid the reasons for her descent of the last few days. The reason for her downward descent out in California was easy to remember, but here ... anyone would think making a new home of her own, with prospects for the future wide open, she would feel nothing but positive. But ... *were* her prospects 'wide open?'

Maybe she shouldn't be too hard on herself. It was all so much at once. She had closed the door on an old life in a very final way, leaving her no choice but to make a life here. And she hadn't yet come to terms with the fact that life here might not be perfect after all.

But what could she do except ride the waves? She placed her head in her hands. *Sigh. Waves, records, grooves, tangled twine—peace ...*

She turned her palms upward in submission. Her eyes searched the sky. Gray clouds rolled past pushed along by an early winter wind. And she made a request with tear-filled eyes, "Please ... *please* grant me lasting peace ..." She trusted the answer would come ...

She opened her eyes. She'd spent the past days resting physically *and* mentally, but her problems hadn't solved themselves. Maybe the answer was simpler than she thought. Maybe she should try the opposite and get busy with something positive.

She hadn't visited the cottages since moving into the gray house. She could really use the income from their rental. Yes, she had sold her condo, but those funds only helped to defray the cost of this place. She was still without an income. Much was needed to make the smaller houses livable—repairing and cleaning at the very least.

Today would be the day she'd make a to-do list for them. She poured the last drops into her coffee cup from the coffee pot. With her laptop tucked under her arm and Karma tagging along at her feet—her tail a happy question-mark in the air, as if she asked, "What are we up to today?" —the two of them trotted off toward the cottage to the east of the main house whose roof peeked through the trees.

"Oh Karma it's cold in here …" *Goodness she'd started talking to the cat as if she were a person!* "… and damp," she said. She ran her hand along a thick, knotty pine plank of wall paneling. These would be the envy of many these days, though time had dulled the varnished finish. She wondered whether termites inhabited any of the wood. The floors were concrete and cold and had paint chipping off here and there.

She stepped into the bathroom and pushed the door closed to determine the usefulness of the shelves behind the door. Her eyes wandered down the length of the cubby and met the floor where she saw one of those—*ugh*—spiders with cricket-like, folded legs poised and ready to jump at her.

"Kar-m-m-a-a," she called—she could use the cat's help now! She eyed the spider and the spider eyed her. Who would move first? She heard Karma's nose snuffling at the space underneath the door. The spider, sensing the cat on the other side of the door, scrunched down and backed toward the corner, giving Lark room to act. She jerked open the door and dashed out while Karma darted out of her way.

Again, Karma had come to her rescue, making her feel not so alone.

Rather than feeling discouraged after looking around, Lark's mouth curved into a smile at the promise of a new friend living in the cottage. In her minds' eye, she saw shared lives and impromptu drop-in visits. Maybe another single woman could live here, someone who needed a new start in life … like herself. Someone she could talk to, rather than a cat.

It would be too much to keep working on the main house and to do anything at all here, alone. She could use some help. *But who?* She typed 'research local contractors' onto the to-do list she'd started on her laptop.

"Karma, let's go see the other cottage." *Would it be in any better shape?* She shooed the cat out, and closed fast the squeaky door. The second cottage seemed sturdy, but just as needful of updating. Discouragement crept toward Lark's optimism.

"Well, first things first, Karma, I have to get a quote for all the work." That would have to be her project for the rest of the day. She locked Karma away in the gray house and headed to the building supply store to get advice on area contractors. She had been there several times now, and many of the workers knew her by name and knew about her projects at home. And she had yet to be treated with disrespect or rudeness there. Although she suspected she was a source of amusement for some of the men. She was sure they didn't think her capable of much and imagined her home projects going all awry. *Well, she'd just have to show them.*

Proud of the work she'd done thus far, her house, if not there yet, was on its way to being a lovely, special place. Today she would find someone else to share the work and the bruises, along with her.

And to take care of spiders—those missing legs *and* those that jumped.

Chapter 31
Worthy of Recognition

During the third week in December, the day of her appointment with a possible building contractor arrived. As she dressed for their meeting, she thought about the impression she needed to make.

Just as she learned to consider how others should see her in her professional life, she needed to be seen now as just another working guy. So she wore clean khakis, a dark blue blouse, and a blue jean jacket, hoping to keep all the construction workers, from their supervisor on down, from behaving condescendingly toward her—she would find that hard to take. She had held the respect of men for many years out in California, until—oh, when would she stop remembering?! *Thump ... ride the waves ... unravel the twine ... peace ... only this moment.*

Sigh.

She put everything she needed into a backpack to carry with her, and went out the door with Karma right behind her, as usual. Parked in front of the inlet cottage was a clean white pick-up truck. He was early—a good sign.

She'd left the cottage unlocked and found him standing in the open living area, gazing up at the vaulted, pine-clad ceiling, dressed in the typical work khakis, thermal and flannel shirts against the late fall weather, work boots and a baseball cap. He turned when she came in. They stared at one another in disbelief.

Hartmann Worth, her boyfriend from high school.

A gasp of a laugh burst from her chest and he shook his head as they stepped toward one another. She reached out her hand for his, but he stepped closer and pulled her into a hug instead.

They stepped apart to look at each other. She was sure that he was considering the changes time had wrought, just as she was.

Of course, she had no makeup on and had hurriedly pulled back her hair with her intent to not seem too girlish today. And she'd noticed in the mirror recently, she had more worry-lines on her face since going through big changes.

Time had been kind to him, though. His gray-green eyes creased with pleasing wrinkles at the corners when he smiled. His light brown hair hadn't grayed much, although his hairline had receded a little. He seemed fit, as one might expect of a man who moved heavy things around as part of his work.

"Lark! How've you been?" he asked.

"Good, Hart. And you?" She was embarrassed to find her hand still held his. She let hers fall away, and took it into her other one behind her back. She looked at the floor and turned the toes of her boot in the dust.

Hart answered her question. "I've been pretty good. Lark, I can't believe it's you!" He looked at her sideways, maybe with shyness. "It's been a long time, hasn't it?"

"Yeah." She nodded unnecessarily and smiled. "So, you're a building contractor?"

"I've been building or remodeling houses for more than ten years now. This place is yours?" he raised his eyebrows as if surprised by that too.

"Yes. I own this cottage, the main house on the point, the cottage on the other side of it, and the land you drove through to get here."

"Wow, you're quite a property owner!"

This roused her temper—couldn't other people succeed? Maybe he recalled her humble beginnings from high school days. She supposed that's all he knew of her after she left. She was wrong.

"I heard you'd become a success out in California, but I didn't know what that meant, exactly." His eyes flickered away, his expression sheepish, as if he didn't say all he'd heard.

She decided to take him at his spoken word.

"Well, it's meant that I could make a change, a rather big one, and come back here to be near Mama and Wren. I bought the gray house for myself and hope to rent out the two cottages for income. But, as you can see, this one's going to need some work, and the other cottage even more, probably. That's why I am looking for a contractor." She blushed at her clumsy effort to bring their focus to the work.

"I can see you need some help. What do you have in mind for this place?"

She removed her laptop from her backpack—she'd outlined the entire job for the two cottages on a spreadsheet. She opened the file and handed the computer over to Hart, relieved to be getting down to business now the greetings were over. She didn't want to delve into memories of two decades ago. Not right now.

While Hart looked over her project plan, Lark poured two cups of coffee from the Thermos she'd brought over. He gratefully took his, and she clutched hers in both hands to warm them up. As she'd expected, the inside of the cottage felt damp and chilly again today.

"Well, you've got it together! If you put this on a flash drive, I have my own laptop and—" She pulled a flash drive from her backpack and handed it to him. He promptly plugged it into his laptop. "I'll make my notes right on your spreadsheet," he said.

They were thinking alike. Things looked good, very good.

They spent a couple of hours walking through both cottages. When they finished, she wanted to give him the go-ahead right then. But like a professional, he told her he would work up an estimate for each cottage as a separate job, and get back to her by the end of the next week.

They shook hands while his gray-green eyes held her dark ones, his expression serious and thoughtful. Yet, neither of them returned to speaking on a personal level.

He climbed into his shiny white truck, and drove away.

Her stomach rumbled with hunger as she walked slowly homeward. She hadn't thought of Hart in a long time, until she'd taken Duff by her old high school and its baseball field. High school seemed so very long ago and far away, and the intense feeling she and Hart had for each other had been erased by time. They'd been able to get right down to business, and she had felt no electricity, no chemistry flowing between them, only surprise to see him. In high school, she'd felt like they were connected by some invisible thread. He'd represented safety and security to her, coming from a stable, well-to-do home, with both a mother and a father. But now … everything was different. She had created stability for herself. That was far better … wasn't it?

As she made a sandwich, she let more memories come forward. She hadn't met anyone since, who was as genuinely nice as Hart. They'd fallen in love and spent the rest of high school mostly with each other, letting their other friendships fade into the background. Everyone had begun to assume that marriage and work would be in the near future for them. He wasn't interested in college, and her family didn't have the money.

But then her scholarship to a university out west surprised them all. Everything else, including Hart and any assumptions they'd made about the future, faded into the background. She'd become so single-minded. *Had she become selfish?* She'd gotten busy making plans for moving to California and assumed that he would understand and be accepting of her going away. They'd agreed to keep in touch, but her ambition won out over trying to maintain a romantic relationship over several thousand miles. The internet wasn't around then, and she had no money for long distance calls, much less for return visits home. Letters helped for a while, and she thought she still had them somewhere in a box, but upper-level classes eventually left her with little motivation for writing letters.

Then job offers came along, and more money than she ever dreamed possible. Hart changed his mind and decided to go away to a state college, and letters between them became few and far between, until they lost touch completely, and twenty years flowed past for both of them.

She hadn't been unfeeling about losing Hart. She could remember pangs of loneliness, and even disbelief, that she had let go her end of the invisible thread connecting them. But at the time, she felt the sensible thing was for her to finish college. And she also remembered a vague feeling of relief, as if she'd narrowly escaped …

She lay in bed that night, more relaxed and at ease than she'd felt in a long while—decision made. There was no one she could trust more than Hart.

The girl in the painting downstairs, forgotten, a part of the scenery now to Lark, wore a peaceful expression.

Chapter 32
Getting to Work

⁓⁓⁓⁓

In the kitchen of the gray house, Lark plunked down the tools she needed—pliers, claw-hammer, and a crow bar. She found a classic rock channel to listen to, as this job called for loud, fast music.

She climbed on top of the lower cabinets and stood shakily, then tested the decorative molding along the top of the upper ones by tapping it lightly with a hammer to find out where and how it attached. It pulled away, but hung on tenaciously with finishing nails from behind. She grabbed each tiny nail with pliers, and wiggled and pulled, while awkwardly trying not to fall, until each one stubbornly released its hold.

She stored all the trim in the back of her kitchen in the breakfast area, a space she didn't use now, as she ate her meals at the library table she bought before Thanksgiving.

Next, she would remove the cabinet doors. She'd forgotten the power drill, so climbed down and retrieved it from a still-unpacked shopping bag from the hardware store. Of course, it was at the bottom. *Sigh.*

She had to read instructions about how to use the drill, which thankfully were easy to understand, then backed out the screws from the door hinges, and stacked all the cabinet doors she took down in the breakfast area too. She rubbed her hands together, quite satisfied with her accomplishments.

The upper cabinet frames—the boxes that held the shelves—would be heavy and attached securely. This part would be the hardest, yet she felt excited because she could already visualize bookshelves for her library built from the parts and pieces of wood she'd stacked in the back of the kitchen. The kitchen was changing before her eyes, already more cheerful without that dark cabinetry hovering over her.

She backed-out every screw in the first frame, leaving only two at diagonal corners to hold it up. As she considered her next move, the structure began to creak and the two remaining screws began to pull from the wall with its weight.

She couldn't hold it up! She squealed and jumped off the counter and out of the way. The frame crashed first onto the countertop, and then down to the floor. As the dust settled she studied the broken frame lying face down on the floor, coming apart at the seams, in total surrender. It reminded her of something—

"Hello? Lark? You okay?"

The greeting pulled her thoughts back to where she stood in the kitchen. She remembered she'd left her front door unlocked as she'd been carrying tools to and from the basement. She grimaced and peeked around the door jamb. *Hart.* Why did he have to choose this moment to show up?

"Oh, hi!" she said, conscious of her messy appearance, brushing at the dust all over the front of her jeans. "I'm working on my kitchen," she tried to sound nonchalant and as if she knew exactly what she was doing.

"I can hear that. Are you building or destroying?"

"Well ... I'm destroying, so I can build."

He chuckled when he saw her handiwork—two glaring holes left in the sheetrock where the screws and bolts had ripped out, the cabinet lying brokenly on the floor. He lifted the fallen piece easily.

"Where do you want this?"

She pointed to the breakfast area.

"Are you going to take all these out?"

"Yes ..." she sounded much less confident than she'd been when she started the job.

He eyed her skeptically and said, "Why don't I hold the next one up while you remove the screws?" He had a derisive grin on his face, though unknown to Lark it was directed internally. He looked at her standing there—her hair a mess, chest heaving, nose and face red from effort—in her little jeans and t-shirt. Feeling warm, he unbuttoned his flannel shirt, pulled it off, and threw it around the corner toward the front door so he wouldn't forget it when he left.

She took his smile of derision personally. Offended by it, she imagined him stepping in and pushing her aside as if he thought her incapable and to show he was stronger and smarter! She pulled her shoulders back and stood straighter, saying, "I can do this—"

"I *know*. But I've got time, and we can talk about the work on the cottages in the meantime, which is why I'm here." He leaned back against her lower cabinets and crossed his arms against his chest, his expression showing some respect for her now.

She considered his explanation, his obviously capable biceps visible through his thermal shirt, his now more passive body language, and the gentle respect in his eyes. She felt chagrined. He was right. She could use help, and they did need to talk about the cottages.

"Okay then," she said, as if it was no big deal, and she attempted a smile to take the edge off the defensive stance she'd taken. Inwardly relieved to have the help, she climbed back up onto the lower cabinets and—practiced now—easily removed the screws from the next frame, while Hart supported it to keep it from falling. When the last screw was out, she slid over while he took on the entire weight of the thing and carried it away.

She didn't like to admit that she had needed his help, but the only way she could've gotten that down on her own would be to let it fall, like the first, leaving holes in the wall that she would have to repair later. While she waited for him, she decided that she would draw up a design of the library shelves she wanted to build. That evening she would sit at her library table with a cup of tea, a pad of graph paper, a sharpened pencil … a thrill of anticipation rippled through her till Hart's voice reminded her there was still work to do.

"While you're sitting there how about looking over this estimate?" He handed her a printout of the spreadsheet she'd made up. She noticed it now included columns for material and labor costs and notes he'd made to clarify her specifications.

"I'm surprised. The estimate is more than I expected."

"It always is. But you have to consider that you're making two homes habitable that no one has occupied for years."

"Can't we reuse some of what's already there?"

"Well there isn't much there, Lark, and what's there is old."

"Yes, well. I'm going to have to think about this."

"Sure. I wouldn't have it any other way. Take as long as you need. We've finished the upper cabinets. You want to work on the lower ones?"

"*Um* … I think not today." She looked at the clock on the kitchen wall. "I'm supposed to be at my mother's soon."

"Okay. Just call me when you've made a decision."

"I will. And thanks for your help today." Shyly, she let her eyes meet his. He smiled, his eyes creasing downward at the corners, in that way she found irresistible when he was a boy. She couldn't help smiling back.

Chapter 33

Lark is Questioned

When she arrived at Pearline's, the front door's three tiny rectangular windows glowed with welcoming light. She had to push hard against it with her whole body as the wood had expanded with the moisture and heat of Pearline's busy kitchen. The reward for her effort was a wonderful aroma when she stepped over the threshold—roast beef and gravy? She was starved after running this morning and taking down cabinetry, too. She heard voices in the kitchen.

When she stepped in, Pearline and Wren turned toward her with expressions animated with recent laughter, and Lark saw they had company—Cricket, whose hair without her hat was shorn close to her head in a thin layer of tiny curls. Lark hadn't seen her since before she moved into the gray house.

"Hey girl! Come here and give Cricket a hug!"

Lark thought her ribs would crack when the woman squeezed her, and she had to giggle. Cricket just did that to people—made them feel like laughing. All she had to do was smile, but then she sometimes took it … so … much … further … *oomph!*

Cricket released her at last, and Pearline said, "We're ready to eat, honey. Let's all sit down." Her mother couldn't stand for any hot dish she prepared to get cold.

They settled in at the squeaky metal table, set with ironstone plates atop blue and white checked kitchen towels for placemats, with a fork on the left, knife on the right, and the good old, dependable glass of sweet iced tea.

Pearline reached for Lark's right hand, Wren reached for her left, and Cricket smiled a toothy white smile right across from her. Pearline said her usual simple prayer.

"Thank you, Lord, for saving us for this day. Please bless what we're about to receive and please bless each one of us here." She squeezed Lark's hand before releasing it.

"Tell me what you're up to at your house now, Lark," Cricket said, as they passed tender roast, potatoes, and carrots around the table.

Lark sipped her tea before she said, "I've painted the walls—and I love them—in grays, like the rain. It's a little empty of furniture though. And ..." she hesitated, knowing protests would be coming her way, "today, I started taking out my kitchen cabinets."

Pearline paused in passing the potatoes, holding them in midair. "Lark! Not all by yourself!" she said.

Lark hesitated again, not sure she wanted to tell them about Hart yet, then decided she had no choice, unless she wanted the ladies to descend on her tomorrow to help. Which wouldn't necessarily be a bad thing, she just wouldn't be able to do things completely *her* way. She smiled sheepishly and fed them the least amount of information she could.

"I ... had some help."

That set them to thinking. "Who?" they asked all at once.

There was no holding them back, so she gave in completely and said, "You remember Hart Worth?"

"Lark! Are you seeing him again?" Pearline clasped her dimpled hands together, eyes lit with delight.

"Mama, no. I've only been here for a short while, I'm not—"

"Well Lark, what about that waiter over in Forestlee?" Wren asked.

Lark knew they'd just been waiting for an opportunity to ask her about that one.

"*What* waiter? An' *who's* Hart?" asked Cricket, looking from one to the other.

Lark huffed—she would not let them get away with interrogating her! She chewed her roast beef slowly, enjoying its savor, sipping her tea, cutting another bite ...

"Lark!" Pearline said, in the way she had when they were children and she demanded an answer.

"We-e-l-l-l, who do you want to hear about first?" Lark asked, and sipped her tea again.

"It doesn't matter! Just t-e-l-l-l us!" Wren said.

Even Wren! Lark sighed. She would have to satisfy their curiosity.

"I've consulted Hart as a contractor for the renovations to my cottages. He stopped by today to drop off the estimate and ... ended up helping me remove some of my kitchen cabinets." She shrugged her shoulders.

"That's all?" asked Pearline.

"Yes, that's all."

"What about the waiter?" Wren persisted.

What was *with* Wren? Lark stated the simple truth.

"Well, we've had some … *um* … longish phone conversations, but I haven't seen him since you guys sent me off with him—a total stranger, I might add—to have coffee. Remember, just before Thanksgiving?" She wouldn't let them forget their lack of protective feelings for her that day!

She recalled snippets of her conversations with Charles as they were relayed back and forth across the air waves in recent weeks. She had spent hours talking with him. He had a kind of fly-by-the-seat-of-his-pants lifestyle—very different from the way she tended to live her life.

"Why not?"

"What? I'm sorry?" Lark asked.

Pearline brought her back to the present with her insistence. "*Why* haven't you seen the waiter again?"

"Well, he went to New Orleans—which is where he's from—for about a week, and I had to go to San Francisco, and I've been busy thinking about the cottages, and doing some other things. Actually, he asked to see me tonight, but, I had plans to come here."

"Now Lark, we could've changed our plans!"

"I know, but I wanted to come here. I haven't seen y'all so much lately. And … I don't know that I'm so very interested in a relationship, right now."

"Well, I don't want to hurt your feelings, honey, but neither you nor Wren is gettin' any younger," her mother said.

Lark turned her head to look at Wren. Their eyes locked and their mouths quirked in silent sympathy.

"Now, Pearline, y'all leave this girl alone. Can't you see she's kinda' confused right now? She'll sort things out. She's had a lot goin' on lately. Haven't you, Lark?"

Lark nodded and looked down at her plate.

"I'm sorry, Lark. Goodness, you *have* had a lot on your plate lately, haven't you?" Pearline said—maybe a tad ashamedly.

Yes, I have had a lot on my plate—and in more ways than one—Lark thought, as she eyed yet another of Pearline's rich meals on the plate before her. But she looked up and smiled, having forgiven them already. "How was your family at Thanksgiving, Cricket?" she asked, to change the subject.

"Oh my! All the kids have grown, don't you know?! I got to see my brother Martin—you know, 'Doodlebug?' An' we had the best meal—

turkey, cranberry sauce, an' that sweet potato stuff with the marshmallows on top? Yes, *yes!*"

They listened, without anyone's feathers getting ruffled for a while, to Cricket talk—with discretion of course—about her own family's happinesses and trials.

While Pearline and Wren were distracted by Cricket's stories, Lark was distracted by her own thoughts. Why were they so curious about her life? Considering her treatment at the paint store not so long ago and Lucy's treatment of her—which she still hadn't gotten over—it seemed that not only did her own family focus on it, but some in the community too. How did someone like *her* become such a focus? What went on, or *didn't* go on in other people's lives that caused them to pay attention to her?

Of course, in the case of her mother and Wren, their involvement was legitimate and out of caring, but others … who knew what their motives were? Avoidance of pain in their own lives? To keep others interested in their conversation? For another selfish—she shivered—or even malicious reason?

She shook her head. She couldn't understand it.

Chapter 34
Cricket Tells a Story: Flightless Souls

Across the table from Lark, Cricket had grown silent and was watching her.

Cricket's intuitiveness about people—her ability to read them—was her special skill. She considered it a blessing sometimes, but most of the time … yes, most of the time it was a curse. She could see and feel so much hurt. She'd been like that all her life, and it had led her to choose counseling as a career. Nowadays, without a career to focus on, and with those skills honed by years of use, she read most everyone she came in contact with—whether she wanted to or not.

Lark looked bewildered right now. At the beauty parlor Cricket had been overhearing the whispered congratulations some in the community gave each other over, for example, driving too close behind Lark's car, shop ladies ignoring her, others cutting her off with their cars in parking lots. Instead of intervening, Cricket had adopted the approach of just listening, to see what all was bein' said. But now, it was time to take action. Lark needed help.

The clatter of Pearline setting a heavy cake plate on the table interrupted Cricket's thoughts. Under a glass dome sat a buttercream-icing-covered chocolate cake—tall, the icing thick, creamy, and perfectly swirled by Pearline's expert hand. Wren filled the coffee cups at each place with fragrant coffee, while Pearline plopped generous slices of cake onto dessert plates that Lark held out, each lowering when the heavy cake dropped onto them.

Cricket reached her hand across the table for the slice Lark handed her.

"I have to tell y'all 'bout something I've been thinkin' on here lately," she said, watching Lark take a bite of her cake and close her eyes in pleasure. She went on, "See, while I was workin' my way through college, I cleaned house every week for this woman. A wealthy woman. Big ol' southern mansion, you know. And it was a *job* to clean, let me tell you! Anyway, that woman is dead now ...

"But, the first time I walked in that house I could hear birds chirpin' and it sounded charmin', you know? The woman walked me through that big ol' house from room to room, tellin' me she wanted this done here an' that done there, but all I could think about was finding those birds. I stretched my neck around this way an' that, trying to see where that beautiful bird chatter was comin' from!

"Finally, we got to the back of the house—a garden room, walls of windows, plants that had to be watered every week—and there stood a big ol' bird cage. It was just beautiful! I couldn't help myself—I didn't ask her if it was all right—I just walked closer to that cage and stood there gazin' at those pretty little birds—white ones and brown ones, all with orange beaks—finches, she called 'em. They seemed like the happiest birds I had ever seen.

"Well, I couldn't wait to go back and clean for that woman and see those birds. I kind of wanted some for myself. I would go to clean that room and have to stop and watch them. I thought they were enchantin'.

"But over time, I began to notice things when I watched 'em. At first I thought they just hopped about, all happy, some of 'em even sittin' right beside each other like they loved each other! But then I looked closer. Two sittin' in a corner, one leanin' over with its sharp little beak, peckin' and peckin' at the other one's head. That was not love!

"And the other two or three scattered about, fussin'—not stretchin' their necks out happy and sleek and calm, but rufflin' their feathers, shakin' themselves, flittin' about from place to place all nervous and agitated like. They were not happy at all!

"All of a sudden one day, it struck me—they began to seem downright neurotic! I stepped back, and as I did I got a picture of their whole little world. They were not happy, and they were in ... a prison!

"Now, those birds looked beautiful. They had everything they needed for basic gettin' by. But they were bored and finding somethin'—anythin'—to do. Even if it meant hurtin' each other.

"An' I began to realize that's just how people can be. Like this situation you're in, Lark? I'm sorry to bring it up! But I hear people talkin' at the beauty parlor, and I think some of 'em are bored to death, don't know what to do about their own problems, maybe even feel like they're in prison in their own lives. And it makes 'em angry, and they start lookin' for something to … peck! They get their feathers all ruffled, hop about from one to the other and chatter an' fuss!"

Cricket looked around the table at the other ladies. Pearline nodded in agreement, Wren looked resigned, and Lark just looked sad, like a wet dog, her head hanging down, face looking tired and older than it had seemed before. Cricket reached across the table and patted Lark's hand.

"Honey, I think you need to get out there and have fun." She leaned forward to see into Lark's eyes. "*You* are *not* in a prison, child! Be happy and free. Let your light shine in spite of them—*to* spite them if you have to! You go and see this waiter—what was his name? Charles? All right?! You go see him and just forget everything. Make a new friend, okay? That'd be good medicine for you!"

Lark smiled weakly and said, "Okay, I'll think about it, Cricket."

Chapter 35

Regaining Perspective

She ran furiously and far, fast and with strength. Surely if she could run past the pain in her legs and in her lungs, she could do anything?! *If only this confidence would stay with her always.*

Lark slowed to a walk. Instead of walking back to the house, she veered to the right and stalked along the perimeter of her property.

She had greeted the first rays of sun this morning with frustration, and disgust for herself. After dinner at Pearline's last night, she had tossed and turned yet again and lay sleepless, allowing her troubles to overtake her mind yet again.

Hopelessness caused her lower lip to quiver. Even if she succeeded in redirecting her thoughts and acting positively, someone brought her troubles to her.

And now her mother and sister were getting into her business! Pearline mentioned that she was getting old, implying that she needed a 'relationship' before it was too late. *Uugghh!* Lark wrapped her hands around her head, trying futilely to stop her circling, clamoring thoughts.

She breathed deeply. The scent of wood smoke hung on the air. Now only a few days from the official beginning of winter, with most leaves fallen from the trees and covering the ground, land around the creek was being cleared and leaves and debris set to burn.

The sound of crunching leaves came from behind her. She turned, expecting Karma. Instead there were a mother mink and three babies trotting along behind her. The mother didn't pause when she saw Lark, but continued on her way, as if she understood Lark wasn't a threatening presence. The adorable babies were dark brown, almost black. Lark could've held one in her palm.

Her thoughts were no longer on anything except that moment. Her blood pressure continued to slow, her breathing continued to deepen, she sighed, and tears filled her eyes. This time the tears were out of gratefulness, instead of hurt or sadness. There was such blessing in this moment. Under a canopy of huge trees, surrounded by creatures who were concerned only with their own existence, she realized how insignificant she was. How inconsequential her life was in the scheme of things. And that felt right. If *only* she could carry this moment of presence, of knowing, everywhere with her ... *always!* (Tolle 1999)

She had reached the property's distant point. She needed that running path she'd imagined not so long ago. It was boring to run the length of her drive and back, and repeat over and over. This was a day when she could work, and she wanted to be out here. She looked behind her. She could only see underbrush and tree trunks, and that ... was the problem. She couldn't run through that.

Her steps quickened as she walked back to the house purposefully to get tools.

Chapter 36

Fresh Ground

Despite knowing Christmas was only days away, Lark couldn't bring herself to go shopping. Although she dearly wanted to find gifts for Pearline, Wren, and Cricket too, the idea of shopping, going out into the community, filled her with dread.

She found leaving the peace of the gray house and going out into public something to bear rather than a pleasure and at the worst times, she felt such hostility around her that it made her fearful. Maybe she had become to some here a representation of all that was wrong with the world—a convenient receptacle for casting others' stories onto, or the stories of others they knew, or even the stories from television or books.

She couldn't spend every moment outdoors, or in a meditative state, so when those thoughts threatened to overtake her mind she got to work. She made her way around the corner of the house to the basement door. Pushing it open on its tight, stiff hinges, she peeked inside. Spider webs hung from the ceiling and corners, and it was dank and musty.

She flipped on the light switch, and the single bulb in center of the ceiling came on, giving off so little light that the first order of business had to be opening the dusty, plastic-lined drapes closed across the wall of windows on the creek side of the room. She gingerly stepped over boxes, odd and ends of furniture, and who knows what else, while making her way across the room. Pulling the drapes open released clouds of dust and moths into the air. The dim sunlight that shone through cheered the room a bit. She crawled over more boxes to pull open all the panels, until there was enough light to have a good look around the room.

It was a disheartening mess. Her love of making something out of nothing stirred only slightly. Mostly she felt discouraged in the face of another overwhelming task.

A thud in a far corner of the room caused her to jump and cover her mouth with her hand after letting out a squeal. It was only the kitten.

"Karma! Can't you meow or … or something to make your presence known?" In response, the kitten sneezed, dispelling the eerie air in the room.

Lark shook herself, pulled back her shoulders, and took a deep breath. She would not let herself be discouraged by a little, *ahem* a *lot*, more work, even in this dark place.

It made the most sense to begin at the corner where there was an overhead door that could be raised for moving large objects in and out. She scooted a few smaller boxes toward the door, but soon arrived at boxes that she couldn't move alone. Her mind wandered among her very few acquaintances for someone who could help.

Hart had already done her a favor by helping her with the cabinets. To ask him for another favor would seem to be presuming a familiarity to their relationship that time and distance had erased. Pearline, Wren, Cricket? No—another woman wouldn't provide enough muscle power No one else came to mind, until … her heart lurched—*Charles*. She hadn't seen him in a while, but certainly hadn't forgotten him. She had enjoyed their talks over the phone. Maybe it was time to find out if there was more there. As an idea began forming in her mind, she moved toward the door.

"C'mon Karma, we're gonna to have to save this job for another day." She gathered the small cat into her arms, burying her face in the soft fur. She would find time to visit Charles at the restaurant and hopefully enlist his help. His answer to her invitation to help her work down here might be interesting. And there was his coffee … and those blue eyes that she hadn't been able to see when they spoke on the phone …

She didn't call Charles to let him know she was coming. She showed up at Latour's at the time of morning he'd said to come in for beignets and freshly ground coffee. How much would the Divine come into play? Would Charles be there or would he not, if she just showed up?

She felt nervous for several reasons—she might be seeing him again, and it had been a while. Also, she was pursuing *him* this time.

The restaurant was decorated for Christmas with a *'Joyeux Noel'* sign on the door, and just inside was a tree draped with gold tinsel and *fleur de lis* ornaments. Red lights in the shape of hot peppers were strung around the kitchen ceiling.

The hostess, one of the young girls she had seen here before, smiled a welcome and Lark told her she was only one, and asked her to tell Charles that 'Lark' was there. The hostess's eyebrows raised a bit before she hid her surprise, and led Lark to one of the tables for two in the back. She handed Lark a menu, and turned toward the office hallway at the back of the restaurant. Lark looked down at her menu to hide her nervousness, while her foot bounced jerkily under the table, and her breath came so quickly she thought she would hyperventilate. The aroma of coffee and sugar wafted through the air, turning her focus to something other than that she would soon see Charles.

She didn't have to wait long. He arrived at her table with the hostess following close behind him. He knelt beside Lark, smiling gorgeously.

"I'm glad you're here!" he said. "I have a few things to take care of and then I'll be with you, but I want you to go back to the office. Ashley will show you." With his hand under her elbow, he gently guided Lark to standing, and she dumbly nodded, seemingly incapable of speech, and followed Ashley to the office where she and Charles had shared their first conversation—before she'd said goodbye to San Francisco and Duff, before she'd seen Hart again, before she'd started running again.

She felt like a different person than she'd been then, just a month ago—stronger, more her old self. The old self of before-Russert, but with something else added too. Her thoughts were interrupted by Charles.

"Hey *beb!*" Without hesitation and certainly without shyness, he stepped in and pulled her up out of the chair and against him. Time stood still while he enveloped her in his warm, strong embrace. He seemed even more ... everything than she remembered. His hair was wavier and darker. He was taller, broader in a good way, and more handsome, if possible.

"I've wished you would come back in. I've been watching for you," he said.

She blinked. He had watched for her? She was surprised he'd been thinking of her at all.

"Really?" she asked, eyebrows lifted. She was sure it was obvious she was shaky on her feet. "Well, I came in for that chicory coffee!" *Hmm,* she had belittled his feelings. *Why had she done that?* She grinned showing all her teeth, feeling fake and disingenuous in her effort to hide her nervousness and lack of confidence. *What was this side of herself that being with Charles brought out?*

Unfazed, he said, "You came in for the coffee, yes? Come with me." He took her hand and pulled her from the room toward the open kitchen without waiting for her answer. She took tiny steps, trying not to fall into his back, feeling she must look very silly being dragged along by him.

He helped himself in the beverage area as if he owned the place, which, of course, he did.

She shyly watched waiters pass through, going about their business and eyeing her curiously. Charles paid them no mind. Though self-conscious she tried to seem nonchalant, and leaned an elbow against the counter while she watched him. He wasn't just pouring black coffee. He poured grounds into a metal cone-shaped thing, leveled off the top and tamped them down with a metal presser thing. Then he put the cone-thing into a big machine and light brown liquid came out into two white ironstone cups. He poured milk into a metal pitcher and put it under another machine, one of those very loud ones she often heard in coffee shops, where a wand stuck down into the milk. Then after banging the milk pitcher on the counter a few times, he poured the hot milk over the light brown liquid in the cups, taking a stirrer and pulling it through the cream. With his fingers he sprinkled cinnamon over the foamy white tops. He put the coffees on the tray and dumped powdered sugar over the top of the beignets. *"Allons, cher!"* he said, as he picked up the tray and started back to the office.

She didn't know what that meant, but she liked the way it sounded coming out of his mouth, and followed after him.

He pulled his chair to the end of the L-extension of the desk, so their chairs were at the same corner, and together they set everything from the tray in front of them. When they sat down he leaned forward over the table, not touching his coffee or pastry, and gazed at her with a slight smile lifting the corners of his mouth.

Embarrassed again, she looked down at her coffee. On its top, Charles had formed a shape in the cream … a snowflake! A heart would've been pushy on his part, of course.

"So how was San Francisco?" he asked.

"Beautiful as always. And I was able to say goodbye to my friends. My condo there is sold and everything is wrapped up," Lark answered.

"You've put to rest that part of your life now?"

"I suppose so." She hadn't thought of it in those terms, but that is what she'd done. She looked up at him. Perhaps there was more to him than those blue eyes—insightfulness. She became lost in studying them. Used to looking in the mirror at her dark brown ones, his—of such a different and intense color—never ceased to grab her attention. In need of a distraction, she tasted her coffee. Creamy yet with a strong coffee flavor. She picked up her beignet, unable to resist any longer. While she delicately tried to take a bite without leaving traces of sugar around her mouth, she watched him furtively. He took a big bite of his beignet, not seeming to care that powdered sugar fell onto the table and was left on his lips. Everything he did, including making coffee and eating, was done passionately, without self-consciousness. It was very … appealing.

She noticed the warmth radiating from his arm lying on the table next to hers and wondered whether he felt the energy flowing between them too. She sat up straighter and cleared her throat, then asked, "Did you enjoy your holiday, and New Orleans?"

"Oh … yeah. Yeah, I did. So, what have you worked on lately at your house?"

She was startled by his brief answer and abrupt change of the subject, but described in detail the changes she'd made and the upcoming work on her cottages, finishing with, "And yesterday I took a look at my basement. It's full of what's probably only junk." She noticed he seemed to turn one ear toward the kitchen—the noise level out there had risen. The lunch crowd must be arriving. "I've just realized you probably need to get back to work," she said.

"*Ahhhgggh!* Yes, I'm afraid so! They come in before eleven, even. But I don't want you to go!" His disappointment seemed genuine.

"I have an idea. If you have some free time after Christmas, would you help me move some things out of my basement?"

"*You* would be there, right?" he asked, followed by a devilish grin and one raised eyebrow.

"Of course, working right alongside you and ordering you around!"

"Then I'm there! My slowest day is Mondays, so I could come by on the Monday after Christmas. I could take the whole day."

"That would be great! I don't suppose you have a truck?"

"I might be able to borrow one," he said, as he began to gather their empty cups and plates onto the tray. "Listen, I am glad you came in. And I'm looking forward to next Monday." He pulled her to him for another hug, and surprised her by lightly kissing the corner of her mouth. She hoped he wouldn't try that on Monday—at least not more than once—because it might greatly hinder the amount of work they'd get done.

Chapter 37
Ophelia's

After leaving Latour's Lark meandered along the sidewalk in the direction of her car—still thinking of Charles. Today the Divine seemed to be on the side of 'Lark + Charles.' After all, he had been at the restaurant and had accepted her invitation to *work* on his day off. And his encore coffee performance was quite good.

Clothing hanging inside a shop window caught her attention. She stopped to read the name above the door—'*Ophelia's*.' She climbed two stone steps and pushed open a weathered wooden door as bells tinkled overhead and the scent of orange and evergreen greeted her, reminding her that Christmas was only days away.

She was transported to another world. Hanging from racks and draped on wire-frame mannequins was clothing cut from fine fabrics in colors of faded brown, dark green, burgundy, and navy blue—fitting colors for the fall and winter seasons.

"Hello." Lark turned toward the woman's voice. Her most striking feature was her long, steely gray hair. Her blouse was of tobacco-brown lace, a necklace of peach and green crocheted flowers lay against her throat, and her smile was friendly and sincere.

Lark's own smile came naturally, without the usual effort.

"Welcome, I'm Ophelia ... can I help you find something?"

"No, I'd just like to have a look around."

The woman inclined her head, never losing her smile. As she turned away, Lark saw that she used a cane on her right side and her stride was stiff and halting.

Lark's gaze drifted upward toward the ceiling's wooden rafters, and then down the crumbly and irregular brick walls. The wooden floor creaked beneath her as she turned about to take in the whole room. Tiny lights in muted colors were strung along the beams. Paintings in gold frames hung on the walls.

Gossamer-like dresses and skirts floated in the air as she pulled them along a rack. She fingered a card of handmade paper pinned to the front of a dress—on it, were words handwritten in beautiful calligraphy:

> *"Your beauty should not come from outward adornment, such as braided hair and the wearing of gold jewelry and fine clothes. Instead, it should be that of your inner self, the unfading beauty of a gentle and quiet spirit, which is of great worth in God's sight."* 1 Peter 3:3-4, NIV

Lark's heart swelled and her throat closed up. Her eyes looked up for the woman who must have made this card, given as if a blessing. Behind the register, Ophelia gazed out the window, looking as if her thoughts were far away.

Lark's hand fell on a skirt of ruffled tiers, each a shade darker than the one above, until it ended at the bottom in bronzy gold. She lifted it from the rack and turned to find something that might look interesting with it. A stand of finely knit sweaters caught her eye. She found one shaped in an irregular fashion, coming to points at the ends of its sleeves. One lapel was longer than the other.

How does one describe the feeling a woman gets when she finds something to wear that absolutely delights her? Lark put a hand to her mouth, self-conscious about the thrill that nearly bubbled over in laughter.

Ophelia approached her and before she was near, Lark blurted out, "I'm confused! This card ... this quote ... would seem to contradict the purpose of your shop—selling the adornment of women?" Lark turned the card and its verse, so that Ophelia could see.

"It would seem so, wouldn't it?" Ophelia smiled knowingly. "I believe that even if a woman chose the most beautiful, most precious, item in my shop, her real beauty would have to come from inside her ... from her spirit. And I cannot sell that kind of beauty." Ophelia turned and motioned for Lark to follow her.

In the dressing rooms, light sparkled from ornate crystal sconces on each side of mirrors in gilded frames. Etched along the top and sides of the mirror glass were more words about the authentic beauty of women.

> *"Beauty is [not found in] in things themselves: It exists merely in the mind which contemplates them ..."* (Hume 1711-1776)

and,

"You. Are. Beautiful."

This woman, who so generously shared these words—so loving of the inner spirit of other women—was someone who embodied Duff's advice, given just before Lark left San Francisco:

> *"Lark, remember something you learned from us here: ... a soul that has freed itself from the bondage others try to impose, that can express itself freely, be true to itself, is safer to be friends with, to trust, than a soul that is in torture, captive to the labels others—that the world—tries to place on it, or even to the ones it tries to place on itself."*

This shop was an expression of a loving, creative soul—a person who could give of herself from the heart, without fear, with sincerity, trust, and no expectation of receiving anything in return.

> *What strength it must take to gently coax out the most tender offerings of one's soul—to present them for the world to see, perhaps even to judge and criticize. For not every person to whom a gift of such sincerity is extended can receive it.*

> *Far too often human beings, wishing only to cling for safety to the solid ground beneath them, feel pain when they encounter sincerity and love, and want to strike out, humiliate the giver, and mock the sincerity.*

Lark's eyes scanned her face in the dressing room mirror. Her last thoughts had hardened her expression and it now showed fear, her jaw set in anger. She took a deep breath, closed her eyes, and chastised herself for nearly ruining the blessing of peace this place had been giving her. She was reminded that if she dwelt on evil, she would be taking it into herself ...

She turned her focus to the beautiful clothes and slipped them on. She ran her palms down her waist and hips, swinging slightly from side to side, watching the skirt swirl around her legs, then she backed up to the bench seat in the little dressing room and sat down, her eyes lost focus, and she leant back against the wooden wall behind her, letting the memory of a sunlit day from childhood come forward.

One hand held her father's and her other hand held Wren's, while they danced in a circle in the yard of the little red-brick rancher. She was wearing her forest fairy costume, her skirt fanned out around her — its colors the same orange, red, and brown as the leaves falling down around them. Her father had told them that they had beautiful spirits …

She stood and drew near the mirror again, her eyes focused on her reflection. The decision to take the sweater and skirt home with her was easy.

Her earlier thoughts about giving with sincerity reminded her of the Christmas gifts she had yet to find.

Back in the shop she found a wrap for Wren with three-dimensional rosettes crocheted along its edges, a colorful scarf for Cricket, and for Pearline she had in mind gifts from a kitchen shop across the street.

She benefited from the shop's quietness, and Ophelia helped her choose earrings, a blouse, and boots to complete her own outfit.

"Where are you from?" Ophelia asked with simple curiosity, from behind the counter where she wrapped Lark's gifts in tissue paper.

"Well, I'm from here now. I live at Echo Creek. But until recently, I lived in San Francisco for about twenty years," Lark said. Here in Forestlee, talking with Ophelia, she felt none of the tension she did when facing those in her hometown. Though lately, even in Pressfield, not everyone made her uncomfortable. Scattered here and there among the tense, angry souls, were some who returned her own tentative look with expressions of sympathy—as if they would say, if they could put it into words, that they had been in the same dark place themselves. She was able to relax around those people, and her spirit flowed to meet theirs with love and grace, as her spirit had met Ophelia's today.

Ophelia said, "Oh, you lived in San Francisco? I'm originally from Los Angeles myself."

"Where do you find the clothing you offer here? I would expect to find it back in San Francisco, but here?!"

Ophelia's smile broadened and Lark could see she had opened a door to the woman's heart. "It comes mostly from friends. Artists, don't you think?"

"Absolutely."

"These days I sell more online than I do here in the store. But I

decided to keep the store open because I need a place to ship from, and …
I like to be amongst people."

"I have a friend in San Francisco, who is in the fashion design
industry," Lark said.

"It's amazing—the internet has done so much for creatives—a
designer can do her work from anywhere, and only travel when she has
to. That works for me as a buyer, too. This is my home. My husband was
from here. I haven't wanted to leave since he passed away—I still feel
closer to him here. I'm content."

"I'm sorry about your husband." Lark looked into Ophelia's eyes
to show that the sentiment was genuine. "But I sense you *have* found
contentment." Lark's sight then fell on yet more words, posted on the back
of the checkout computer monitor, they said:

> *"Your only role is to represent what God created you to be—so be
> true to yourself—you are His creation, after all. The others you
> needn't worry about, for He has given them other roles, and they are
> trying to be true to them. But if you are true to yourself, it is likely
> you will find another soul, or souls, with whom you chime."*

As Ophelia handed over her purchases, she said, "I hope you'll come
back and visit sometime and have a cup of tea with me." She swept her
hand toward a comfortable-looking sofa, its cushions rumpled, as if well-
sat-in.

"I'd like that," Lark said, distractedly, her mind still on the words
she'd just read.

She stepped out into the watery, early-winter sunshine, a smile framing
her face that echoed the contentment she'd found inside *Ophelia's*.

Chapter 38

Under the Tree

⁓⁓⁓⁓⁓

Just as Thanksgiving had been, Christmas was a quiet day, except this time the family shared the holiday dinner at Pearline's. Again, the three of them prepared the meal together—a new tradition had been born that would carry on for years. None of them could foresee the future, but *we* know that others would be added to their gathering over time.

Still, they didn't compare themselves to a famous painting of the traditional American family. There were no grandfather, no grandmother, no aunts, uncles, cousins—only the three of them—but they made it special, and except for a moment or two when their thoughts turned to Joe and Duff, they were happy.

They took their after-dinner coffee and desserts into the den to enjoy while they opened their gifts by the Christmas tree. Pearline always insisted on a real tree, so the scent of evergreen would waft through the house for several weeks around the holiday. This year she chose a humble cedar, cut from Lark's place, and decorated with ornaments from the girls' childhood.

Pearline was delighted with Lark's gift of a cookbook, written by a famous southern lady chef, along with a piece of fancy French cookware.

Wren's eyes sparkled when Lark handed her a gift. Lark draped the wrap from Ophelia's, hand-knit by an unknown but talented artist, around Wren's shoulders. She knew Wren rarely bought anything to wear that spoke to her heart, being ever-practical, and with a librarian's salary at that.

Duff's gifts, which had been placed under the tree the day they arrived in a big box marked, 'Do not open till Christmas!' were mirrors whose frames she embellished with mosaics of special meaning for each of them.

Pearline's had tiny kitchen tool charms, tucked in amongst blue and white china shards. Wren's had tiny books and letters scattered amongst rose-pattern china shards. And Duff covered Lark's mirror with mementos to remind her of San Francisco—sea shells, pieces of sea glass, a fish, ocean waves—amongst china shards of gray and cream to look well in her home.

When Lark crawled into bed that night at the gray house, around her shoulders was the vintage crocheted poncho that Pearline had given her, in her hands she held a book from Wren that she'd been longing to read, and Karma curled around her feet, contentedly purring and wearing her own gift of a velvet collar.

Chapter 39

Bonne Nuit … A Good Night

On the Monday after Christmas, Lark woke early for her run, then hurried back inside, grabbed a yogurt from the refrigerator, and wolfed down spoonfuls on her way upstairs for a shower. Afterward she rummaged through her closet for jeans, a gray t-shirt, and a zip-up jacket lined with fleece—she needed warm working clothes today.

Back downstairs, she eyed her coffee machine. She might be embarrassed by her coffee. It wouldn't compare to Charles's. She made a pot of the coffee Duff sent her—fully caffeinated for her company today. It was the least she could do. Actually, it smelled pretty good. Maybe Charles wouldn't be disappointed after all. She poured it into a thermos and grabbed two cups that wouldn't make her sad if broken while things got moved around in the basement.

She wrapped a knit scarf around her neck and pulled on fingerless gloves before stepping out into the cold to circle round to the basement door. The cluttered room was cold and damp as usual. When she'd cleared a space, she would buy a heater to warm and dry the air down here.

She stamped her feet and blew on her fingertips, picturing Karma upstairs snugly curled into a ball on a soft cushion, likely in a spot of sunshine. The cat had wisely refused to come outside with her this morning. It seemed she'd changed from a wild thing to a creature of comfort as fall changed into winter.

A vehicle rumbled up, so she stepped back out into the sun which, in its wintry weakness, didn't offer much warmth. Charles climbed out of a rusty green pick-up, and met her as she walked toward him, grabbing her up in a hug—all their cold-weather wrappings keeping it platonic. He stepped back and clapped his gloved hands together.

"Where's the work? Wow—this place is great!" This was the first time he'd seen it in daylight. "Can we walk down to the water first?"

They walked down the slope to the dock. The creek was calm without fishermen in fast motorboats zooming back and forth. Water birds fussed about the cold. A fish rose to the surface of the water and splashed, making tiny waves wash against the shoreline. Charles's boots clomped heavily to the end of the dock, where he stood with his hands in his jacket pockets.

Lark waited just where the dock joined the shore and watched him. He looked quite out of place. With his black leather jacket and boots and his striking good looks, he would look more at home in a city, surrounded by other strikingly good-looking people.

He turned and caught her watching him. Hesitating for a moment, he looked down at his feet, and then walked toward her. He stopped so near he brushed against her.

She shivered, and said weakly, "Ready to get to work?" She turned toward the path, leading him back to the basement.

"Well, here it is," she said, pushing the door open and standing back to let him step in. "It's a mess huh?"

"Wow … look at all the cool stuff in here!" He grabbed the handle of a metal box, snapped the latch open, and looked inside.

"When I bought the place at auction, everything down here was part of the deal. I guess the previous owners considered it junk. It's going to take me some time to go through it all. I want to make this a workshop so that I can build some bookshelves and take my books out of boxes upstairs. To me, it's not home without my books."

"So now I can add 'reader' and 'carpenter' to the list of things I already know about you—land owner, remodeler, former techie—have I forgotten anything?"

Lark thought *definitely*. She never planned to stop learning new things or transforming into whatever took her fancy, out loud she only said, "Maybe." She didn't like to be labeled and felt he thought her ridiculous for trying so many things. Maybe he thought she had adult ADD. She'd wondered about that herself at times, since buying this place. She leaned over to move some things around and hide her embarrassment at the possibility she might not be perfectly normal. But she reminded herself that, after all *no one* was perfectly 'normal.'

"I'm beginning to feel lazy … compared to you I'm a one-trick-pony!" he said.

"I don't see you that way. I imagine that running a successful restaurant wouldn't leave time for much else. I've admired you for what you do."

"You've admired *me*?" His smile looked sly and made her stomach turn over.

He was flirting today. She needed to put him to work.

"Hey, help me with these tables over here," she said. Together they moved two small tables outside. Charles said that his own vehicles, other than the black sports car, were motorcycles. She nodded—that fit his image.

They sorted things to keep, donate, and throw away, until Lark's hands became too cold and stiff to hold onto anything.

"How about some coffee?" she asked. She poured two cups from the thermos, and they stepped out into the sunshine where they'd set the two small tables earlier, settled side-by-side on them.

Charles sipped his coffee and gazed at the water. Lark allowed her eyes to drift upward and follow the strong line of his jaw, shadowed by a light beard. Her eye rested at his temple where the hair grew thicker into a sideburn, and was messy and damp from working. A reckless feeling took over her good senses as she imagined her hand reaching upward to touch the places her eyes had been, but he turned to look at her, and the moment was lost. She looked away, but not before he saw her looking.

He smiled bemusedly. "What?" he asked.

"Nothing." She grinned sheepishly, wishing she could control the turmoil in her stomach.

He said, "Remember when you asked if I was married and you said you'd tell me why later?"

"I remember." But she wasn't sure she wanted to talk about that. She hadn't dwelt on the troubles she left behind in California in several days. She shrugged further into her jacket and pulled her gloves down over her exposed fingers.

"Well, why did you ask? Do I look like the kind of guy who would run around on his wife?"

Did he? She wasn't sure. Had Russert looked like that kind of guy? No—absolutely not.

"I'm sorry, Charles. I had a bad experience out in California, and I believe it's made me gun-shy. I wanted to be sure you *weren't* married, before we went any further."

"Will you tell me what happened?"

"Well …" She looked away from him, then went on, resignedly, "… a man who worked at the same company I worked for asked me out. Over time I found that we weren't … meant for each other … you know? And I let the relationship end. Then things started going wrong at work and, in time, I found out he had been married all along, with kids. People at work, colleagues, had been turning away from me all the while, my reputation was severely damaged. And I lost my job."

"You lost your job because of—"

"No, I can't say that for sure, but I suspect a connection. I'll never know. And to be completely open with you, I think—no, I *know*—the whole thing followed me here. And it frightens me. People get very angry when they think you've broken up a family. Not only that, the thing that baffles me the most, is a person in my situation never gets a chance to defend herself. Never gets her day in court so to speak, and it's like being accused and convicted of a crime, without ever having a chance to prove one's innocence."

"But what's so bad about that? I mean, if you've tried to do the right thing, what does it matter what people think?"

"It affects a person's life. Jobs can be lost. People can be hostile, hurtful. You're given the wrong paint color at the paint store, the wrong dish at a restaurant. People drive too closely behind you on the road. It can actually be frightening. Since being here, at times I've even felt my life has been in danger."

Charles fell silent, a look of genuine concern on his face.

"Lark, it seems to me, all anyone would have to do is to look at you. You are far from the family wrecker type."

"I know—or at least I thought I knew that. I don't know anymore. I don't understand how others perceive me that way, when that's not in my heart."

"Well, one approach—maybe the only one—would be to accept it. Accept the label they've handed you." He turned to face her with a mock-serious expression. "Lark, you're a *femme fatale*, face it! *Tsk, tsk, tsk.*" He shook his head in mock scorn and chuckled, as a picture of Lark dressed in the cliché fashion of a man-killer entered his head—four inch heels, short-shorts, halter-top, and lots of make-up. But the look on Lark's face stopped his laughter cold.

"Not funny, Charles," Lark said grimly, as her eyes filled with tears. "I've never done anything even remote to that, I mean preyed on … *anyone*. And that's what hurts the most—that someone—*anyone* would think that of me!"

"*Je suis désolé!* I'm sorry! I'm trying to get you to find some humor in the situation. To see the way some people judge others based on their own perceptions—thinking their way is the only way of seeing things, even when judging someone they don't know, is … laughable! *Non?* You gotta love 'em, right?"

"I *wish* I could laugh about it!" Lark closed her eyes and dropped her head into her hands.

"You have to rise above it, Lark. Leave 'em down in da *crotte* where they belong. Fly free of them, but forgive them or bitterness will kill you, for true." He paused, a serious expression on his face. Then a smile lifted his mouth again, making his eyes sparkle, and he said teasingly, "Now me, I'd be easier to love than those folks, and 'dat's 'for true,' too."

She couldn't take her eyes away from his face. *Wasn't it far too soon to use the word 'love?'* He had teased her, but his face turned serious again and he leaned toward her and wrapped her in his arms, hugging her tightly.

"*Cher*, you are stronger than you know. Sometimes you have to be stronger than you want to be. When you get up tomorrow, take a deep breath, step forward. Even if you don't feel strong, stepping forward in your fear, and maybe even weakness, makes you so. *Le bon Dieu* is with you. All you can do is be who you are, Lark. And who you are is a good person I think."

His words made her feel stronger. *What was it about him that allowed this devotion so soon? Ah, why think about it? Just enjoy it, Lark. Remember, you told yourself you would try to give in to it? Try to do that. Try not to analyze. Let him be who he is.*

Tired of delving into her troubles, she stood up, took his hands into hers and tugged so that he would stand in front of her, and said, "Let's see if we can get the back of the truck full." The basement would never be cleaned out if she didn't start letting stuff go. It was simple—she had to stop analyzing each item. "Let's just start putting stuff on there," she said decisively.

They worked to fill the truck, fitting objects together like puzzle pieces. At last they had cleared a large corner of the basement, enough room for her workshop for now. Charles swung the heavy tailgate up, slammed it, and latched the corners.

Lark's stomach growled. If she felt hungry, he probably did too.

"How would it be if I fix us an omelet? And I have some arugula for a salad." *Goodness, she sounded … pleading.*

"If you're gonna feed me, I promise I'll get rid of the stuff on my way home!"

"It's a deal!" she said.

The sight of her gutted kitchen took Charles aback. "Whoa! You *did* rip out your kitchen cabinets!" he said.

"I know—it's a mess!" Lark said laughingly. She'd had to buy metal shelving racks for temporary storage in her kitchen, but planned to move them to the basement to store tools and projects, after her new cabinets were installed—which she needed to get to work on too.

The old stove was still in its place though, and Charles stood next to her as she made an omelet with shaking hands. She tried not to see him out of the corner of her eye, tried not to sense his masculinity. She told herself her nervousness was because of his skill in the kitchen, and he might be judging hers.

But the omelet turned out fluffy and lightly brown on the outside. And the salad would be refreshing with a simple dressing of olive oil, freshly squeezed lemon, and salt and pepper.

As they carried their plates to the library table, Lark said, "Watch your step—I've had carpet pulled up and all the nailing strips are still here. My cat and I have learned where they are, and we step over them.

Charles scanned the room—its high beamed ceiling, the stone fireplace, and the view from the windows where the creek could be seen past the trees, barren of leaves now. "How did you find this great place?" he asked.

"An auctioneer's website, and it didn't seem so great when I found it. I've put some work into it, along with my family and a friend or two. It's still in progress, as you can see."

"Yes, but anyone could see the potential. Don't you get lonely out here?"

"Sometimes. But I enjoy solitude. If I get lonely, I go to Pressfield and have dinner with my mother and sister. And I have Karma, my cat, here with me ..." She glanced around the room ... where *was* Karma?

"*Mmm*, nice work on the omelet." He was silent for a time, and hungrily consumed most of the omelet before he went on. "I've done my share of remodeling. I live around the corner from the restaurant in what used to be a gas station."

"Do you?"

"Yeah. It's pretty great. Even though I can appreciate a remote place like this, I love living in the city. If not for the restaurant, and my Pop, I'd probably be back in New Orleans."

"How did you come to be in this part of the South?"

"My parents divorced when I was fifteen and my Pop moved here. His cousin lived here, and he must've wanted a new life, in a new place."

Lark's assumption had been that everything in life went Charles's way. But the lines that appeared in his face when he wasn't smiling showed that he bore some cares on his shoulders—if not now, in the past.

"Having a business like yours must carry a good deal of responsibility."

"It does. Employees can be hard to keep. We hire college students mostly, and they move on just as their value as employees is paying off, and then we have to train someone new—all the while trying to keep food quality up and customer service excellent. And my Pop isn't doing well these days, so I'm helping with the financial side too." He leaned back in his chair. She cringed when he leaned so far back it stood on only two legs. He said, "I didn't mean to bring us down! Tell me about your plans for this place." He swept his hand to encompass the house and the view.

And Lark did, struck again by how lengthy her to-do list had grown. She'd better get busy-er.

Daylight was fading and shadows forming under the trees when Charles left.

"Thank you for your help today," Lark said.

"Thank you for the omelet and for the guy stuff from the basement. I'd like for you to see my gas station sometime." He stopped abruptly with his hand on the doorknob and she bumped into him. He wrapped one arm around her waist, pulled her tighter, leaned down, and brushed his warm, rough lips against hers. "*Bonne nuit,*" he said, and walked out the door.

Though Lark was blissfully unaware of the painting over the fireplace, the wind blew the girl's hair harder than ever, and her expression was aloof, uninterested.

Chapter 40

Lost Cats

Now that the holidays were over and things had settled down, and she'd been mildly embarrassed when company saw the state of her kitchen, *and* she'd had to ask Charles to step over the nail strips in her floor, it seemed time to bump some things to the top of her to do list. She paid a visit to the hardware store, and chose new flooring—aged hickory hardwoods to be installed throughout the house, and Marmoleum for the kitchen and bath that would bear water splashes and feel soft underfoot. All of it had to have a touch of gray. She also ordered kitchen cabinets, though weeks lay ahead before their delivery, leaving time for her own project—library shelves.

She and Charles had cleared a usable corner of the basement, and it needed a good cleaning before she could work there. She headed out the front door with a bucket full of cleaning supplies. She remembered that she had nudged a reluctant Karma onto the back deck earlier that morning.

About to descend her front steps, she paused with her foot on the first one, when a buzzing sound drew her attention to the bushes beside her porch. As her eyes searched for the source, a horrible stench wafted past.

Her heart leapt to her throat at the sight of a gray paw, unmoving, sticking out from beneath a bush. Her bucket clattered to the porch. Her hand flew up to cover her mouth and nose, as she hurried over to the bush. She bent down and pushed the branches aside, pulse pounding in her ears, breathless—a cat. She exhaled with relief—*not* Karma. This cat had white fur mixed in with the gray, and was older. Its lips were curled back over its teeth in the grin of death. Though it appeared to be stiff, its fur was unmarred.

She walked away from the house and around the yard, calling for Karma, who at last came along at her own cat-like, meandering pace. Lark scooped the cat up and buried her face in the warm fur, tears filling her eyes while the silly cat purred loudly—as if nothing in the world was wrong. Holding Karma tightly in her arms, Lark stepped back inside the screened porch, then closed and latched the door. Why would a dead cat be lying beside her porch? What had happened to it?

She reasoned with herself to calm her fear—fear that threatened to send her thoughts in an irrational direction. Likely, the cat had died of natural causes. After all it was cold outside. It wasn't a young cat. But for caution's sake, she would keep Karma inside for now.

She set aside her plans for the day, and found a large trash bag and a shovel in the basement. When she lifted the dead cat with the shovel, its fur moved with the wind, and reminded her again of Karma. She managed to get it into the bag without having to touch it. She couldn't help imagining how she would feel if she *had* found Karma in this state. She shook her head, her jaw set stubbornly. She refused to fall into despair.

She and Karma stayed inside for the rest of the day with the doors locked tight.

By next morning Lark realized it was unrealistic to hide out inside. If she did, she would only be repeating the self-destructive pattern she had formed in California. But finding the dead cat strengthened her desire for company here—whether in the form of Hart's work crew or renters for her cottages.

It was time to put Hart to work. And time to store his number in memory, she thought, while she dialed his number on her cell phone. When he answered she rushed to say, "Hello, Hart ... I've gone over your estimate, and I have no reservations whatsoever. I'd like for you to start the work on the cottages, as soon as possible."

"Okay. I've looked at my schedule and we can start the third week in January."

That was weeks away! She said, "*Um* ... also, I need some work done here at the gray house. Would you—"

He interrupted, "Is it major work?"

"Installing kitchen cabinets and flooring."

"If we take that on, it might push your other project's timeline and finish-date out. And it would still be the third week in January before we could get to that. Do you want to wait?"

"Well, I am sort of … anxious to get started."

"Then how about I recommend some contractors and you give them a call for those two jobs?"

"Well …" she said, sounding as lacking in confidence as she felt, remembering her simple request for paint at the paint store and how misjudgment could become hostility, which in turn resulted in her not getting what she needed. She trusted Hart, but unknown contractors? She wondered what it would be like to have a similar situation happen when thousands of dollars were involved.

And the experience of finding the dead cat shadowed her mind with fear now. She'd had haunting dreams last night after finding the cat yesterday. Her thoughts threatened to run rampant today. What if someone had left the cat to scare her? Or worse—to send her a message her loved ones might be in danger? And Hart … might working for her cause trouble for him?

"Is everything okay, Lark?"

Lark groaned, her stomach twisting with anxiety. "Goodness Hart, I think we need to have a serious talk before you begin work at my place."

"Okay … do you want to talk now?"

She was causing confusion for Hart, and she'd be surprised if he still wanted to work here after she talked with him. "I don't want to talk about it on the phone," she said. "Can you come here? Or could I come to your office, and talk to you privately?"

"If we need privacy, your place would be best. We're pretty busy this week. My crews will be in and out of the office because we're wrapping up several jobs before starting yours. How about Friday evening around six o'clock?"

"Okay. That would be good." Lark hung up the phone and rubbed the back of her neck, arching her back to relieve the tension there. Her wish to have Hart's crew working here for company had changed to concern for Hart. She bent her head into her hands and rubbed her eyes. Things were getting so complicated.

Charles knew about her troubles—although he didn't know about the dead cat—but she sensed he would be undisturbed. Somehow he seemed untouchable and removed from the situation over in Forestlee.

But the nature of Hart's work made him more vulnerable. Did she owe him the allegiance of protecting him if taking on her work would turn people away from his business? Her conscience wouldn't let her do that to him.

In the afternoon she returned to the basement and worked half-heartedly, stopping for a time when the cold stiffened her hands, to make a trip to the hardware store. She bought a fireplace heater to bring warmth and a bright spot to the room.

She continued her work there next day, taking up Cricket's old-fashioned method for cleaning the windows that overlooked the creek. She marveled at how the room cheered with each window she cleared of grime, allowing natural light in. Debussy played in the background and she hummed along with the music, while she imagined taking each beloved book out of its packing box and sliding it onto her new shelves. She'd brought Karma down for company and the cat sat near the new fireplace heater, gazing out the large windows. It must be the best of all worlds for Karma—a warm, dry place inside where she had a panoramic view of the outdoors.

Lark's hand paused in its wiping and she gasped at the sight of white things floating down. *Snowflakes?* She stepped outside, leaving Karma by the heater. When she looked up into the white-gray sky, the small flakes disappeared, but if she looked hard at the gray tree trunks she could *just* see them. She forgot her work and wandered down to the dock, enjoying the beauty of the rare event.

She stopped in her tracks as she drew near the waterfront. Something lay on the bank, near the dock. She haltingly moved closer. Another cat. This one black, its mouth pulled back like the other in a grin. Lark's body began to quiver and she gasped. What was going on?!

She turned and hurried up the slope to the basement. She scooped Karma up, flicked off the heater, closed the door tight, and hurried around the corner with the cat bouncing against her chest, and through her front door, locking it behind her. Karma scooted off, tail bushed out like a bottlebrush, disturbed by Lark's unexpected behavior.

She paced back and forth. Call Charles? No, too far away. She would have to call Hart.

"I know we're not supposed to meet until Friday, but could you *please* come over here now? I'm sorry! I know you are busy." She hoped he could hear her desperation.

"No, it's okay. It must be important ..." Hart could hear her voice trembling and she sounded ... fearful?

"Yes. It is important."

"Let me give some instructions to my guys and I'll come right over, okay?"

She hung up the phone and waited for him to arrive, arms wrapped around her knees, rocking, staring into space.

Chapter 41

Hart Steps In

When he arrived at the gray house Hart could tell right away that Lark wasn't herself. She burst out of the door before he even set foot on the porch, her body leaning forward like an arrow with vengeful purpose.

"Follow me," she said.

Baffled, he did what Lark asked and followed her down the slope. Near the water's edge, she stopped and pointed toward the dock. His eyes followed her gesture toward a black shape on the ground. He picked up a stick and nudged the dead cat. Though covered with a sprinkling of snowflakes, the body was soft and pliable. There was no obvious cause of death—no puncture wounds, no blood. It must've happened only hours ago. He walked back to where Lark stood waiting at a distance, and said, "It's a cat. It probably—"

"It's the second one in two days."

"You found another one?"

"Yes, by the front porch."

"*Hm.*" His eyes scanned Lark's face. She was very anxious. Her mouth trembled and her eyes nervously scanned the landscape. She stood stiffly upright, her arms crossed over her chest protectively.

So ... he did what any man would do. He said, "Lark, you go inside and I'll take care of this." He walked with her back up the slope to find a shovel and a trash bag just inside the basement, and returned to the water's edge to get rid of the dead cat while Lark obediently went into the house.

When he finished the grisly job, he went inside too, and closed the door against the cold and the grisly scene. He found Lark sitting at a table at the back of the living room, and asked where he should wash his hands. He left in the direction she pointed to find the laundry room sink.

Returning, he ran his hand across the smoothly curved back of a chair at the table, and the corner of his mouth twitched with a smile.

Looking toward the kitchen to his left, he noticed some of the scrap wood from the cabinets was gone. She'd been busy.

The gray cat wrapped itself around his legs and meowed at him. He bent over and ran a hand along its back, and it responded by arching its back against his palm and purring loudly.

He looked over at Lark where she nervously fidgeted, some part of her body moving constantly. She bounced her foot, tapped her fingers, sat forward, leaned back, then got up to pace, sighed, and sat down again.

"Lark, do you have something strong to drink?"

"No. Sorry, no alcohol."

"I wasn't asking for myself." He looked at her face, wishing that she would look at him. "You seem pretty shaken up."

She nodded. "I'm afraid now," she said.

"You're afraid now? What are you afraid of?"

"Afraid of finding another dead cat. Afraid of someone crashing into me on the road. Afraid of someone running over me in a parking lot or hurting someone I love or talking about me or not speaking to me!" Her chest heaved with dry sobs and her face twisted. She wrapped her arms around her stomach and leaned forward in her chair.

Hart patiently waited for her to regain her composure.

When calm again, she said, "This is such an unpleasant situation, Hart. I don't want to talk about it, but I feel it's only fair that I warn you."

"*Warn* me?" he said.

"I fear that working for me might … be harmful for you."

"Lark—*what* are you talking about?"

"It's such a long story, and I wish … I *wish* it would just go away!" She pushed her palms into her eye sockets as if to shut everything out.

Hart leaned toward her, his elbows resting on his knees, his hands clasped together.

"Hart … out in California, I got into a mess." She stopped and sat up in her chair with a puzzled expression. How had it become *she* who had gotten into a mess? *Was* she somehow to blame—based on the fact others seemed to think so? Because, after all, with so *many* believing it?

She shook her head, and when her expression cleared, she fingered the rough grain of the table and talked at length about the ordeal that ended her time in California. How it made her feel. How it changed her life. How it changed her.

He listened and watched while she talked. He tried to hear her words without judging her, without trying to explain her predicament away, without denying it … or most importantly, without trying to blame her.

As her story drew to a close, she said, "It's just the *years,* you know? Years of doing the right thing, building a good reputation, building … *a secure life,* having the respect of others—all that *work!*—taken away from me. Stolen. What was it all for?!"

She explained how she thought that the judgment and condemnation from others had followed her even here–to this place where she had hoped to find refuge. She once again lost her composure and cried inconsolably, like a lost child. One badly hurt—who had lost its innocence.

Hart felt a pain in his gut, as if her words shredded a place inside him that had remained innocent too … until now. He reached out his hand and touched her hair, then stopped, surprised.

His touch stopped Lark's crying momentarily, but then she began afresh, even harder if possible. He yielded to his instincts and moved to kneel beside her, stroking her hair to comfort her, just as he would a child's.

He … didn't know what to do. He just hoped his presence comforted her. There was much sadness in life. Sometimes women had to cry just to get it out and could go on and be stronger afterward.

Seeing Lark was struggling to breathe through the tears that ran into her nose and mouth, he pressed a white cotton handkerchief to her clenched hand, peeling her fingers back to push the cloth within.

Lark's tears stopped and she grew quiet. She looked at the soft cloth in her hand. It was exactly like the ones her father folded into a square and carried in his back pocket. She wiped at her tears with it, till she could breathe and her eyes stopped tearing. The handkerchief smelled like her father too … of work and pipe tobacco.

Exhausted, she laid her cheek flat on the cool surface of the table, one hand holding the handkerchief to her nose, the other arm stretched out on the table above her head, dark eyes blinking, hiccupping.

If Lark had looked at the painting right then, she might have perceived a startled widening of the girl's eyes, the red, bow-shaped mouth opening the slightest bit in amazement.

Chapter 42

Hart Speaks

"Do you smoke a pipe?" Lark asked, eyes staring into space, voice squeaky from a throat swollen and tight from crying.

"Sometimes ..." Hart answered.

She nodded. She really hadn't needed to ask.

For the last several minutes, Hart had been trying to formulate words in answer to her story. Since she seemed to have a hold on her emotions now, he began, "Lark, I don't want you to waste one minute worrying about me. You got that?"

She nodded and hiccupped. "I'll try," she said.

"By the way, I'm kinda glad that you *would* worry about me."

She gifted him with a weak smile.

He cleared his throat. "I'm very sorry for all that happened to you." He looked into her eyes, hoping she could see that he meant that. "But now ... you have to live here. You have to find a way to live with all that's happened to you, and with the fall-out. It's unfair, I know. I'm not gonna lie to you, Lark, I don't think that it will be easy. People can be hard on each other. Seems like especially these days. I'm not sure some of them care how you feel, or how their lack of reasoning and good judgment, or how their downright meanness affects you. In fact, if I was a bettin' man, I'd say some of them don't care at all. But others ... I've lived here all my life, and I wouldn't have stayed here if I didn't know there was some kindness around here. Most folks mean well. I suspect those people don't know what's been happenin' to you, and if they did, they'd do somethin' about it."

"But what if someone is trying to make me feel *threatened*—like leaving dead cats here?"

"Well, I think it couldn't hurt to notify local law enforcement. I know the police chief, and I know they'll keep an eye on things if they know about it."

"That'll help, but it won't take away all my fear."

"Do you know what the word courage means?" Hart asked.

"I think so."

"Seems like you hear a lot of people talking about it these days—it means you go ahead and do whatever it is you're afraid of, despite your fear. It doesn't matter if people see that you're afraid. Don't be ashamed of it. Everybody is afraid sometimes.

"Just say your prayers and then, stand tall. You're a fine person, Lark. Don't let those people take away what you've earned—what's good in your life, the reward ... your *peace* ... Just keep bein' who you are, keep doing the right thing.

"You may not want to hear it, but it could be that having a reputation that's been damaged was given to you as a ... lesson to show you what's important—to show you who your real friends are. Security is important, yes—and you still have that. But respect, a good reputation ... I'm not sure that's worth despairing over.

"Think about the Man who died on the Cross ... he didn't have the respect of everyone when he died."

He sighed, "It may take a while, but they'll see, with time. You don't think you're the only one in this town who gets talked about, do you?" He looked at her from under his brows, a sardonic smile on his face. "Do you think my family hasn't been talked about? Do you think *I* haven't been talked about? Sometimes, it seems like the quieter the life you lead, the more you tend to what you should, mind your own business, the more attention you draw. It's paradoxical, isn't it? But there it is. And I'll handle those guys at the paint store. I know them, they'll be sorry they didn't treat you right."

"You're not going to—"

"I'm not gonna be mean, but they need to know that how they treat a person's friends—a person who's given them a lot of business over the years—well, that might affect his use of their services. They'll learn a lesson, and then you and I will be able to do our business there. They're not bad guys, just maybe not capable of looking at a situation more than one way. People like that, I guess we have to give 'em some leeway."

He stood up, groaning as his legs unfolded, and stretched his back. When he grasped the back of the chair to push it back under the table, he said, "Where'd you get these chairs?"

Lark sniffed and sighed before answering, looking relieved to talk about something ordinary. She said, "I found them at a folk-art gallery in Forestlee. They're works of art, don't you think?"

"Well," he shook his head, "these are my chairs."

"*Your* chairs?" Lark asked with raised eyebrows. "You mean you made these chairs, Hart?"

"Yeah."

"They're beautiful! I love them!" She leaned forward in her own chair, her sadness forgotten. "When did you have time to work on these? And where?"

"You could say it's my hobby, when I'm not doing my real job. And I have an old barn that I work in."

"I'd love to see your place," she said, without guile.

He grinned. "How about if we grab a burger and go now?"

Her mouth trembled into a watery smile. She said, "That sounds wonderful! *Really*, I would like that."

Lark made sure the fire in the fireplace had died down. The little girl in the painting might have appeared to turn her eyes to watch them as they put on their coats and went out the door—a pleased smile tilting the corners of her mouth.

If only Lark would notice.

Chapter 43

Collapse Creates a Vacuum

After Hart dropped her off at the gray house later that night, Lark straightened the chairs at her table. She admired the attention he had paid to each detail, the careful selection of varied woods for the different parts that he'd joined securely together with pegs, and the seats molded as comfortably as any chair a person might sit in.

She remembered the words he had spoken earlier at this table. He had given her much to think about, as had Charles. Each man had his own take on her situation. Hart helped her see things from the perspective of someone who loved this community. Before tonight she had only seen the unfairness of it all and how it made her feel. She hadn't tried to see herself—the outsider—through the eyes of the community.

She beckoned to Karma with soft words and a gentle hand movement. The energetic cat bounded ahead of her, jumped onto the bed, and curled up while Lark trailed behind, drained from tension and emotion.

When she too crawled into bed, tired though she was, rest didn't come easily. She tossed and turned—Hart's crinkly-cornered, calm gray eyes changed to Charles' provocative, snapping blue ones, and changed again to the darkly angry eyes of a woman who had cut her off in a parking lot earlier in the week.

At last she drifted off to sleep and into a dream.

She walked down a long hallway alone. People she trusted, who she had thought were good and kind, stood crowded in the doorways she walked past, their hands shielding their mouths. Bits of whispered sentences hissed through the air, "she … getting … deserves" and "her, not me." Fingers pointing … harsh, twisted faces … mocking laughter …

The setting changed to an age-old scene in a far-away land, a terraced hillside surrounded by mountains silhouetted against a red sunset, and the faces changed to those of Incan warriors chanting rhythmically, lips pulled back in terrible grins. The horrid stench of death hung in the air while the crowd celebrated her vulnerability and humiliation—an Incan woman, who had committed no misdeed. Against her back pressed a hard, unyielding, unrelenting surface. Beside her a warrior raised a blade above his head, ready to let it fall.

Though surrounded by other souls, she felt so alone.

In disbelief, she turned her head to look at the crowd of *her* people. And then closed her eyes, her heart pounding, and waited for her sacrifice.

She felt beside her … a presence. She dared turn her head only slightly and saw—her father! His appearance was ethereal—not of this world. He was a force to be reckoned with, something more than flesh and bone. He smiled at her—the love in his eyes unmistakable. He moved to stand steadfastly by her side.

Then Pearline—face glowing with a mother's reassuring smile—came to stand beside him, gazing his way in tearful wonder. Wren took her place beside Pearline. As ever, Wren's expression was peaceful, angelic. On Lark's other side, Duff arrived and took a place looking surprisingly composed, but gave a wink only Lark could see. Edwin appeared beside Duff, and Lark saw that these stalwart beings were forming a barrier around her. Ophelia haltingly drew near, using her cane with Cricket's supportive hand on her arm. The two of them stood together, and looked all-knowing—as if familiar with this place. Charles arrived—a fierce warrior—handsome and clad in armor as if ready to fight. And then … Hart. He was beautiful. A white knight—a peacemaker—who would fight only as a last resort. But his face told her that fight he would, if need be.

Everyone she loved had come to her aid. Tears of joy flowed down her face. But wait … there was someone else.

Someone small. Lark didn't recognize her at first. The others parted and stepped back so the small one could draw nearer. And then— recognition shot like a bolt of electricity through Lark. It was the little girl from the painting. And now Lark knew her—she was the child Lark. The frail, dark-haired, elfin child took a place very near, looking uncannily peaceful and unafraid.

The tortured souls closed ranks in their effort to intimidate and cause fear, swaying back and forth as one body, gnashing their teeth in protest. Their chanting turned to howls of frustration, as Lark's loved ones drew near to her.

Despite the threat they posed, Lark felt a warmth and security she hadn't felt since before her father left this world. She craned her head to look at him. Yes, he was still there. He leaned over and whispered in her ear.

"Do not be afraid, Lark. Their hatred is about to collapse upon itself. It cannot continue in the light of our love. And here is why: the more hatred they direct toward you, the more *our* love for you grows. And see the child you were? You love her, don't you? Your love for yourself has grown as well. She is the strongest of us all for she is pure innocence. I have watched you Lark, from the place where I reside now. I have seen the strength it has taken for you to stand against your detractors. It hasn't been easy has it?"

"No, but I've had help." Gratitude shone from her eyes as she looked at each loving face near her.

"Yes, you have continued loving, despite your difficulties. There is one thing remaining, Lark. *Your own* acceptance of the truth that—no matter how good you try to be, no matter how *acceptable* you try to make yourself to others—there is evil out there. It will find you and try to change you, diminish you, make you feel rejected, and *unacceptable*. It will do all it can to turn your love to hate. By simply *acknowledging* evil's existence—not yielding to it, mind you—but *accepting* its existence, not denying it anymore, you will become a whole being. Light itself. You will move through life gently, a being at peace here on earth. A rarity. This is happening because you have shown yourself love by standing up for yourself, for your own innocence, by rejecting what the world tried to cast onto you—what they tried to make you. You are one of the lucky ones who have learned to quiet *their* voices." He inclined his head toward the vicious rabble. Lark listened—yes, they were still there—but quieter now. Her father continued.

"The innocence, self-love, and self-acceptance of your childhood have come forward in the form of this child, so that together you can become one, a whole being. For her part, she became stronger as you stood against the bad for her. She saw you would help her, protect her. Our inner children—the innocence and grace with which God blessed us—can slowly die, as we are hurt in life. All of us are created with His love and blessed with understanding and acceptance of ourselves, but are taught discontent with ourselves, *non-acceptance*, judgment. This happens because others are unaware that through others' judgment of us, they attempt to cast *themselves* onto us, cast their *own* hurts onto us. They do not do this with malice, but unconsciously. They simply 'know not what they do,' as the Good Book says. Give me your hand." Lark's father took her hand and joined it with the girl's.

A wind began to blow. The girl's hair blew to the side. At that moment, she was the image of the girl in the painting exactly. She looked so fragile, Lark feared for her. Lark gripped her hand harder. The child's innocence and unconditional love joined with Lark's knowledge and wisdom. The wind howled, swirled around them, tornadic in its strength. The voices of the tortured souls clamored yet higher in one last, desperate effort to prevent this wonderful thing from happening. Her loved ones braced themselves too, staying steadfastly by her side.

Aiding the effort and unseen by Lark, were good, quiet, right-thinking souls, at first only a pale glow, moving among the tortured ones, whispering kind, rational words about Lark into their ears. The whispers of the good souls' words overrode the howling, rose higher and higher, louder and louder to a crescendo. All the while, the light that shone from these good souls grew stronger too, until it joined with the light Lark's loved ones generated and all were blinded by it. The intense sound and light created nearly unbearable pain in Lark's chest, exploding around her heart ... and then ... nothing. Suddenly all fell silent.

Lark's eyes opened. She gasped. *Was* it a dream?! *Was it?*

Chapter 44

The Warrior and the Peacemaker

Charles continued to live his life, clad in the leather armor of a motorcycle rider, for a time at a distance—he was busy, and Lark was too, though Lark occasionally ran across him in her *good* dreams.

And then there was Hart—the White Knight, the Peacemaker.

His quiet strength was present in a tangible, touchable way. He had taken on the role of her protector, in the here and now. Lark thought he saw himself as her big brother. Hart ... perhaps he saw things a little differently. But no matter, the result was that Lark was relieved of the worry that being associated with her would cause trouble for him in the community. Fortunately, that didn't materialize, as worries so often don't. In fact without any action on her own part, she'd received some friendly smiles from people around town, making her feel that public opinion about her was changing, in part due to Hart's friendship and influence.

It was time to order paint for the cottages. Lark chose colors from a decorator's fan deck that Hart placed in her hands, but he said he wanted Lark to come with him when he placed the order at the Pressfield store. He said, "Come with me, and I'll take care of things."

When they pulled up to the store, she looked across the cab of the truck at him worriedly.

"It'll be okay, you'll see," he said.

Hart strode confidently to the counter and greeted the clerks by name as they looked confusedly from him, to Lark, and back again. Hart said that he needed to order paint for a job he was doing and handed over Lark's lengthy written list—she'd chosen a colorful mix of paints for the cottages. Then Hart carefully called out each number and name alongside the actual paint chips from the store's own cards as the clerks looked on, and he ended with a warning.

"Now Mayfield, my friend has said that you've had some trouble mixing paint colors here lately. It would be unfortunate, Mayfield, if our long-standing business relationship were damaged because of a mistake like that, so y'all take extra care mixing up our paint today. Do we understand one another?" His eyes were serious as they looked directly into the clerk's, leaving no doubt that he would carry out the implication of his words and withdraw his company's business, if need be.

"Yes, Mr. Worth," the clerk called Mayfield said, and the clerk beside him nodded too, both of them blushing hotly in embarrassment and chagrin.

Hart made Lark feel both protected and vindicated in a very real way.

Chapter 45

Is Peace Lasting?

Lark jokingly called out to Hart's crew before she closed the door of the inlet cottage.

"Okay guys, no slacking off today. I want to see some progress when I bring coffee over tomorrow morning!" Then she set off between the tree trunks toward the gray house. She crossed her arms over her chest and rubbed her hands up and down her sleeves for warmth. Above her the wind knocked the barren branches together, a sound that would be particularly spooky at night.

Tonight though, she would feel safe even if the wind kept up its mischief, because Hart would be nearby in the ridge cottage. In yet another gesture that showed true friendship, he had moved there so she would have someone nearby at night after she'd been so frightened upon finding the dead cats.

He had started some of his crew on her projects too. Their presence gave her security in the daytime. She opened the front door from time to time and could hear the sound of their hammers, saws, loud talk, and playful kidding around. Like today, she carried coffee to them nearly every morning and stayed for a while to inspect their work and chat with them before returning home to her own work.

Also helping was the distance of time from the fright that January brought. Her determination to keep her thoughts out of bad grooves had stayed with her. That strategy was working swimmingly, and was working ... literally.

Yes, she was riding a high on the crest of a wave ... she snorted scornfully. It hadn't been easy. There were still times she had to thump her thoughts to prevent herself sliding down a wave crest into the trough.

Still ... that dream. It had brought about a change deep inside her—in a place beyond where her worst doubts and fears could reach.

Her path through the trees ended when she pushed open the door of the gray house so that she could take care of a few things before heading down to the basement. She hurried to toss a load of clothes into the dryer and in the kitchen grab a snack and a bottle of water to carry down to the basement. The transformations that had taken place during the last few weeks were helping to make the gray house her own. With its new gray-toned cabinetry with a tiny alcove of six shallow shelves for her collection of coffee cups, open shelves for her plates and glasses, the island Hart's crew built from weathered barn wood, and the gray-veined marble countertops, the kitchen was near-perfect.

In the basement she switched on the fireplace heater and turned to worriedly eye the large plywood sheets that today she would cut into the side panels for her new library shelves.

She grabbed a tall sheet of wood and walked it on its end a short way across the floor to her sawhorses, while reassuring herself that she *could* do this alone. She laid it against one sawhorse that was braced against the basement wall while she walked to the other end to lift and slide the panel over both sawhorse tops until it was securely centered across both. With the lead of a carpenter's pencil placed against the straight line of a T-square, she carefully marked the wood all along its eight-foot length for cutting.

She stopped to eat her energy bar while she watched an online how-to video about her new power saw one more time out of caution. Then she took a deep breath, wiped her sweaty palms down her jeans legs, put plugs into her ears, lowered her safety glasses to her eyes, grabbed the saw and chanted, '*You can do this, you can do this.*' She held the saw tightly braced against the end of the plywood sheet, switched it on to a high-pitched whir, and fiercely gritting her teeth while controlling its forward movement, allowed it to eat along the line she'd marked.

By the time dusk arrived, she had cut all four side panels for the cases. She was about to start smoothing the ends with sandpaper when a vehicle pulled up outside. She knew it was Hart before she heard his knock on the door.

"Thought I might find you down here."

"You came to help?"

"No, I'm done working for the day. I think I'll just watch you."

"Hmm," she said. It was a good thing she had finished with the saw, because with a woodworking expert like him watching her, she might have been too nervous to cut a straight line. She reached for her sanding block and wrapped a sheet of sandpaper around it.

While she rasped at the rough end of the panel, Hart inspected the work she'd done earlier that day and said, "I'm impressed. You used a power saw?"

"Yep," she said.

Hart picked up a sheet of sandpaper, folded it till it fit into his palm, and began to rasp it across the length of the panel. It seemed he wasn't able to stand by and watch someone else work. They worked in companionable silence until he said, "The guys are nearly finished with the inlet cottage."

"I was over there this morning. They were going to paint inside today."

"They'll be ready to start on the ridge cottage next week. Looks like I'm going to have to find other accommodations."

That was right. He wouldn't be able to stay in the ridge cottage when his crew started work up there. And from where she lay in her own bed at night she would no longer see his lights shining up the ridge. She would be alone again—her only company Karma, and the branches bumping together, and the occasional hooting of an owl in the darkness outside.

She could ask him to move over to the inlet cottage, as it would be finished. But, how would he feel about that? She looked over at him. He had taken off his jacket and rolled up his sleeves. She let her eyes wander from his plaid-shirted shoulder down to his left forearm where it braced his weight against the wood panel while he sanded with his right hand. The edge of the muscle formed a line above the bone. How beneficial the strength of that arm would be against a night-time intruder.

She looked up at his face, his calm, unfurrowed brow and forehead, seemingly unworried despite having employees and clients who depended on him, or that his mother's health wasn't so good lately and that his father depended on him to help with her at times.

He had his own life. Being here for her likely had been a burden he didn't need. Wasn't she an adult, one who had been living and behaving responsibly for decades now? *What had come over her? How had she let herself become so dependent?*

As if he'd read her thoughts, he voiced her earlier thought, "I could move over to the inlet cottage."

Of course he would offer, thinking only of how she might feel. His face was impassive, not giving her a clue as to how he really felt.

"I … think it's time I bucked up my courage, Hart—like you said I should. Remember? Right after I found the cats?" She put her sanding block against the wood's edge and began thoughtfully rasping again. "I think I should let you get back to your own place."

"You think you're ready to be alone out here?"

"I'm ready." She rasped more determinedly along the wood.

"And how have people in town been treating you lately?"

She blushed and cleared her throat. His question reminded her just how much of her heart she'd shared with him.

"Oh mostly good," she said. *That dream … seemed to have given her a vision to carry with her as she went about her business—one of light, and strength, and love.*

To Hart, she went on, "Lately, I've been trying to shine light on negativity and hostility when I run into it. The other day, a car was following behind me far too closely so, I calmly pulled over, and let them pass on by. And when a store clerk seems hostile, I make an effort to speak and smile gently, hoping that their anger will collapse. If they've turned away from me completely, over too long a time, then I have to protect myself and turn away too, and I find a place to do business where I find kindness always. I'm only human after all!" She looked up at him and smiled.

"Sounds like you're taking control again."

"I have at least some control through the choices I make."

"You haven't given up. You're winning against it."

"But what is *it*, Hart?" She shivered, remembering the grimacing faces in her dream. *What made others want to condemn her?* Out loud, she said, "What is this *thing* that has felt like real danger? Bad luck? Bad Karma? Evil?"

"The nature of this fallen world—*all* of those things," he said.

"I don't understand how I was able to avoid bad luck for so long, and then … it took over my life. At times I've been quite angry at those who've damned me without really knowing me." Her stomach tightened and her heart fluttered. This conversation was heading in the wrong direction and threatening her peace.

Hart said, "Sometimes when people lead charmed lives—they don't know what it's like to lose. Don't know what it's like to be treated unfairly—to have bad luck. They haven't had to take love wherever they could find it or struggle against a reputation unfairly damaged, and they level judgment here, there, and everywhere, satisfied that they are leveling them at the right people and for the right reasons. It protects their psyche—makes 'em believe it can't happen to them."

"And how are you not one of those people, Hart? You've been fortunate, haven't you? You grew up with everything you needed. I remember you told me once that you had everything you wanted, so how is it you aren't walking around in the same shoes they are?"

"There was a time when I had everything I wanted. But that was … a long time ago." He tossed aside the sandpaper he'd been using, and said, "I'm beat now, I think I'll go up the ridge. I don't want you using that power saw any more tonight, hear?"

"Okay."

He pulled on his jacket and headed for the door, his eyes meeting hers for only an instant before he closed the door behind him.

Chapter 46

A Widening Circle of Friends

Lark hadn't seen Charles since they'd worked on her basement just after Christmas, though they'd talked on the phone. She had been busy with work at home. He had been busy too. The restaurant was taking more of his time, but he hadn't said why. The last time they'd spoken, it seemed he needed a distraction as much as she did, and he promised her dinner at Latour's tonight. Afterward they would walk around to his gas station.

She felt pretty wearing the sweater and tobacco-colored skirt that she'd found at *Ophelia's* before Christmas. She was filled with anticipation and excitement to see Charles, to feel the promise of spring in the air, and to see the lights of a city at night—even one as small as Forestlee. Her foot was quite heavy on her little car's gas pedal.

Before she saw Charles she had a few things to take care of.

She found a pair of serious running shoes. Because she was running up to twenty miles a week on her new trail, she'd lost all her extra pounds, was as lean as she'd ever been and, more importantly, felt energetic and healthy. She took Hart's advice and found a landscaping crew whose lighter workload during the winter months allowed them time to take down some of her trees, clear and level a path, and put down a soft layer of pea-sized gravel around the perimeter of her property, perfect for running on.

After leaving the shoe store, she walked with purpose to the next doorway along the row of shops. Inside, the scent of handmade paper, paints, the lead of pencils, and the soft wax of crayons hung heavy in the air. Browsing up one aisle and down the other, her eyes and fingertips took in the tools, colors, the smooth and uneven surfaces of papers, for every sort of creative pursuit.

A box of watercolor paints reminded her of a childhood birthday gift from her father. She picked up the box and opened it, put her nose to it, and breathed in. She remembered her father sitting beside her, white sheets of paper in front of them, the box of paints between them. He encouraged her to let her paintbrush do what it would, admired what she put onto the paper, made her feel … as if what was inside her was okay, special even. His acceptance of her had been more a gift than the paints.

"Are you an artist?"

She turned toward the voice, shaking her head, and said, "Oh no—I'm not an artist." Before her stood a man—short in stature, with gray beard and hair.

"Do you have any questions then?" he asked.

She looked away down the aisle at the mind-boggling choices. "Well … I would like to try painting, and I'm not sure what I need."

"I'll ask some questions, and I'll help you find what you need."

As she followed along behind him, he told her his name was Mr. Schlemmer, and he quizzed her—*'which tools did she see herself working with,' 'what kind of surface did she want to paint on,' 'which masters did she find inspiring?'*— he pulled from the shelves fine brushes, tubes of oil paint, a palette, canvases, and even an easel. She already knew where she would make her studio.

Mr. Schlemmer helped her to get the easel to her car as both her arms were laden with packages.

"Thank you for helping me!" she said.

"Please come back when you need more supplies. You are going to need them—I feel it!" He clenched his fist and rapped it against his heart.

Though she wanted to hug him for his kindness, she felt it more proper to take his hand in both of hers and shake it warmly.

Checking her watch, she saw that she still had time before Charles expected her. Hoping Ophelia wouldn't be busy, she intended to accept at last the kind invitation she had extended before Christmas. The bells above the door rang out, and she was greeted by a floral scent—for spring she supposed.

"Hello … oh!" Ophelia said, as she came straight to Lark and laid her hand on her arm. "It's good to see you!"

Pleased that Ophelia remembered her, Lark said, "It's good to see you too!" and patted the other woman's hand where it lay on her arm.

"Did you come in to shop or to have tea with me?"

"I came in to have tea … is it a good time?"

"Couldn't be better. It's been quiet today and I would love your company. Please have a seat and I'll get our tea." Ophelia leaned her cane against the sofa and, limping only slightly, walked down a hallway toward the back of the store.

Lark noticed springtime colors filled the racks. Maybe there would be time to have a look around for something new for herself, and for Pearline and Wren, too.

Ophelia returned, trying to keep the tea tray level which looked more than a little challenging, but Lark was hesitant to offer help. Ophelia was surely capable—after all she took care of this shop with minimal help—and although she suspected Ophelia was not easily offended, Lark didn't want to take the chance.

They settled into the sofa, Lark at one end and Ophelia at the other, blew on their tea, and sipped cautiously. Lark was thankful for its calming effect—she felt jumpy, a bit nervous.

"So tell me Lark, how was your Christmas?" Ophelia said.

"Nice. Quiet, with just my mother, sister, and I, but we celebrated in our own small way. How about yours?"

"Well, since my husband is gone and I have no children, it's quiet at holidays. This is the first time in the three years since I lost him that I haven't gone to friends'. I decided to see how I would do on my own."

Lark was concerned that Ophelia may not have had anyone to celebrate with, and felt a shade of guilt over her own celebration—small though it was. Maybe her expression showed her concern because Ophelia went on and reassured her.

"But I celebrated—I prepared food that only *I* would like, watched old Christmas movies and had to consult no one else, and gave myself a fabulous present!"

Her laughter eased Lark's concern. She knew that Ophelia was making the best of a difficult situation, but she could also see that Ophelia was being truthful and had relished the holiday. Good for her!

Lark said, "I sometimes see the idealized, large extended families on television or in magazines and am tempted to compare my small one with them, but I remind myself that everyone's situation is different. We have to make the best of where we are at any particular moment in life, don't we?"

"Yes, that is my belief exactly. And never more so than since my loss and too, since I discovered that I have Multiple Sclerosis."

"*Ah,* that's the reason for the cane."

Ophelia nodded, and said, "I am in a stage where I have periods of remission. I have recently been able to walk without my cane a bit. Hopefully, the improvement will continue. There are medications now that can help so much. I am lucky to have them."

Lark's admiration grew for this woman who had been visited with so much misfortune in recent years, and who was trying to make the best of her situation. *Had she been thinking that she was the only one who experienced misfortune?* Ophelia inspired her to continue in a positive direction. That she also had been trying to make the best of a bad situation was something they had in common. Still, Lark didn't want to burden her new friend with her own problems. Anyway, since sharing her troubles with Charles and Hart, and especially since her dream, she had felt freer of them. If she brought them up, she might only be perpetuating them.

She deflected conversation away from herself and said, "I've been very busy since Christmas with work at home." And she told Ophelia of all that had been done. Of course Hart's name came up often.

"And this Hart, is he ... special in your life?"

"He's mostly my contractor, but he is an old friend as well. A very good friend." So much had changed in the last couple of months—he had become a constant in her life. His protection of her, her visit to his workshop in an amazing loft of a barn, the friendship he'd shown when he'd moved nearby when she was afraid, his integrity in his work—all flashed through her thoughts. Flustered, she set her empty tea cup down and stood.

"Ophelia, I've enjoyed visiting with you, but I'm supposed to meet a friend at Latour's soon, and I would like to have a quick look around before leaving ..."

"Of course, let me show you some new things I've been sent for spring."

And so, Ophelia gave Lark yet another reason to believe she was not easily offended, as she might have been for her abrupt change of the subject.

She found something for everyone on her list, including herself, attended to all the while by Ophelia, who then packaged her purchases, and surprised her with an invitation.

"Lark, I wonder whether you might like to come to my house next Saturday. I'm hosting a get-together with some other friends, and I'd love for you to come. You can bring someone with you, if you like."

"That sounds wonderful! Yes, and I will bring someone—although I don't know who ..." Again she blushed.

"Good! I'll write down my address for you and you can go on the internet. You'll find the directions from there much easier to follow than my own. Dress in something semi-casual and come to have fun."

They hugged with mutual gratitude over the new friendship they were growing, and Lark stepped out into the evening. The city lights that Lark loved were flickering on, and the sun was setting down the hill behind her. When she turned the corner toward Latour's, she saw that already there was standing room only inside, because a crowd, chatting cheerily in anticipation, had gathered outside.

She walked past them and into the restaurant with her own sense of anticipation.

Chapter 47

The Gas Station

This time she found Charles waiting for her just inside the door of Latour's. Without a word he grasped her hand and pulled her through the Mardi Gras celebration that was in full swing. Bright decorations of purple, green, and gold hung throughout the restaurant and the crowd cheered while a waiter paraded out of the kitchen, holding a king cake high above his head.

After they stepped into his office, Charles wrapped his arms around her and rocked her back and forth in a tight hug. He said, "I've celebrated Mardi Gras many times in my life—I think I can let this one go by. Let's go to the station."

Who was she to argue with such an invitation?

He pulled on his jacket and pushed open the door at the back of the restaurant for her. She shivered when she stepped out into the dark, colder now that the sun had gone down. Charles swung his arm around her shoulders and pulled her close against his side. It was awkward walking like that, but she liked the warmth … and the thrills that crept all over her skin.

Where the back alley met the street they turned right, walked for a block and a half, turned toward the college campus, and there with blue and pink neon signs lit in the two large front windows announcing the goods once for sale there—'ice' and 'soft drinks'—was Charles's gas station. Pumps, refurbished and looking like new, stood in the same place where fin-tailed cars had once filled up. Engraved on a historic district marker at the door was 'est. 1952.'

Charles unlocked the door and flipped on the light of an expansive room whose walls were painted bright white. To the left was a modern kitchen, stainless steel glinting brightly. To the right near the front windows were clustered a retro-modern sofa and chairs in front of an extra-large plasma television. The only vivid color in the white, black, and gray room was a vintage pinball machine in the corner and a motorcycle, trimmed in red and suspended by thick chains from the ceiling against the back wall.

Charles tossed his jacket carelessly onto a coat rack by the door, and turned to help Lark out of hers. She watched him hang it on its own hook, his movements slow and reverent, and she gulped.

"I thought I would fix us something to eat here, *cher.*" He leaned toward her, capturing her eyes with his own. Lark sensed that tonight would be a turning point for them. She looked toward the kitchen to disrupt the moment.

He straightened and asked, "Do you like grilled tuna?"

"Yes, I love it."

"Good. What can I get you to drink?" They moved into the kitchen.

"Could I have one of those cokes?" She pointed at a vintage soft drink machine that stood in the corner, the bottles lined up vertically and visible through the glass door.

He opened the door and pulled out a bottle, a clink sounding from inside the machine as the next bottle slid into the hole it left behind. He patted the machine and said, "Came with the place." He popped the top off the curvy green bottle and set it in front of Lark who had scooted onto a stool at the old station counter that served as an island.

"What inspired you to make your home in this place?" She sipped her soft drink and her eyes watered. There was nothing like the bite from the ones in the old bottles.

"It was a natural choice—near work and it has a workshop in back where I keep my car and motorcycles. It's perfect!"

He was right—it suited him. She watched him move efficiently around the kitchen, taking butter and tuna steaks from the fridge, gently laying the pink fish onto the grill where it sizzled away. Into boiling water at the back of the stove he tossed pasta, leaving it to cook while he turned back to the tuna steaks, lifting one gently with tongs and checking the underside. He turned them over and wiggled them a little on the grill, treating them lovingly. This was probably why crowds flocked to his restaurant—this care and focus on the food. Turning back to the boiling water, he set a basket on top, tossed in a mix of colorful vegetables, and covered them to steam while the pasta finished.

Everything was ready in less than ten minutes. He expertly plated the food—placed a thick slab of herb butter on top of each tuna steak, and squeezed juice from a fresh lemon over the top. Then, he slid onto a stool beside her.

"Enjoy," he said and, not waiting for her to start first, cut hungrily into his tuna.

A bit shut out while he focused on his food, she turned to her own. The tuna melted in her mouth, but her focus wasn't there. She watched Charles while he ate. He seemed lost in his own thoughts, uncharacteristically quiet. It was unnerving, so different from the way they'd talked freely for hours when he helped with her basement. She looked back at her own plate, turning her body forward and sitting up straighter. Maybe he'd decided because of her troubles with thinking everyone was talking about her, she was paranoid. Maybe he was sorry he'd asked to see her tonight and just wanted to get it over with.

Also, maybe he found her dull and uninteresting compared with other people. He seemed as though he would draw exciting, fun-loving, interesting people to him. She was quiet, could never find enough in her life to effervesce about like those bubbly, life-of-the-party girls, who thought even the smallest details of their lives interesting. And they usually were, at least the way they could talk about them. She sighed.

Charles looked at her and said, "I'm sorry, Lark. Am I boring you?"

"No, I thought you might be thinking the same thing about me!"

"*I'm* not bored Lark." Again the intense eyes.

"Neither am I," she said.

"It's actually nice to be quiet with someone for a change. My life is all about people and noise, I think." He smiled, then rose and took their plates to the sink, saying, "Come out back, I want to show you my cycles."

They pulled their coats on and walked through a short hallway, passed a bathroom, his bedroom. Lark looked but turned her head quickly away, embarrassed to see such private spaces. Out back under the glare of two tall streetlights was a paved area, once the parking lot of a car repair shop Charles said. Shelves of motorcycle parts and old motorcycles leaned against the wall of the building.

"Wow, this is quite a hobby you have, Charles."

"I work out here every chance I get," he said.

She knew nothing about motorcycles, had never ridden one. She followed him to the garage where he reached down to grasp the handle of the door. It squeaked and groaned with effort as he rolled it back to reveal a surprisingly dust- and oil-free interior. Standing in the center was a beautiful, special-looking bike. A machine from another era. Black with shiny chrome front and back fenders curved at the outer ends, and many-spoked wheels.

"My favorite. A '58 Honda Benly that I restored. Want to go for a ride?"

"*Um ...*" she should've known this would happen when he brought her out here. "The seat doesn't look big enough."

"Are you kidding?" He stepped behind her and she felt her face and neck grow hot as she supposed he was sizing up her ... posterior. "There's room, *beb*."

"You probably don't have a helmet that'll fit me." He stepped to shelves along the front wall where six or seven helmets sat in a row. He pulled off a silver one, settled it onto her head, wiggled it, and adjusted the chin strap for her, running his finger under it along her jaw line to be sure it wasn't too tight. She made one last effort, saying, "Not to mention, we should probably wait for a while after eating."

"Let's go," was his reply. He rolled the cycle out of the garage while she reluctantly followed.

She watched him swing one leg over, scoot forward on the seat, and pull on a helmet. He turned to watch her, waiting for her to climb on behind him.

Her stomach churned and her legs felt like jelly while she stepped over to place her left hand on his leather-jacketed shoulder, steadying herself. "Turn around please," she said, and awkwardly pulled her skirt above her knees to climb on. *Hmmph*, he could have told her they would be doing this, and she would have worn jeans! "Okay. I'm ready," she said weakly once she was settled behind him.

He turned the key and the cycle started, surprising Lark with its whirring, sounding like a sewing machine instead of a loud rumbly motorcycle. She tightened her arms around him, trying to join her hands together, but instead had to grab onto his shirt inside his jacket, clutching as much fabric in each hand as she could.

He drove out onto the street, and wound slowly through the college campus, where students walked to restaurants on the square and to each other's places and milled around the fountain on the campus green, staring as she and Charles passed by. Several of the guys shouted out in admiration of the cycle.

Charles picked up speed and they left the congested downtown streets behind. She rested her face against his back, praying she would be able to lean with him. She clung to him as tightly as possible, so that she would move with him as they took the curves. She quickly got the hang of it, and squealed and laughed when Charles sped up and the front wheel left the ground briefly. The air rushing past was exhilarating.

Charles settled to a steady speed and she relaxed. Her breathing slowed. Through the night they rode and she watched the lights blur past, until the sound of the motor and the warmth of Charles lulled her to sleepiness.

She had to force her eyes open as they slowed and pulled back into the garage. She stiffly got off the bike, stepped back and shook out her skirt, then pulled her helmet off, hair popping and flying outward with static. Trying to pat it down with her gloved hands, she feared she was only making it worse.

Charles stepped up to her.

"Let's go back inside and warm up," he said, taking her helmet.

He showed her to the restroom, calling it the 'cahbin.' In the mirror she looked frostbitten—her nose red and dripping, cheeks blown into redness rather than rosiness from the wind. She patted her face and nose with warm water and a towel to thaw it, and stepped out to find him.

He was at the pinball machine, his back to her, his entire body moving as he pressed the flipper buttons on the side. She stopped beside him to watch as he made the bells ring and lights flash

"Wow," she said, when he stopped and turned toward her.

"Your turn."

Her first bouncy silver ball rolled down the exit alley.

"Let me help," he said, and she could feel the warmth of him as he stood behind her and placed his rough hands over hers on the flipper buttons, lowering his mouth to her ear. "It's a timing thing." For a minute he pressed her fingers onto the buttons, then both distracted by their closeness, watched as the silver balls rolled, one-by-one between the flippers and disappeared. They remained motionless, the only sound their breathing. He leaned to press his lips to her neck, Lark's stomach lurched, and she gasped.

She scooted sideways, pulling his arm away from its grip on the pinball machine beside her, and ducked out of his embrace.

"What?" he asked.

She defensively folded her arms across her chest and strode to the other side of the room. She expected anger when she turned back to look at him, but he surprised her with an apology instead.

"I'm sorry Lark. I guess you're not ready?"

"No, I'm not." She hoped he wouldn't ask why. How could she explain her inexperience at the age of forty? *How humiliating.* She'd kept Russert at arms' length and there'd been no other opportunities … There would have to be a long, embarrassing explanation. And she'd already had to tell not only him, but Hart, about her recent misfortunes. How *pathetic* would she sound?! Not only had she been duped by a married guy, lost her job, told Charles—and Hart—her sad story, but now she had to tell him she'd pretty much been a non-participant in the romance department all her adult life?! She doubted he would believe it had been her choice.

It was hopeless. She unfolded her arms, strode to the coat stand by the door, and lifted her jacket off the hook where Charles had tenderly hung it earlier. Charles appeared at her side.

"You don't have to go. I'll leave you alone, for true."

She could see it was 'for true,' and that he regretted the way the evening was turning out. Looking down at the floor rather than at him, she said, "Charles, you can have any girl you want in that way, I'm sure. But, I'm different. I take more time. I hope that's not all you want from me. But if it is, I guess that's it for us."

"I'll walk you back to your car." He pulled on his jacket and they walked back toward the square in silence. As they neared Latour's they saw the crowd from the restaurant had spilled out onto the sidewalk, now wearing beads and hats from the Mardi Gras celebration. They were laughingly littering the air and the sidewalk with confetti and gold coins.

"Charles!" a man called out from the crowd, except it sounded like 'Chaalz.'

"My Pop," Charles said wryly out of the corner of his mouth. It was easy to see which man spoke as he stood out from the crowd because of his height and breadth.

A woman's voice called out, "Make him come to the party, Shrimp!"

The big man's frame swayed dangerously as he draped his arm around Charles' shoulder and pulled him toward the crowd.

"Where you been podnah?! These gulls been talking 'bout puttin' the gree gree on you. Git on ova' here!"

Charles pulled away from him and touched Lark's arm. He had to shout so she could hear him.

"Lark, I'm sorry! There's not gonna be anything for me but to humor him! Can you make it to your car from here?"

She nodded her head, and shouted back, "Yes—I'm just down here." She pointed toward the end of the row of cars, but he had already turned away—the big man and the girls drawing him into the party. She turned away, confused, and even less certain about herself and Charles than she'd been at the beginning of the evening.

Then she remembered her purchases in the back of her car, and she couldn't wait to get home.

———

She painted until the morning light shone through her windows, all the while pure joy sparkling from the dark eyes of the little girl in the painting over the fireplace.

Chapter 48

Hoping for a Different Sort of Help

Lark closed the front door of the gray house behind her and went in search of Hart. She groggily considered painting in the daytime rather than playing at being an artist way into the night as she had again last night.

From a distance she saw that Hart's truck was not parked at the ridge cottage as she had thought it might be, but she walked up anyway. He had moved back to his own place but stopped by nearly every day to inspect the renovations his crew had well underway.

As she stepped onto the porch, the scent of new wood wafted up from the steps they had constructed. Inside, they had pulled out damp-damaged paneling from corners here and there, and had installed new plumbing and duct work for a central system. She was most interested though in the new bath fixtures. A lovely white claw foot tub, pedestal sink and toilet had been installed and Lark envied them, as her own gray house still had the pink marble ones from the '70s with which she had yet to 'make friends.' Maybe she would get new ones there too, eventually.

She heard heavy footsteps along with a scritching sound on the porch, and turned to watch Hart come in, and hold the door open for someone … or some*thing* behind him.

"C'mon boy!" he said, and into the room tumbled a golden yellow puppy, fur fluffed out like a new chick's.

Lark bent down and held out her hands. The puppy part ran, stumbled, and rolled to her. He was already bigger than some dogs, and she speculated that one day he would be a force to be reckoned with.

"When did you get him?" she asked.

"Friday—which you'd have known, had you been here. I came by that afternoon to oversee the installation of the bath fixtures and planned to introduce you two."

Lark easily remembered where she'd gone Friday afternoon and evening—to Forestlee to visit, shop, and … ride a motorcycle. She delayed her response to Hart's remark and caressed the puppy's soft ears, gazed into his big brown eyes, and plopped down on the floor to let him into her lap. She buried her face in the fur of his ruff. There was no smell quite like a new puppy. Finally she glanced up at Hart said, "I'm sorry I missed you … I'd gone into Forestlee." She didn't want to elaborate, so she changed the subject. "What's his name?" she asked.

"Puddles—I expect you'll find out why soon enough."

Lark turned her attention fully on Hart. He was dressed in a flannel shirt over his t-shirt and jeans. Probably glad, like she was, not to have to wear a jacket, and to see the first warm front of the coming season bring a hint of spring to the air. He still had the build of an athlete. She'd seen him swing a two-by-four like a baseball bat while he took a break from working.

He grinned widely and Lark looked away embarrassed. He probably realized that she'd been thinking about how he looked. She blushed and stood, brushing off the back of her jeans.

"I came up here to see the …" she cleared her throat, "new bathroom installations."

"Oh yeah? What do you think?" The twinkle in his eye and quirk of his mouth made her wonder whether he was trying to flirt with her.

"They look great. I'm thinking I need new ones in the gray house someday." There was a tension in the air. She felt a need to keep things moving. "What's on the schedule for today?"

"Delivery of the kitchen cabinets."

"That's exciting … what else?" She watched him grimace. He had told her that her expectations were often too high—that she wanted things to happen, 'boom … boom … boom—like that.'

"That's enough for one day—don't you think?" he asked.

"I suppose so," she said. "Maybe I'll walk over to the other cottage and have a look around. It'll make me feel hopeful about this one. I can remember when it was at the same stage, and now it's finished! Want to come?"

Hart clicked his tongue and the puppy obediently darted, then stumbled, away from the corner where he'd been sniffing the floor, and he and Hart followed Lark out the door, where they heard a vehicle drawing near. Was that the whirring of a small engine? Her heart lurched. She tried to see around Hart and down the drive to confirm her hunch. Craning her neck she saw a flash of sunlight against chrome near the gray house. She and Hart crunched through dry leaves toward the black motorcycle.

Her good manners covered the turmoil inside her.

"Charles!" She was truly surprised to see him, especially with such uncertainty about their relationship hanging in the air when they parted the other night. Forgiving and ever-hopeful soul that she was, she stepped without hesitation to his side and placed her hand on his leather-clad upper arm. He surprised her and leaned over to kiss the corner of her mouth. She sensed Hart's surprise behind her.

With her hand still on Charles' arm, she turned and said, "Hart, I'd like you to meet Charles Latour." Words to explain the nature of her relationship with Charles failed her. She would have to leave Hart to draw his own conclusions. She turned back to Charles. "Charles, this is Hart Worth. He's the contractor for the work on my cottages, and a friend as well." Giving Hart his due, she advanced his status from 'old' to current friend.

Charles climbed off his cycle to shake Hart's hand and he and Hart exchanged a few cursory words. *Was there wariness between them?*

Charles's blue eyes were uncertain when he turned them on her. He seemed to take a settling breath then possessively looped his arm around her waist.

"Do you have a minute?"

"Sure," she answered, and turned to Hart to say she'd meet him at the cottage later, but he'd already started to walk back toward the ridge. Puddles hopped and jumped along beside him, stopping to look back to see if Lark was coming too. She noticed Hart's downturned head and slumped shoulders. Frustrated that things had gone off rudely toward him, she sighed.

To Charles she said, "Let's go inside."

The canopy of tree limbs above was thick enough even while bare to shade the house from the weak winter sunlight. She'd found that the inside always seemed chilly without a fire. She stirred the still warm ashes in the fireplace, set a small log on top. She motioned for Charles to sit on the sofa and settled beside him, curling her feet underneath her.

"When you left the other night, we had some unfinished business, didn't we?" he asked.

She nodded. He looked especially handsome today. His face was flushed and his jaw set. His blue eyes sparked with electricity. She shivered and swallowed.

He said, "You asked me a question that I hadn't answered yet when I was pulled away by my Pop."

It occurred to her that if he'd really wanted to answer the question she'd asked, he would've stayed with her rather than *let* himself be pulled away, but she tried to give him the benefit of the doubt. It was possible that, as he'd said, he hadn't formed an answer to her question at the time. She said, "Yes … we did part with some uncertainty."

"Yeah. Lark, what I think is that … I like to talk to you and just *be* with you. I'd like to keep doing those things if there's a chance for more in the future? Maybe the not too distant future?"

A gratified blush warmed her face. She leaned toward him.

"If we could just give it a little more time, Charles? Get to know each other better? I know that will have to come first for me." Her conscience prickled. Her answer really did nothing but delay what would have to be faced eventually. She didn't know how much time she needed. She certainly wasn't inclined to discuss marriage which her mother had always taught her was a precursor to a physical relationship.

With Russert, there hadn't been the spark in the air that existed between her and Charles. There hadn't been the problem of a strong physical attraction pitted against her upbringing. Putting Russert off hadn't been difficult at all, come to think of it. When she looked at Charles again he smiled and looked relieved. She bowed her head shyly and felt his lips touch her hair.

"So, tell me about this guy … Hart?" he said.

"What about him?"

Looking into the fire Charles said, "Just something I sensed. He seemed a little territorial. A little bit like his hackles were up."

"Well, I can't speak for Hart," she said, "but maybe he is a little protective. We go way back. We knew each other in high school."

"That leads me to the next question."

She guessed what his question was.

"Yes, we were involved back then," she said. "But I left him to go to school in California. Maybe hurt him? We have a working relationship now … although, I do consider him a friend as well."

"*Hm,*" he mused. "That'll have to do, I guess."

"Now *Charles.* I know that you have 'friends' as well. You're around attractive young women all the time at the restaurant. Right?"

"Yeah, but I haven't noticed them so much lately." He looked as if this had just occurred to him. "My mind seems to be sort of filled with *you.*"

A rush of heat infused her face. Some physical distance was needed, and fast. She rose and headed to the kitchen, "Can I get you a cup of tea?"

"*Grrrrr,*" Charles growled as he followed her.

She laughed. Frustrating him was kind of fun.

"I don't drink hot tea, but I'll have something cold." He leaned back against the countertop.

"I'm sorry—I don't keep beer, but I have bottled water." She had avoided alcohol completely and had returned to the ways her mother taught her, avoiding any temptation to rely on it for escape from worries as she had during her low time in California.

"That's okay," Charles said.

She handed him a water bottle. "Was that your father who called out to you at the restaurant the other night?"

"Yeah, that's Shrimp Latour," he said, sounding resigned.

She couldn't help the smile tugging at the corner of her mouth at the incongruity of the name for such a hulking man. "How did he get the name Shrimp?" she asked.

"It's one of those cases of getting nicknamed just the opposite of what's obvious about you—it's tongue-in-cheek." A shadow fell over Charles' face. "I imagine you could tell he was drunk as a lord."

She understood what he meant. "I could see that yes."

"It's a problem lately and an old habit. He's relied on alcohol to ease some health troubles … chronic pain, but he's using it more and more now, and he's messing up the books at the restaurant because of it. I've been tryin' to sort through it—that is, when I can look at the books without him knowing it. He's pretty possessive about them—thinks I'm tryin' to boot him out of the business."

Lark's forehead wrinkled with concern. A troubled life did not fit her image of Charles. It always surprised her to realize others had troubles too, and eased her embarrassment over sharing her own.

To comfort Charles she moved to where he stood against the counter and leaned against him, wrapping her arms around his back. Then she kissed him for the first time by her own choice. As she pulled away, legs weak, heart lub-dubbing heavily, she glanced at his face. From the serious intensity in his eyes that quickly changed to amusement and then revenge, she saw that she was in for it and took off running.

"You *can't* kiss me like that *beb*, and then run away!"

"You're right—I won't do it again!" she squealed. He caught up to her and tackled her onto the sofa, pinning her underneath him. Their laughter was interrupted by a loud knock. She pushed herself to her feet and weakly and breathlessly stumbled to the door.

Her smile froze then faded as she opened the door and saw Hart's stormy face on the other side.

"I came to tell you that the cabinets are here. Thought you might want to make sure they're right before the guys install them," Hart said, his words short and clipped off at the ends.

She blushed as if she'd been caught doing something she shouldn't by a parent. Her own hackles rose and her head snapped back as if he'd slapped her. She stood up straight and, trying to look a little more dignified, ran a hand through her hair and tugged at her shirt that was twisted from her tussle with Charles.

"Yes, I *would* like to see them," she said, primly with tight lips.

"Good." He turned, without waiting for her to walk with him.

Hmmph, she thought. Turning back into the room, she watched Charles rise from the sofa and reach for his jacket. "Charles?"

"I think I'll head on back to Forestlee. It looks like you're about to get busy." He stopped beside her at the door. "I don't have to be at the restaurant this Saturday. Can I see you then?"

Lark remembered that she'd promised Ophelia that she would come to her dinner party and that she could bring someone.

"Well, I have a dinner party to go to. Would you come with me?"

He looked delighted. "Sure, where?" he asked.

They made the necessary plans and he left, revving his motorcycle a little challengingly, for Hart's benefit, Lark supposed, before he drove away down the treed drive.

She walked slowly toward the second cottage, less anxious to see the new kitchen cabinets than she had been earlier. Things were certainly getting complicated. She puzzled over Hart's behavior and something in the air between him and Charles.

She already had quite enough on her mind. There was a new tension between her and Hart. She had received no romantic overtures from him since she'd arrived back here, only a great working partner and renewed friendship but, as a woman will, she had begun to pick up a flirtatious edge to their interactions.

She was going to carefully observe her feelings. Again, she decided to trust that the Divine would show her the way.

Chapter 49

Ophelia's Party

The day of the party was beautiful and the warmest yet. Lark listened to upbeat music and dusted her new wooden floors. The chore turned into a game when Karma hid under the furniture and sprang out, front paws splayed, and attacked the soft strings of the mop, as if it was the most shockingly evil creature ever. She left her warm spots in the sun more often to play, now that spring was in the air. By the time Lark finished the downstairs floors, she was breathless with laughter over the cat's antics, and the cat was just breathless.

With a sigh Lark collapsed onto the sofa for a rest. She was pleased with her home even though it was still only sparsely furnished. And that might be remedied soon. With the work on the cottages near completion, she would have time to indulge her love of shopping and find some things to fill the empty spaces—maybe some new projects by way of furniture to refurbish. If only she could find a local Duff to go with her.

As the light faded outside and evening drew near, Lark went upstairs to dress for the party—something she didn't get to do often. Excitement trilled through her in anticipation of meeting Ophelia's friends who, if anything like Ophelia, would be interesting company. And there was Charles too—how would things go with *him*?

A Zen-like spa atmosphere was impossible to achieve while the cat sat on the edge of the tub and reached a paw toward the wavelets Lark's movements made in the water. If Karma fell in she would make a big mess trying to scramble out, probably scratching Lark. Fortunately for both of them, the silly cat at last jumped down and ran away. She had a new habit of making trouble as Lark got ready to leave the house. *How on earth did she know?*

When Lark turned on the hair dryer, Karma returned to lie on the rug. She rolled over to expose her soft belly which she well knew was irresistible. Lark tried to ignore her until the cat's green eyes closed drowsily from the warmth in the room and the white noise of the dryer. Lark could resist no longer and got down on her knees to bury her face in the soft fur—a mistake, since it woke the cat, who then followed right at her heels as she went to the closet.

Much larger than the one she'd made do with in San Francisco, this closet was mostly given over to clothing she loved. Raggedy, paint-spotted work shirts and jeans replaced her business clothes. When she wasn't working and grubby from head to toe, she dressed in whatever made her happy—usually something whimsical—giving fuel to the talk roundabout she was 'different.' *Well, so be it.*

Since the dream—the one in which her father had come to her—she was able to calm her worries much more easily. She'd had moments of pure joy again—unlike any she had experienced since she was a child and before her father died.

Other things helped too. When worries about what others thought of her circled round her mind, she reminded herself of the words she'd read at Ophelia's—

> *"Your only role is to represent what God created you to be—so be true to yourself—you are His creation, after all. The others you needn't worry about, for He has given them other roles, and they are trying to be true to them. But if you are true to yourself, it is likely you will find another soul, or souls, with whom you chime."*

She had written the quote on a piece of paper and had taped it above her full-length mirror. When she looked at her reflection in the mirror, the words reminded her not to censor her heart—or who she was.

She looked around for inspiration for what to wear to the party. In the far corner of the closet stood a wooden mannequin and, for illumination, an antique floor lamp of curvy iron. The iron table topped with stone she'd found while fleaing in San Francisco, on which she'd kept her collections, was now here in her closet, laden with makeup, lotions, and jewelry.

On several coat racks she kept scarves, wraps, necklaces, belts, and handbags all in a jumble. Karma, who loved to paw at the straps and fringes that cascaded down, was having a try at pulling a rack over. Lark put out her hand to stop its wobbling. *Goodness*—she would never be ready to go out if Karma didn't behave, and if she didn't keep her own thoughts focused.

She shooed the cat out the door, then pulled clothes hangers past her, considering each item. No, no … *no*. Her hand stopped on a silk dress of a muted rose, gray, and cream floral print with dolman sleeves. Its asymmetrical hemline stopped at the knee and its neckline plunged more than something she would normally wear, though she would still feel tastefully modest wearing it.

She slipped it over her head and let it float down around her, then found a long necklace of silver and gold disks and slipped that over her head too. She sat on a stool to pull on dark tights and short boots—the latest trend for wearing with dresses—or so the fashion magazines told her. She grabbed a cashmere shawl to slip into in case the evening got too cool.

As she passed by her bed on the way downstairs she tweaked the cover smooth. She had finally paid it some attention and found beautiful bedding online in midnight blue velvet—striking against her rain-colored walls. Before starting down the twisting spiral stairs, she turned to catch Karma eyeing the bed.

"Don't even think about it," she warned, shaking her finger at the cat, who played innocent by arching her back and skirting sideways around the bed to follow Lark down the twisting spiral stairs.

Thankfully Charles arrived in his car, and not on his motorcycle. He wore dark gray dress pants and a charcoal hound's tooth sport coat, his shirt collar casually open. He looked perfect for a dinner party … *although she was finding she really preferred a man in jeans.*

Ophelia's house in Forestlee was easily found. Like Charles she lived near her business, only a block from Charles's station, her red-bricked Queen Anne fronting the fountain green of the college campus. Lark expected to find the interior done up in the period of the house. Instead her eyes snapped open to an eclectic mix of mid-century modern furniture, upholstered in bright colors and patterns, very different from the style of Ophelia's dress shop. Two statues of cartoon characters sat underneath a parson's table in the foyer. She had to introduce Duff to this woman who seemed to share her sensibilities! Ophelia and Charles greeted each other like old friends. Lark supposed she shouldn't be surprised, after all the two owned businesses within steps of each other.

"It's wonderful to know two of my friends have become friends, as well!" Ophelia said. Charles accepted a glass of wine and Ophelia introduced them to five other guests who had arrived before them, and asked all of them to follow her to the back yard.

They stepped out onto a patio where a fire was lit in a brick-hearth fireplace to ward off the chilly night air. The setting was enchanting. A large tree draped its limbs over them and created a canopy above. A wooden table stretched long to allow all of them to sit comfortably with just enough elbow room to keep them close and encourage conversation. Candles nestled inside Mason jars hung at different heights from the tree branches all along the table—a breeze gently swayed them, making their shadows drift to and fro across the table. Along the table were small plates for olive oil and baskets for bread—clues they would be having Italian.

A couple of guests helped Ophelia to bring the food to the table while Lark, Charles, and the others settled around it.

The food was simple and well-made. There was roast chicken, homemade pasta, vegetables tossed with freshly grated parmesan, butter and lemon juice, and crunchy bread to dip into olive oil laden with rosemary, garlic and black pepper.

Ophelia told stories of her former life in Los Angeles. There was a guest from Seattle, one from New York, and Lark was able to share her own stories of life in San Francisco. There were a few comfortingly southern guests too. Lark's glance met Ophelia's across the table from her and a smile passed between them when Charles told a colorful New Orleans story.

Lark brought her wrap closer around her shoulders when Charles moved their chairs closer to the fireplace to have dessert and coffee there. The others joined them and arranged their chairs in a semicircle in front of the fire. The dessert was a lovely tiramisu flavored with almond, espresso, and chocolate. Lark coddled her coffee cup beneath her face, her hands wrapped around it for warmth, and listened to the others talk.

Vanessa was a writer of romance novels and was being teased by some of the other guests for her vocation. She said in her own defense, "Well, there might be a stereotype of women who write the sort of novels I do … but you should let me explain!

"Most women need some romance in their life. Am I wrong?" She smiled as she looked around at the faces of the other women for affirmation. Although Lark silently reserved her opinion, the other women nodded and murmured in agreement.

Vanessa clasped her hands under her chin and said dreamily, "When I was a girl my favorite author was Barbara Cartland. She wrote *wonderful* historical romance. My mother, who was concerned with my emotional development, of course, would fuss at me—she'd say, 'I wish you wouldn't read those, Vanessa. They will fill your head with fairy tales and the real world will not measure up!'

"But, you know, those novels made me believe the right man was out there for me, just like he was for the girls in those stories I read. I was able to *relax* about the whole thing and to just allow romance to happen for me when the time was right.

"My friends worried and obsessed over boyfriends—upset when they didn't have one and dissatisfied with them when they did. Tired of hearing her complaints, I scolded one friend for that and told her, 'If you make yourself happy, and just be yourself, stop worrying so much about it … the right guy will come along.'

"I remember that she asked me, 'So where's *your* guy?'

"I said, 'I'm not going to worry about it! He will come along, I *know* it.'

"And I didn't! And he did! And I've been married to 'the right man' for twenty-five years now!"

Charles caught Lark's glance and smiled. Laughter, applause, and chatter broke out around them.

Lark didn't want the evening to end, but because her eyelids were heavy, she yawned and stood to see whether moving about might help her become more alert. She lifted several dinner plates and drinking glasses and headed to the kitchen with them. Ophelia, who had joined her in gathering the dishes, followed her into the kitchen.

"Lark, have you enjoyed yourself?"

"Absolutely, Ophelia! Thank you for inviting me," Lark juggled dishes to turn and smile at her.

"Charles is something, isn't he? I should've thought to invite him myself!" Ophelia said.

"He has an interesting lifestyle. And he is so … confident," Lark said.

Ophelia responded with laughter and sounded affectionate when she said, "Charles is one of those *lucky* people so into what they're doing—their own passions—they don't notice others' preoccupations, even if their preoccupations happen to be with him!

"But … he isn't selfish, like I may have made him sound. Part of being into his own passions is, doing for others. His business often contributes to community needs.

"Somehow his focus lends him confidence, as you mentioned, and keeps him above the pettiness that goes on around all of us. Oh, it swirls around him too—he *is* a handsome guy—but he's totally unconcerned. It must make his life much easier." Ophelia became silent as several of the others joined them in the kitchen to say good night.

While her hostess saw the departing guests out, Lark was left alone to think about what she'd said. As for lucky people, unconcerned with what others thought—she suspected Ophelia herself was one of them, and Duff too. Though, it had to be easier for Duff, in a big city like San Francisco. That thought reminded her of Duff's now familiar words, '*...a soul that has freed itself from the bondage others try to impose, that can express itself freely, be true to itself, is safer to be friends with, to trust, than a soul that is in torture, captive to the labels others—that the world—tries to place on it, or even to the ones it tries to place on itself.*'

Could it be that Ophelia and Duff were talking about the same thing? Duff's soul that could 'express itself freely,' was similar to Ophelia's description of Charles, 'lucky people so into what they're doing—their own passions.' Those souls who expressed themselves openly and honestly, who followed their own passions, had to be free from labels, had to be unconcerned with what others thought of them. She had found painting allowed her to express herself. And she was passionate about it, finding herself frustrated when chores or commitments pulled her away from it.

When Ophelia returned with a halting step to the kitchen, Lark saw that her eyes were shadowed with fatigue and her back bowed with the strain of staying upright through the long evening. She and Charles really should be going, so that Ophelia could rest. *Where was Charles?*

At the still-open doorway to the patio, Lark almost stepped over the threshold when she was taken in by the scene before her. If she stepped outside she would intrude on a private moment. Charles had one foot propped on the fireplace hearth, his knee supporting his elbow, leaning close to the pretty guest who had come alone to the party. The woman looked up into Charles' face, enrapt.

What was she to do—interrupt or stay inside and wait? Fortunately, Ophelia passed by her where she hovered in the doorway, and spoke out before she reached the two, breaking the spell that was over them.

"Well you two, I am going to have to call it a night. I'm afraid I am *quite* tired!"

Flustered, the pretty guest named Elizabeth rose to give her hostess a light hug. "Thank you for a lovely evening, Ophelia!" she said.

Charles' gaze met Lark's questioning, confused one. He raised his eyebrows. "Ready to go?" he asked.

Lark nodded, and they said their goodbyes to Ophelia too.

They drove through the moonlit landscape toward Lark's gray house. After a long silence, hoping to relieve her confusion and the tightness around her heart, Lark said, "Charles, do you know Elizabeth from somewhere before?"

"No, tonight was the first time I've met her."

"She's quite beautiful."

"Yes. Lark, let's not do this. I told you I haven't noticed other women since I met you, and that's for true."

"But you did seem to notice her." She said the words gently, without anger, and smiled in his direction. She did not like this conversation or the vision in her mind of herself as she said these things.

Charles said, "She is beautiful. It would be difficult not to notice, wouldn't it?"

Neither moved to get out when the car stopped in front of the gray house, and instead they stared at the water sparkling through the tree trunks, rather than at each other.

"We haven't made a commitment I'm not aware of, have we Lark?"

"No, of course not, Charles. But I'm not sure where this leaves us."

"Neither am I. Seems like we're at a standstill again, no? Maybe time is the only thing that will answer this question, too."

A part of Lark wanted to grab his hand, look into his eyes, invite him inside, and give him what she knew he wanted. *She didn't want the evening to end this way!* Instead, they would again part with uncertainty between them. Why were they so out of sync with one another?

Hiding her frustration, she said, "Yes, you're right, Charles, time will tell." She stepped out of the car and walked alone to her door, while behind her the sound of Charles's car faded into the distance.

Maybe some of those lucky people she and Ophelia talked about—like Charles—were so focused on doing their own thing, they had nothing left for a committed, romantic relationship?

No, Lark argued with herself, after all she had recently rebuffed him physically. Instead, maybe those lucky people like Charles knew most what they wanted, and maybe Lark wasn't it for Charles—maybe he wasn't it for Lark. As they had agreed—time *would* tell.

As usual, the little girl's face in the painting was expressive, though unseen by Lark, as she walked past toward the stairway, her shoulders slumped.

She stood in her closet awkwardly putting one foot at a time into old-fashioned, one-piece pajamas with feet in them—*might as well be warm*—when her eye fell on the quotation taped to her door. The mirror reflected her open-mouthed surprise as she realized the words said almost exactly the same thing Ophelia said, that Duff said, that Charles lived, and that she'd been trying to live herself … about being what God created her to be, fulfilling His role for her, not worrying about the others, who were fulfilling their own. She climbed into her beautifully made bed alone.

Astonishment that the same message kept coming at her from different directions kept her from falling asleep right away. She determined to concentrate her efforts toward doing her own thing *with far less concern for what was on the minds of others.* Maybe that effort should include not troubling her mind with what Charles would decide about their relationship. She felt glad she hadn't clung to him. To have promised things or done things contrary to her wishes would have also been contrary to that effort. Peace settled over her and her eyes began to close. She had faith that the way would become clear.

Chapter 50

Ridge Cottages on Echo Creek

Duff had arrived for her second visit since Lark left 'San Fran,' Lark persuaded her to have breakfast down at the dock. The two of them walked slowly down the slope, carefully balancing their lidded cups so as not to spill the precious coffee inside. On Lark's forearm hung a basket of napkin-wrapped pastries that she'd picked up at a bakery especially for this morning. Fragile tufts of spring-green grass poked through the leaves and twigs on the path.

She'd found a chair, matching in style and vintage, to place alongside her own at the end of the dock, and had arranged them at an angle to each other, with a small table between, so they had a view of the creek and could see each other as well.

"Take care going around the chair, there's not much room along the edge ..." she warned Duff.

" 'Not much room?' You can say that again! Just let me set my coffee down ... and I'll ..." Duff fussed, as she scooted along the edge of the dock, her feet only inches from the edge, to make it to the front of the chair and sit down. Once she was sitting and gazing outward over the water, she said, "Lark, I have to say, this is a *beautiful* place. The great outdoors is not my thing, but I can appreciate why you wanted to live here."

"I am loving it here," Lark said. She didn't mention her uneasiness in the not-so-distant past—it was fading into the distance. Why not leave it there?

They sipped their coffee and watched the fog rise above the trees, revealing fresh leaves that tinted the gray-brown branches green.

When fully awake, with the fog burned completely away, and caffeine coursing through her veins, Lark asked. "How is San Francisco?"

"It hasn't changed, except it's lonelier. I haven't found anyone to replace you." She looked at Lark to show she was sincere.

"There's certainly no one here like you, Duff! I've wished for it, but no one has shown up."

"Well, I'm here now! By the way, what do you have planned for us?"

"I want to advertise that the cottages will be available for rental in May, and I want you to help me furnish them. That'll keep us quite busy. I have friends I want you to meet. And I just ... I've missed your company." She sighed and looked over at Duff, feeling awkward after all their sentimental declarations.

"When do we get started on shopping?" Duff asked, leaning forward in her chair.

Lark grinned. "Very soon. This morning I want us to look over the cottages and make a list of what they need."

It didn't take much prompting to get Duff moving when Lark held shopping like a carrot in front of her. After they finished their pastries and coffee, they stopped by the gray house so that Lark could fetch her laptop.

When they neared the inlet cottage, Duff exclaimed, "Cuuuute, Lark!"

Hart's crew had replaced rotted, warped, and loose board-and-batten siding, leaving as much of the original as possible, then painted the exterior gray to match her own house and the tree trunks around it. Lark had added a cheerful touch by choosing turquoise, pink, and goldenrod yellow for the trim.

Duff was enthusiastic over the fresh, new interior. The knotty-pine paneling remained, but it was now painted creamy white, and brightened the inside. Although the concrete floors had been a challenge, Lark had decided for practical reasons to leave them, but had them painted in mottled grays, so that they resembled stone now, and had their surface protected with a clear finish.

Duff was already forming her opinions. "Ya know, I think you're gonna want to bring those cheerful colors from the exterior trim indoors."

"I agree, but I think the bare minimum in furniture for now. I can add things later as tenants let me know their needs. So a sofa, an armchair, a side table ..."

Their enthusiasm lasted through the first cottage without flagging and then to the second cottage up on the ridge.

This one, Lark had painted in more subdued tones with the same gray on the outside, but with a green door and white trim.

"I think the colors here will have to lean mostly toward the gray and green, don't you?" Lark said.

"Yes, and you know that mixing greens is the thing these days, so let's do some of that in here. We can use the same list from the other cottage, except add a small dining table as this one has an area for that." Duff clapped her hands twice. "Do we have time to shop today?"

"Aren't you tired from traveling? I thought you could rest and we would have Mama and Wren over tonight. But let's do make a list of stores we want to visit."

"Okay then, sweetie. Let's go tomorrow, and stop for coffee on the way."

Before Duff returned to San Francisco, the cottages were 'pretty as a picture,' she said, and Lark decided they were ready for renters. She perched in front of her laptop to design a flyer for the local newspaper. The summer rental season was upon her and she wanted to get word out as soon as possible. Now that the time had arrived, she was anxious to see who would show up to rent them.

'For Rent:
Ridge Cottages on Echo Creek
Newly Remodeled Waterfront Cottages for Weekly or
Monthly Rental, beautifully situated on Echo Creek,
with a screened porch, or a high-ridge view.
Two Available
Both are One Bedroom, One Bath, and equipped to sleep four.
Call: XXX-XXX-XXXX for rates and availability'

With the advertisement in hand, she met with the classifieds clerk at the newspaper office—an officious, gray-haired lady who wore cat-eye glasses on a chain, and whose stooped posture allowed only her head and shoulders to show over the counter.

"From your experience … do you think I can expect a good response to my advertisement?" Lark asked.

"Dear, your chances for renting your cottages seem *very* good. There is a shortage of such properties hereabout. Unfortunately, that's not good for the paper, as it means your advertisement won't have to run as often. But that is the newspaper business, isn't it?" she smiled, her head wobbling slightly with palsy.

"Yes. Well, I am sorry about the paper, but thank you."

"It was a pleasure doing business with you. Good luck to you, dear." The woman raised her hand as Lark leaned into the swinging door and waved back at her. She was just turning when she ran into a solid object.

"Oof!"

"Oh! I'm sorry!" She pushed against the wide chest she'd run into and looked up. Hart. They stepped apart and moved aside as a man tried to get past them.

"It's good to see—" they said at the same time.

"No, you—" again they spoke simultaneously. Hart closed his mouth determinedly and nodded at Lark to speak.

"It's good to see you, Hart!"

"You too. Are you here to advertise your cottages?"

"Yes. A friend and I have furnished them, and they're all ready. They look great, Hart." She smiled to show her pride of ownership and gratitude for his work. "I'm thinking now would be a good time to let people know about them. Summer break is near and the kids will be out of school, families will need a get-away…"

"Good possibilities. I'm sure you'll have no trouble." Hart ran his hand around the back of his neck, shifting from one foot to the other. "I've fished at Echo Creek several weekends lately. I go by your dock most of the time. Never seen you out there though."

"No? What time do you go by?"

"Usually about six-thirty … in the morning."

She had to laugh. "Well, no wonder. If I'm out there, it's usually later in the day."

"The fishing's better early." His smile was teasing.

"Yes … well…" An awkward silence yawned between them, but both seemed reluctant to make a move to leave. "Maybe I'll try to get up earlier," Lark said.

"Hope to see you out there."

They backed apart, waved, and he went inside. Lark climbed into her car. She didn't see him look out the door to see her leave. And he didn't see her look wistfully toward the door before she pulled away.

Chapter 51
Reelin' 'em in

Down on the dock Lark settled into a chair. She leaned her head against the back and looked across the water at the cottage lights on the opposite shore—the only light other than the stars. She pulled her hands up into her jacket sleeves, curled her arms around herself, and pulled her feet up underneath her, trying to make herself as small as possible to preserve her body warmth. She grew drowsy and began to drift back to sleep.

At the sound of a motor in the distance, she opened her eyes to a squint. At first she wondered where she was, and her heart thudded, slow with sleepiness, but hard. *Was she dreaming?* Goodness knew her dreams could be frightening.

The sound of the motor grew louder and she sat up straighter in her chair. The sky to the east had lightened and she could now see the outline of the shoreline and trees on the other side of the creek. A yellow light moved in her direction along the main channel. She waited.

The sun rose just enough during the few moments it took the boat to draw near for her to see a lone figure guiding the outboard motor. At a distance of several yards, the motor was silenced, leaving the only sound the small splashes caused by wavelets rippling against the dock pilings and the shoreline.

She knelt at the edge of the dock. To steady its rocking and to keep it from drifting away again, she grasped the boat's wale. Hart braced his hand against the dock, his strong arm clothed in a flannel shirt within inches of hers.

"Good morning," he said in a voice pitched low, as if afraid he would wake someone. "Come fishing with me," he stated, rather than asked. The quiet that encircled them made it feel as if they were the only humans awake.

She hadn't come out here while it was still dark to turn him down, so she took the warm, rough hand he held out for her, and stepped unsteadily into the wooden boat, leaning into his body against the sway of it.

"I think the fish'll be biting back up the creek a bit," he said. He kept hold of her hand until she settled on the wooden seat in the front of the boat. Then he sat down in the back, started the motor, and eased away from the dock.

Lark held her jacket closed with one hand and her hat on her head with the other. She squinted into the wind as the boat cut through the smooth surface of the water along the shoreline. She turned and watched her dock recede behind them. Floating past were the lights of the gray house, then the white trim of the ridge cottage, high above the rocky bluffs, glowing through the early light. This was the first time she had seen the water aspect of her property and it took her breath away. *It was beautiful and it was hers.*

Hart veered away from the shoreline, guiding the boat past islands bristled with evergreens, and crossed the channel. He cut the motor and allowed the boat to drift nearer the rocky bluffs that towered over the western shoreline across the creek from her property. He said, "This is a good spot. We might catch a bass or two, a catfish, definitely some bream." He lifted a rod and reel, extending its handle toward her. "Do you know how to cast?"

"No," was her answer. There'd been no fishing in California for her.

He moved to kneel behind her and she held the sides of the boat against its rocking. He covered her hand that held the rod with his own, and pulled her arm backward.

"You want to cast to the side. Press this button down and hold it." He pressed his thumb down over hers. "Don't release it until you're pointing at the spot where you want your line to end up. Keep your eye on that spot and you'll cast right to it." He helped her go through the motions a couple of times until she thought she had the hang of it. "Now, you'll have to keep in mind I'm right back here, okay? Try not to hook me!"

"I'll try!" she said, with her own teasing sarcasm.

They grew quiet and listened to the water life that never seemed to sleep—the croak of frogs, comforting just because it was ever-present, and the chirp of crickets who liked to crawl over the bluff's warm rocks and hide in the nooks and crannies between them. There was the mesmerizing slosh and splash of water against the rocky shoreline and against the sides of the boat. Upon casting, there was the winding spin of the reels, the plop of the lure as it landed at a cast point. Then, the winding in again of the line.

Lark cranked her reel slowly and stared at the point where her white fishing line disappeared into the dark and murky water, absent of the sun's rays to illuminate its depth. Suddenly her reel stopped its winding. She felt a tug on the end of her rod, and sat forward quickly, rocking the boat.

"I got one! I got one!" she squeaked, her voice high-pitched with excitement.

"Okay, *shhhh*! Pull back on your line to set the hook, okay? Then—" Hart's loud whisper ceased in mid-sentence as Lark pulled her rod back hard, her line gave, all tension released, and she watched an object leave the water, arc through the air, and strike Hart on the side of the face with a *'thwap'!*

A dark, slimy-skinned fish flopped to the deck and left a red spot on Hart's surprised face. She couldn't help herself—laughter bubbled up from her stomach and burst from her in a loud, *"ha, ha, ha, hee, hee."* Her rod and reel clattered from her hands. Not wishing to humiliate Hart, she tried to control her laughing fit by covering her mouth with one hand and holding her stomach with her other hand, but it was useless. Fearing she would laugh herself right over the edge, she slipped off the wooden seat and sought a more secure place in the bottom of the boat. Through squinting, teary eyes she watched Hart grab a towel and wipe the wet slime from his face. She gasped for air just like the poor, too-small-to-keep fish that he grasped inside the towel. He eased the hook from its mouth, and dropped it back into the water.

At last her laughter quieted to an occasional muffled, *"hee, hee."* She scooted back onto the wooden seat and settled her hat back onto her head. "I'm sorry!" she said, but she cleared her throat and had to press her lips together to keep from laughing again.

"You are messing with my numbers this morning!" he grumbled, although his lips twitched at the corners, as laughter threatened to betray him.

She watched as he cast his line to land just where the rocky shoreline disappeared into the water. The sun was low on the horizon behind him where he sat in back of the boat. It streaked the east golden and purple and pink.

"Look," she nodded that way, and Hart looked behind him.

"Beautiful," he said—yet he didn't linger over the sunrise, but turned to look at her.

She settled back to watch an expert for a while. Over the last few months Hart's ability to do anything and everything well had made an impression on her. There seemed to be nothing he couldn't do. During the work on her cottages, there had been no request she made that intimidated him or his crew. He guided the people who worked for him calmly and with fairness. In return they respected him and worked hard for him. And there was the beautiful furniture he made on his own, which also made him an artist, rightfully. Fishing was just one more thing that he could do well. Any woman who had him by her side for life would be a lucky woman, indeed.

Regret tugged the corners of her mouth downward. She'd known the boy. Baseball was what he did well back then. She'd learned that he'd gone to college on a baseball scholarship.

"Hart, could you have played baseball past college? I mean, were you offered something beyond that?" She waited for his answer. He always took his time, never speaking before considering his words carefully.

"I could've, but … I was *tired* of playing ball. I'd been playing all my life. I'd gotten my degree in business, had worked some during college for a construction company, and they gave me a job as a foreman when I got out. I did that for a while instead. Made pretty good money. But as I saw the housing market pick up in the eighties, I decided to start my own company. It turned out to be a good decision." With a hard flick of his wrist, he cast his line the furthest Lark had seen so far. He leaned back against the boat motor and braced a foot against the wooden seat in front of him.

"No … I left ball behind."

The poignant thought occurred to her that Hart had left boyhood behind, along with baseball, and become a man.

She studied his profile and tried to superimpose upon it the boyish face she remembered—the smooth tan skin, the strong, dark brows, the full lips, the straight nose. All were still there, but small lines were now etched alongside his mouth and at the corners of his eyes by the smiles he so often wore. His eyes were sometimes shadowed underneath—perhaps because of the responsibilities he carried—making him seem tired at times, but wiser too than in boyhood, less tossed about by passions. In fact, Lark doubted passions tossed him about at all anymore.

She couldn't have been more wrong.

215

Chapter 52

Friends, Neighbors, and Lovers

Lark's heart was hopeful that very soon someone would be living nearby, someone who would become a friend, who she could call on in an emergency, who might leave a light on at night that she could see from her kitchen window. She walked toward the inlet cottage to meet with a possible tenant.

Several motorcycle engines could be heard coming down the drive. *Had a motorcycle gang pulled off the main road?*

A huge Harley appeared in black and chrome. Lark's eyes widened as she realized the woman riding it must be the soft-spoken Jude she'd talked to on the phone. She waited in front of the cottage as the short, stocky woman swung her leg over the bike and removed her red, white, and blue helmet, uncovering graying, light-brown hair divided into two braids down her back. She wore boots, jeans, and a sleeveless black leather vest over a t-shirt. Her appearance so riveted Lark's attention that she didn't see that another motorcycle and its rider had pulled up.

"Lark!"

Charles?! She stumbled when she turned to him. He met her in front of the cottage and took her up in a tight hug. She pulled away from him, crossed her arms, and said exasperatedly, "Charles, *where* have you been?!" Weeks had gone by since she had seen or heard from him. She'd gone by Latour's and it was closed—a sign on the door said 'Indefinitely.'

"It's a long story, *beb*. And we'll talk, but first I want you to meet my cousin, Jude."

Lark stepped past Charles toward the woman and extended her hand in welcome.

"Hello, Jude," she said. "You've come to see my cottage?"

"I showed your newspaper ad to Charles and he recognized it from the description and your phone number. He told me I had to come see it and meet you."

"I'm glad. Well!" She looked from the woman to Charles, nonplussed—never ceasing to be surprised by the twists and turns of life. "Let's go have a look." She couldn't resist another glance in Charles's direction, not believing he was walking right beside her. Already she could see that he looked older, more worn than the last time she'd seen him. Her brow creased with concern. Although she would rather hear what he had to tell her right away, she stuck to the plan and invited the two of them into the cottage, standing to one side and holding the door for Jude to come in. Then Charles held the door for her.

Jude looked all around the open living area, moved into the hallway, peeked into the bedroom and bathroom back there, then returned to the main living area, completing the tour. She had nodded her head affirmatively and exclaimed with pleasure the whole while.

"It's real nice. I ... I love it." She sighed, as if relieved.

Jude's voice like her smile so contrasted with her tough biker exterior that a brief silence fell while Lark studied her. She was curious to know this woman's story. She cleared her throat when she realized she was staring rudely while the others waited, and said, "You would like to rent it, then?"

"Yes, I would ... for true!"

Lark glanced at Charles, whose blue eyes sparkled with amusement. He said, "Jude is working for me as head chef. I need her experience in the kitchen at the restaurant because it doesn't look like I'm gonna to be overseeing the kitchen as I used to."

Lark scanned his face for the reason behind this change.

He went on, "I'm taking over the financial side of things." His eyes told her there was more that he wanted to tell her.

"Well, I'll certainly be happy to have a member of Charles's family here, Jude. Why don't we go over to my house? I have papers laid out there for you to sign if you agree with the terms. When do you think you might move in?"

"Tomorrow—is that all right?"

"Good—I mean—yes, that'll be great!"

They completed the paperwork over her library table, and Lark exhaled.

"That's it then!" She made a copy of the papers and handed them to Jude. "I'm happy to let you know a good friend of mine has taken up rental of the other cottage I advertised. She lives in San Francisco, but she'll be coming here to work and stay often—every six weeks or so." She walked

Jude to the door and said, "It will be so nice to have your company here!" With that she leaned over to hug the incongruously dressed, yet sweet-seeming woman who would be her new neighbor.

Charles walked with Jude to her bike. Lark waited by the front steps as they talked, and then Jude pulled on her helmet and swung her leg over her Harley. When she drove away, motor revving, Lark couldn't help smiling at the stuffed frog and bear who sat facing backward on the rear of the bike, goggily waving goodbye and smiling back at her.

Charles turned back toward Lark, smiling in an altogether different way.

Her heart fluttered as she watched him moving toward her, unhurriedly, as if he was formulating words before he reached her. When he neared her he took her into his arms, burying his face against her neck. Overhead the branches clattered together. Dark clouds were moving in.

"Where is Jude staying tonight?" Lark asked, her voice raised over the wind. She pulled her sweater closer.

"My place. She's headed back there now."

"Do you think she'll make it before the rain?"

"Hope so. Do you have someplace where I can stow my bike?"

"Bring it around to the basement." Wasting no time, they hurried the bike down the slope and Lark opened the door so Charles could wheel it in.

They ran back around to the front door, their heads ducked and shoulders hunched, as the first raindrops pelted them. Lark led the way to the window bench in her library. If it was going to rain outside, she wanted a good view. Pillows cushioned the walls against their backs. Charles followed suit when she kicked off her shoes, and they pressed the soles of their socked feet together on the center of the cushioned seat.

"Tell me," she said.

"Well, since I saw you last in ... let's see, it would have been—"

"March," she filled in for him.

"Yes, March. My Pop's health took a dive right after that. I found him at home one day, so sick he couldn't leave the house, and had to take him to the hospital. Turns out, he has liver cancer, and the outlook isn't good." Charles turned his head to look out at the pouring rain.

Lark saw his sadness in the deep shadows around his mouth and eyes.

"I'm sorry, Charles," she said, and reached out her hand for his.

218

"I took him back to New Orleans. He needs more care than I can give him. He has a brother and his wife there—Jude's parents. They'll take good care of him. He told me to come back here and take care of the business, which I'm trying to do now. Jude came back with me, like I said to cook. She's divorced and needs a hand up. She'll be a big help. I also found a source while down there for crawfish, and I've put some new items to the menu to bring people back in. We had to close for a while."

"I know. We were sorry about that—Mama and Wren and I. And we were worried about you."

Charles nodded and went on. "I've paid some employees during my time away a percentage of their wages, hoping to keep them. Most of 'em hung in there."

"Charles, you've been through a terrible time. I wish you had called me, or answered *my* calls." She looked at him from under her brows, not wishing to fuss, but hurt nevertheless.

"There wasn't anything you could do. And I was wrapped up in what I had to do. I'm sorry. I hope you understand."

"Without a doubt." She smiled—she'd already forgiven him—and she scooted closer to comfort him, but the wind had risen outside and drew their attention to the tossing treetops. Lightning flashed and thunder crashed before its light faded. They jumped and moved away from the window at the same moment, laughing in the way people do when they narrowly escape danger.

They moved to the sofa and settled side by side. Lark's thoughts went back over Charles's revelations while her thunder-rattled nerves calmed down. She wouldn't mention the rumor of bankruptcy that Ophelia had told her was spreading in Pressfield about Latour's. It showed rumor and gossip could be so inaccurate—if anyone knew how hurtful that could be, she did. She didn't want to add to Charles's sorrow.

He had changed in these weeks they'd been apart. In the past his spirit had seemed younger than hers, making her feel their relationship was somewhat incongruous, but he was more serious now, more grounded, as if he'd grown up a bit. It was unfortunate it had to happen in this way—brought on by sadness and responsibility.

"I haven't told you everything," he said. "Jude and I came here to get the business back on its feet. Bring it back to its glory days. And then, I'm going to try to find a buyer. I don't want to stay here without my Pop."

He turned his eyes to her and in them she saw sadness. He wouldn't be in Forestlee any longer. Because she hadn't heard from him in the last weeks, she'd ridden a roller coaster of hope, worry, hope again, then anger ... but today had brought finality to his life here.

What future could there be for the two of them, with him in New Orleans and her here? For some moments her mind considered irrational options—they could visit one another, or she could move to New Orleans—either was ridiculous. The truth was that they were finished before they were really started.

Time did indeed tell. She smiled ruefully, and said, "You and I weren't meant to be, Charles."

"Looks that way." His smile was regretful too.

"But, Charles—aside from your father's sickness, of course—you told me once you would be back in New Orleans if you could—"

His eyes lit up. "Yes, and I want to be. But you and I—"

She shook her head. "Charles, you can't change what you want, or force yourself to live somewhere you don't want to. You'd feel miserable. We both would." Her mouth twisted and she turned her head to the side. "Just out of curiosity—Elizabeth? Remember Ophelia's party?"

Charles grinned sheepishly and he nodded to show he remembered the last evening they'd spent together, but his nod changed to a shake.

"No. I meant what I said. I didn't call her. I'm not that shallow, Lark."

Lark felt reassured that all men weren't like Russert—not all of them fit the philandering stereotype. She wished she hadn't asked, because it only made letting him go more difficult.

They grew silent, letting their acknowledgement that it wouldn't work between them sink in.

"I intend to take full advantage of your friendship while you're here, Charles, and maybe come to visit my New Orleans friend one day," Lark said, gently changing the definition of their relationship.

After Charles left and the rain ended, Lark walked down to the dock. Passing the chairs, she sat instead on the wooden planks at the very end, knees pulled up under her chin.

The nightly frog symphony had begun. Tonight they croaked especially loudly in appreciation of the rain-wet earth. She stretched and felt surprisingly happy, despite knowing that a relationship with Charles was out of the question now. She had begun to let him go as the weeks had ticked by and she hadn't known where he had gone, or what he was doing, and he hadn't answered her calls, and Latour's shut down. She was relieved that he was okay and, she was surprised to find herself relieved that the tension their relationship caused was gone. Charles was intriguing, and handsome beyond belief, so there was melancholy too, to know the chapter on Charles had closed 'for true.' But there had always been some thing or another that wouldn't let them be together.

The annoying sound of a boat interrupted her peace. She shrugged her shoulders and rolled her head on her neck. There were times when she could do without the innumerable fishermen who tore up and down the water too fast for her liking. Well, she would have to share. Besides some fishermen were welcome. She watched the light of the boat draw near, but then veer away to stay in the main channel.

She lowered herself back onto her elbows and then down onto her back along the rough planks of the dock, willing to bear the discomfort for a short time to see the stars.

"Star light, star bright, first star I see tonight, I wish I may, I wish I might, get the wish I wish tonight." (Unknown Late 19th c.) She closed her eyes and wished, and opened them again. Out here you could see stars you rarely saw in the city. She wished she knew all the constellations. She did recognize Orion, the Big Dipper, the planet Venus.

Scritch, scritch, scritch … she turned toward the sound.

"Puddles?" The puppy waddled up to her, his entire back end, not just his tail, wagging from side to side. She looked past him. *Wow* —that was the fastest granting of a wish she'd ever received.

"Hart!" she said in surprise.

"Hi—what are you doing out here? I've been knocking and knocking up at the house. I was starting to get worried."

"I'm star gazing. Want to join me?" She moved to a chair and Hart took the one beside her.

"I like that you can see so many of 'em out here on the water," he said. "Look—there goes a satellite." He pointed his finger to show her its steady path across the sky.

"You can *see* a satellite?" Sure enough, an unwavering light arced slowly across the sky. She said, "I'm not sure I like the idea that there are manmade things out there among the stars." Objects like stars set in motion long ago by a higher power seemed infinitely more reliable than an object created by humanity and suspended for what could only be a finite time period.

"Yeah, things have sure changed since we watched the stars back in high school," Hart said.

"Who would've thought twenty years later we'd watch satellites cross the sky?"

"Not me, that's for sure."

"Do you think times were simpler then, Hart?" She looked over at him. Somehow his answer was important to her, closer to home than … stars and satellites.

"In some ways things were simpler then. The most I had to worry about was improving my curve ball or finding a hole in the outfield. But maybe it was just because we were younger."

"We had some good times together … remember coming to the creek?" she said.

"Yeah, but seems like once high school was over … things changed."

He was right. As high school ended things became not so simple. There had been her future to consider. Standing on her own feet and not being a burden on her mother. A strong need to succeed, to ensure … security.

She felt his gaze on her face for the first time since he sat down.

"Remember coming to my games?" he said.

"Even in the rain! I wouldn't miss them for anything back then. My girlfriends were envious of me, you know. Lark's boyfriend, the baseball star …"

"Is that right? And I missed out on all that admiration? I only had eyes for you, though. I still don't understand how you could have gone out to California so easily."

"I was just thinking about that. It wasn't so easy, actually. And, it was more than just one thing. You know? I'm not the same person I was back then, but I'm not sure I thought it all the way through. I didn't think about decades going by before living here again! Back then a decade was a lifetime! But the opportunity to get a wonderful education … well, I couldn't turn that down. And, you and I had gotten so close. My life had been limited by scraping by and living in a small town. I had never been anywhere.

"You seemed right for me, but, then so had my father been right for us. And we depended on him so much. He was our *everything* and we lost him, and nothing was the same again. I saw what my mother went through, having to find a job after she'd been at home with us for so long. I didn't want to be that dependent on another person ever again. It was a helpless feeling … a frightening feeling. I wanted to stand on my own two feet. I knew I would be okay always, if I could do that."

"And you did."

"Yes. And I'm glad I did, now."

"Me too." He took a pipe out of his jacket pocket and filled it with scented tobacco, lit it, and pulled on it.

Did he have to do that? Her father used to smoke a pipe. She laid her head back on her chair and closed her eyes as the scent brought forward memories. There was so much about this man beside her that reminded her of her father. Not just the physical—the pipe and the handkerchiefs he used, so like one of her father's she still kept upstairs in her closet. But the person he was—in times past called an upright man—good, kind, and respectable, who did what he said he would do, was there when you needed him.

Chapter 53

Never Had She Dreamed …

Lark worked hard to have enough paintings to fill a booth at the Forestlee Summer Arts Festival on Fourth of July weekend.

She painted what spoke to her heart—people, especially those with a colorful personality. She loved the challenge of capturing the special qualities that made them different from everyone else. There were several representations of Cricket and Duff.

Should she take to heart the praise that those who passed through her booth that day? She feared they were just being kind. She only knew that painting made her soul fly, made her forget everything that troubled her. She felt most like herself in front of a canvas, paintbrush in hand, simply *happy.*

When evening arrived, most of her paintings were sold. With the help of friends, she closed her booth. It was quick work to put everything away. And then she was free.

There was to be dancing on the town square before the fireworks. Twinkling lights were strung from the roof of the town gazebo to the surrounding buildings. The night looked and felt magical.

Never had she dreamed she would have two men waiting to dance with her. Nor would she have dreamed her heart would be able to expand and hold love for so many people in her life.

She closed her eyes and held out her hand. She knew her partner only when she opened her eyes again.

Lights swirled past as he spun her onto the floor. Her heart raced as always when Charles touched her, but Latour's was sold now, and he would leave for New Orleans in the coming week. She didn't know when she would see him again. She tried to notice everything her senses allowed her in these few moments, to keep something of him with her.

The song ended, as of course it must, and he escorted her to her next partner. His blue eyes held hers while he placed her hand and in the one of her next partner and then turned and walked away. *Gone.*

Lark caught Duff's eye. No worries—her friend wouldn't let her stay melancholy. The lights strung overhead jigged a dance of their own in the warm summer breeze as Lark watched Duff dance alone to the notes of a happy tune. Her teary eyes crinkled with laughter as Duff put her whole self into the dance—just as she did everything else in life. She was leaving too—returning to San Francisco after this visit but would return often to be her neighbor again in the ridge cottage.

The happy notes died away, replaced by the gentle ones of a familiar old song. Lark turned to the man who held her hand, ready to be swept away.

This hand, this man, was steady and sure. He held her close and she laid her head on his shoulder, her heart throbbing with a calm and regular beat. There was nothing about him that made her feel sad or unsteady on her feet. And, although she didn't know it this night, he would never leave her side, not even when the lights went out and the last note faded away.

———

She took down the painting of the little girl from over the fireplace. In its place, she hung her first work of art—a self-portrait. She had worked night and day until it was complete. It might not be everyone's idea of a masterpiece, but it represented her vision of herself, her complete self—unafraid, at peace, whole, and happy, no matter what might come her way.

A woman who was able to forgive, so her heart could be open to love. A woman whose soul was *free.*

The End

Afterword

Thank you, dear reader, for taking the time to read this story!

For those who are interested in its origins ...

I don't know where I heard it, but every story, every book, has something of the author within. And so does this book. However, this story wasn't a stagnant creation. The story took on a life of its own, as many do. The characters took on lives of their own. So while I wrote it, it isn't all *of* me.

In writing, I was inspired by stories we often see in the headlines about those in the public eye, and I thought about how the public in general, passes judgment on their lives based upon a photograph, a headline ... something someone says. And I wondered how all of that attention, the forming of an opinion about them, and the assumption of guilt that often follows, affects them.

And then, I thought about how it would be to be a quiet person, a private person, one who does not live in the public eye, a person who tries to live consciously, thoughtfully, carefully, and morally, who finds herself in a situation, where it would seem to the observer, that she's behaved immorally, when she is actually someone who tries very hard to do the right thing. And she is cast unwillingly into the public eye, never having had the wish to be, not being one to seek attention, perhaps even being one to shy away from attention. Then I took the story further—what would happen if the public then passed judgment on this person, based on distorted information or perceptions influenced by personal bias, resulting in condemnation, and then punishment, through actions carried out by an irrational, misguided individual? The quiet person would become a victim.

What would that domino effect of uttered words, judgment, condemnation, and punishment do to a good life? And what would happen to such a victim? Would she just fade away, as one might wish to do? Would she become a recluse? Would she take her own life? Or would she persevere, and walk through the pain, humbly accept the changes it brought about in her life, and then become a victor rather than a victim? And if so, how?

I tried to leaven the hard realities within the story with love, humor, with examples of good, trusting relationships. Our world needs a touch of all of that.

The story evolved into one that reminds us that every person who walks the earth had one Creator who loves them, who intended them to be unique and special, unlike any other. Maybe the world would be a better place if each of us could learn to love the unique and special qualities within ourselves—that love would then *naturally, effortlessly* shine outward.

In my own life, I found that *creating* can be a wonderful resolution to the impossibility of seeking, achieving, and maintaining the approval of others. And so it is for the main character in this book, who reaches back toward the joy she felt as a child, before judgment altered the way she sees herself, back to that person approved of by her own Creator, before others cast their judgments onto her—who, all the time was after all, *His* creation, and acceptable for that alone.

The story is a fiction shaped by my perceptions of the world—a creation of my mind—in its entirety. And as the copyright page says, in so many words—all characters, and all names, happenings, businesses, and locations (with the exception of major U.S. cities or national landmarks) are fictional, or fictionalized, and products of my creative ability; and any resemblance whatsoever the characters bear to persons living or dead is entirely coincidental.

By the way, the store where I buy my paint? The guys there are great – professional, helpful, and efficient. My hair salon is nothing like Betty's—although Betty's doesn't *really* sound like such a bad place, I think!

Note: Since first writing this story in the year 2010, my impressions of the information traveling to and fro on the internet has altered somewhat. The internet and social media can be used for good … and *not so good*. I suppose it is just another battlefield on which the two forces will wage their battles.

Peace to you,
Angela

I would love to know your thoughts about the book! Visit and reach me through the Contact page on my website at www.angelabrackeen.net.

Bibliography

The following works influenced the story (Kushner and Tolle); or were quoted within (Hume, Richter, and Unknown):

Hume, David. *Of the Standard of Taste*. 1711-1776. http://en.wikisource.org/w/index.php?title=Of_the_Standard_of_Taste&oldid=3741546.

Kushner, Lawrence. *Eyes Remade for Wonder*. Woodstock, VT: Jewish Lights Publishing, 2002 Third Printing.

Richter. "Vol. III, No. 6, The Gold-Mine." *The Cottage Hearth*, June 1876: 167.

Tolle, Eckhart. *The Power of Now*. Novato, CA and Vancouver, B.C., Canada: New World Library and Namaste Publishing, 1999.

Unknown. "Star Light, Star Bright." Late 19th c.